Amazon

of

Previous Books

The Master's Inn

Kay DiBianca, Dec. 2022

When three troubled families find themselves isolated in a Bed & Breakfast during a serious blizzard, the tragedies they've allowed to rule their lives become evident. Deb Gorman has written a powerful story of characters who help one another face their past failures and find forgiveness and hope for the future. A worthwhile book for our unsettled world.

Who Are These People?

Sandy Allen, Dec. 2016

Vivid, well-written stories about lesser-known Biblical characters. The author's reflections add depth, while the study/discussion questions challenge readers to examine themselves and seek God's will for their lives. I enjoyed this book, and will add it to my "read again" list.

Who Are These People, Book 2

J. A. McPhail, June 2022

Deb Gorman has such a gift for taking minor Bible characters and making their lives relevant for today. With great skill she digs into the unwritten story behind a barely-mentioned person in the Bible, and puts the reader into their mind and life. Then she turns the tables by sharing her own

No Tomorrows

A NOVEL FOR TODAY

DEB GORMAN

Edited by Dori Harrell, Breakout Editing

Cover design by Emilie Haney

Author's photograph by Ric Brunstetter, RBIII Studios

Formatting by Colleen Jones

ISBN 978-0-9979587-8-2 (Paperback)
ISBN 978-0-9979587-9-9 (Digital)

Published by Deb Gorman
Debo Publishing

https://debggorman.com

For Holly . . .

I'll see you tomorrow, my sweet sister.

Do not boast about tomorrow,

for you do not know what a day may bring forth.

Proverbs 27:1 (NKJV)

One today is worth two tomorrows.

— Benjamin Franklin

ACKNOWLEDGMENTS

It's hard to remember at the end of the journey all those helpful folks who kicked rocks out of my way, patched a skinned knee, picked me up and dusted me off when I careened off the beaten path, or stood on the sidelines cheering me on. There have been so many.

I thank my God—who has never left me behind, never let me get ahead of Him, and always answers when I call.

I thank my supportive husband, my kids and grandkids, my father, and innumerable friends who encourage my wild, hairy ideas—then rein me in so I can get it all tied up in the pages of a book.

I thank my team—my wonderful editor and cover designer—who have both been with me since the first book was born.

I've had many, many mentors who have taught me much about the craft of writing. I wish I could name them all, but I'd leave someone out for sure. You know who you are.

And . . . yes, you guessed it . . . I can't leave off without thanking the characters in this story, who first lived in my head and then in my heart. They are as real to me as some real people I know.

And they always will be.

Deb Gorman

1

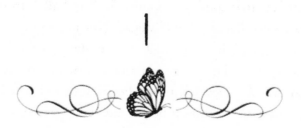

The woman in the mirror tormented her. She stepped back and turned off the light.

Now the woman in the mirror was a frightening shadow, right index finger outstretched, pinning her to guilt.

Of course. It was Thursday.

Annie turned the light back on.

She gasped. The image was herself, but decades older. Face sagging, eyes unnaturally black and unlit, hair sparse and gray, wrinkled hands trembling at her waist.

She needed to stop this madness now, before she became her reflection.

She turned, throwing one last glance at the mirror, losing her breath because the woman in the mirror had not moved.

She locked eyes with herself, then turned and headed to the stairs and dinner with her husband and four children.

Annie Lee reached the bottom of the staircase and glanced at the front door. She heard an odd scratching noise. It wasn't Max wanting in, because he sat across the living room staring at her, tail thumping the carpet.

What was that sound? Gripping the handrail with shaky fingers, she cocked her head and listened. Nothing.

She sagged against the wall. Annie always hoped it would be different, that the dread wouldn't return just because it was Thursday, but she knew what she'd heard. It had slithered in again, and she'd have to confront it before the night was over.

Thursdays were always the same.

Annie let go of the stair railing, smoothed her hair, and tiptoed toward the dining room. She heard the banter and managed to relax and smile as she heard Roger perform his impression of Roadrunner for the kids. She paused to listen.

Her grin broadened at Kimmie's high-pitched voice. "But why does he beep, Daddy?"

Hands clasped together to stop the tremble, Annie continued to the dining room, where her husband and four children waited. Before entering, she stopped at her collection of porcelain monarch butterflies and straightened one. Touching the beautiful creature settled her nerves.

The food was already on the table, and Annie threw Roger a grateful glance.

He stood and pulled her chair out. "There you are. What took you so long?"

She paused to master the shake in her voice. "Doesn't matter. I'm here now."

After the blessing, Annie started the mashed potatoes around the table. "How was your day, kids? Anything interesting happen?"

She asked the same question at dinner every night, never sure what she was getting herself into. Sometimes just blank stares, but other times their comedic creativity flowed.

Like the time a couple of years ago when Hank wove a long story of skipping school and going to the casino with his best friend, Shane. She had to give him an A+ for imagination.

Or when Kymber—Kimmie for short—said school was exciting that day because Elvis had visited. The family had watched a documentary of his life and music the night before, and evidently the seven-year-old had forgotten the part about Elvis having died decades ago.

And then there was Mayra, who had her own imaginative stories—but her fierce teenaged sophistication prevented her from sharing them. Instead, she'd perfected sarcasm to an art form.

It didn't matter to Annie, as long as she asked the question that had become part of her nightly routine. It was like stamping a smiley face on the end of the day, giving tomorrow permission to begin.

Outside, a car horn blared in their central Washington cul-de-sac. Annie and Roger jumped at the sound, but Max didn't even bark. The huge black Lab sat, as he did every night, at the corner of the table between Hank, almost thirteen, and Roger. Max's head topped the table by three inches, tongue hanging out, drooling at the smell of grilled pork chops.

They'd gotten Max seven years ago from a nearby shelter when he was a floppy-eared six-month-old pup with gigantic feet. Hank had won the naming contest. Mayra had never gotten over it, but who had ever heard of a dog named Tweeter? Roger offered to get her a parakeet, but the humor was lost on the then eight-year-old.

Annie and Roger had tried to teach Max table manners, but he'd proven more stubborn than both of them—and as Roger said, they had enough trouble teaching the kids their table manners, let alone the family dog.

Since no one had answered the nightly question yet, Annie prompted them again as she reached for the pork-chop platter. "And you too, Roger. Anything interesting happen today in the world of finance?"

The skin around his dark-brown eyes crinkled. "Nope. Same old, same old, as usual." His standard answer.

Roger always said finance was a world in which six months of dull was followed by three days of sheer terror until the stock market righted itself and people started buying and selling as usual.

Annie thrived on *as usual.* Lord knew her life before Roger—as a navy brat—had been anything but boring. She'd struggled through years of moving from base to base until she was ten, always having to say goodbye to friends and start over. She tried not to dwell on it though, usually successful at keeping her well-developed insecurities down inside where the sun didn't shine.

"Anything else?"

Roger reached for his fork, which caused Max to raise his head, nose twitching. Roger glared, causing the dog's head to go down a notch, resting his furry chin on the table.

"Well, Harv did spring for lunch, the old tightwad. He wants to meet with me tomorrow."

Annie raised an eyebrow. "About what? A partnership?"

"Not sure. We'll see. Probably to give me kudos for landing the Jackson account—you know, that retired couple from California who moved up here with their millions to invest."

"Wow, Dad. Do you get some of their money?"

Roger grinned and handed him the pork-chop platter.

"No, Hank. I invest it for them. Hopefully, make them some more money. At least, that's always the plan."

Hank scowled. "You don't get any of it? That's not fair. What's the use of working there if you don't get any of their money?"

Mayra seared her brother with a superior glare. "Hank, you're so dumb. Dad gets paid."

"But—"

Annie broke in with practiced smoothness. "Kids, you haven't told us about your day yet." She and Roger hated arguments and sniping and took turns putting the brakes on it.

Mayra wrapped a tendril of long hair around one finger. "Oh yeah. Remember I told you we have to write an essay?"

Hank butt in. "Essays are boring. Let me tell you mine."

"Rude—I'm older. I should answer first." At fifteen and the oldest, Mayra had an inflated sense of self-importance.

Roger stilled Mayra's comment with a wave of his hand, reminding Annie of a Jedi knight in *Star Wars*. "Let Hank go first, okay?"

"Fine. It'll probably be just more Hank-ness anyway."

"Funny, Mayra." Roger turned to Hank. "Okay, son, you've got the floor. Make it good."

"It is. So I have a question for you. Mr. Neely asked it today, and we had to write our answers on slips of paper and turn them in."

Mayra sniffed. "Ugh, science—"

"Hey, science is cool."

Roger thumped his forefinger on the table. "The question, Hank."

"Okay, here it is. If the earth stopped spinning—I mean, just stopped dead from spinning all of a sudden—what would happen next?" He looked around the table. "Anybody know?"

Four frowns appeared as everyone—except three-year-old Nora, contemplating the small mound of vegetables on her toddler-sized plate—considered the question.

"Well? Who's gonna guess first?"

"No school!" Kimmie yelled.

"No yelling at the dinner table," Mayra said.

Hank pointed at Kimmie across the table. "You're right. But why, mush-head?"

"Come on, Hank. She's only seven. Give her some credit," Roger said with a grin at Kimmie. He leaned down eye level with her. "Good job, honey."

Kimmie smirked at Hank, folding her arms over her chest like a boardroom boss.

"Dad, aren't you gonna guess?"

"Well, let's see. The earth stops spinning all at once?"

"Yup." Hank sat back in his chair, index finger on his chin, his expression like the Cheshire cat with a secret.

Roger glanced at Annie. "What do you think, Mom? Any ideas for our budding scientist?"

Annie shook her head and looked at her plate, a tight feeling in her chest at the direction the conversation had taken, but unable to think of a graceful way to stop it. She'd started it, after all.

"Okay, Hank," Roger started. "I guess nobody would have a tomorrow, right? It's the rotation of the earth that makes tomorrow arrive. Without that rotation—"

Annie looked at Nora, then back at Roger. She needed to stop this.

"All right, let's change the subject—" She didn't mean to sound gruff, but that was the way the words popped out.

"Mom, don't you want to know the answer?" Hank leaned toward Roger. "You're right, Dad. Tomorrow wouldn't come. But something else would happen right away. There'd be sudden winds, about a thousand miles an hour, the teacher said. And they would flatten everything on earth, except at the poles. So no school the next day, because there wouldn't be any schools or a next day. And Mr. Neely said ocean waves a hundred miles tall. How's that for cool?"

Roger shook his head with a grimace. "Very cool, Hank. Thanks for sharing."

He gestured to Mayra. "You're up."

"Maybe we can just eat now." Annie didn't want to hear about Mayra's essay.

"But, Mom, Hank got to tell his. Why can't I tell mine?"

Annie raised her hands in surrender. "Fine. But let's not let our food get cold, you guys. We can eat and listen at the same time."

"Okay, my essay."

Roger handed her the mashed potatoes. "Uh-huh."

Mayra grabbed for the bowl. "Miss Harris gave us a choice of three questions to answer." Mayra passed the dinner rolls to him without answering.

"Oh?" Roger took the rolls and paused with the basket midair.

She spooned some mashed potatoes onto her plate, dipping her finger in for a taste. "Oh, good. Cheese, no onion."

Roger grunted, clearly exasperated. "Don't keep us in suspense. What question did you choose?"

Mayra speared a pork chop and sawed off a bite while everyone waited. "What would I do today if I knew I'd die tomorrow?" She popped the morsel into her mouth. "Mmm. Good, Mom."

Annie stared at Mayra, who chomped her meat and chased it down with a noisy slurp of milk.

"Kinda goes along with Hank's, huh Mom?"

Hank smirked. "Yeah, but yours is just an essay. Mine's real."

Mayra threw him her best know-it-all glance. "How do you know? It's never happened before. And probably never will, dufus." She drained her glass of milk.

The pounding in Annie's head kept time with the ticking of the grandfather clock in the corner. Her gaze narrowed to Mayra's unperturbed profile, the teen clearly unaware she'd sent her mother tumbling through a decades-old abyss.

Annie was unable to stop her mad descent into the same unreasoning fear she'd suffered all her remembered life, that the other shoe would drop soon and wrench everything good out of her breath and being. Except it wasn't exactly unreasoning. She'd been here before.

She heard the scratching sound again. The old fear hissed behind her, then glided in, serpentlike as the silence enclosed her. Just as it always did.

What she wouldn't give for a week without a Thursday.

2

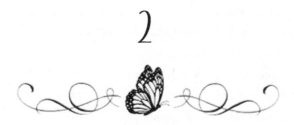

Mayra banged her glass down and looked up at the sudden silence. "What? What'd I say? Why are you all staring at me?"

Annie dropped her fork. It hit her plate with a clang—harsh in the silence—then bounced and skittered under the table. She scooted her chair back and dived to the floor, banging her knee. Stretching, she grabbed the utensil—along with a broccoli floweret—a split second before Max could stick his nose on it. Her hand trembled as she pushed her hair back from her damp forehead. Max dived for the fork again when it slipped out of her fingers.

Annie pushed him away. "Max, behave yourself—"

Roger's face appeared under the lacy tablecloth, one hand on Max's collar. "What are you doing down there?"

"Getting my fork. You writing a book? Leave that chapter out."

Crawling out to a chorus of giggles, she wiped her fork on her napkin and popped the broccoli into her mouth.

"Five-second rule?" Kimmie chirped. She had a habit of pushing her bangs out of the way, and her short reddish-blond hair stuck up all over her head. Of all the children, she was the most mellow, never pushing back. Compared to Nora, the miniature scrapper, Kimmie was a pussycat.

"Yes, honey, five-second rule."

"Hey, that was longer than five seconds!" Hank's indignant expression looked so like his father's, with his black wavy hair, olive skin, and dark eyes.

Roger stopped the argument before it started. "Never mind, you guys. Eat your dinner."

He pulled Max back from the table. "You stay back, Max, ya hear? This is not your dinner—it's mine." He looked down the table at Annie. "You okay, honey?"

"Of course. I just dropped my fork. Let's not make a fuss about it."

The undercurrent of *not usual* danced in the forefront of her mind like a dragonfly on the breeze. "Can we eat now please?"

Roger shrugged and sipped his tea. "You don't have to get so testy."

He looked at Mayra. "Back to your essay. Sounds like a grim subject for a tenth grader. Did anyone else pick that question? And what were your other choices, anyway?"

"I dunno and I dunno."

"Don't know and don't know."

"Yeah, that too."

Annie glared at her. "Mayra, don't be rude to your father—"

"You were."

Hank snickered and mocked a high five at his older sister.

Annie tightened her grip on her knife. Had she ever been fifteen? Not this kind of fifteen. If she'd spoken to her parents that way . . . She stopped herself and relaxed her fingers, meeting Roger's gaze.

Roger shook his head, exasperation wrinkled between his eyes. "Have you got any ideas for your essay—what you're going to say, I mean?"

The queen of teenaged sarcasm groaned and displayed her talent, enunciating each word with a break in between. "I don't know, Dad. Maybe if I knew for sure I'd die tomorrow, I'd say goodbye to people. Family, close friends—"

"Ya think—"

Roger wagged an index finger. "Hank, don't talk with your mouth full. And stop giving Max bites of food."

"—or maybe I'd go off by myself for a long walk or something and just not come back." Mayra scraped up the last of her mashed potatoes. "I don't know."

She looked sideways at Annie. "But I know this. I wouldn't make a federal case out of dying. And anyways, how could I possibly know if I'll die tomorrow? Who cares? I'm only fifteen."

Only fifteen.

Roger leaned toward her. "It's 'anyway,' not 'anyways.'" He sat up again and covered her hand with his. "But you should think about the question."

She jerked her hand away. "Why?"

Hank, bless his heart, was not to be outdone by Mayra's sarcasm. "Yeah, why? It's not like it'll really happen—"

Mayra sent her brother a blistering glare. "Dude! What would you know about it?"

"Hey, sometimes I know stuff. You don't have a corner on the brains market."

Roger lowered his forehead to his palm. "Kids, will you stop bickering. Please?"

Annie felt the walls close in and squeeze the breath from her lungs. At the same time, the table stretched, elongating itself, moving her family away from her. What an odd, frightening sensation.

She pinched her eyes shut, then opened them.

The dining room returned to normal. Sort of, if she didn't count the unnatural conversation. Her usual tight rein on mealtime had slipped tonight. She must get it back.

Roger tried again with Mayra. "Because, honey, life's short. And we never know what might happen the next day or even the next minute."

He lifted his chin and looked over Mayra's head at Annie, pinning her with his stare.

She wondered where he was going with that. Mom and Dad? Abby? *No, not that . . .*

No one said anything, not even smart-mouthed Hank. It was as if they were frozen in time, staring wide eyed at each other. Max was quiet too, on the floor near Hank's chair.

The next minute Mayra snorted her disdain. "Geez, Dad, now you're the one who's grim—"

Annie struggled to keep the irritation out of her voice. "Okay, that'll do—"

"Mommy, what's 'die'?" Nora's breathy whisper blitzed into the room and into Annie's brain, almost drowning out the beating rhythm of the clock in the corner.

But it didn't tick again. Annie jerked her focus from Nora's white face to the clock. It was motionless at one second past six o'clock. It'd never stopped before.

Nora's fingers tapped a beat on Annie's arm, her tone rising in high-voiced desperation. "Mommy, Mommy, what's it *mean*?"

Annie wrenched her gaze from the clock's face back to Nora's. The child's worry-smeared eyes pierced her heart as the fear slid up to the table next to Annie's chair. Next she'd feel it on her pant leg.

How did you tell a three-year-old about death?

She gave a sideways glance at the two photos on the wall. And where the third should've been.

Roger cleared his throat. "Baby—"

Annie rushed to answer first. "It's . . . it's when—"

"Remember when you found that squished bird in the park? It was dead—I mean, it died when it got squished."

Roger slammed his cup down. "Hank! For crying out loud, don't scare your sis—"

Nora grabbed Annie's fingers and shrieked. "Sis . . . Sissie's gonna be squished?"

Hank threw his head back and burst into unbrotherly laughter. "You're so—"

Annie glared at Hank and thrust her palm in his face, causing him to jerk back.

"Ah, Mom, don't be so—"

"Hank!" Roger's voice thundered.

Max slunk under the table.

3

Annie sucked in a deep breath and wiped a slick of sweat from her forehead, desperate to rescue this family time and return it to some semblance of *as usual*.

She faced Nora and leaned over her booster chair so they were eye to eye, gentling her voice. "No, Nora. No one is going to squish Mayra. Hank's just teasing you." She unwound Nora's fingers and stroked them.

"When people die, they go live with God. Mayra just has to write an essay—a story—about it. It's only a school assignment. It's not real. Understand?"

"Yeah, Nora—"

Roger gripped Hank's forearm. "Let your mother handle this. Not another word, son."

"Promise, Mommy? She won't d . . . die . . . be squished?" Nora's anxious eyes, blue as the summer sky, searched Annie's face, her plump fingers gripping her mother's thumb like a vise.

"I promise, honey. Now let's finish dinner, okay? Mayra, we

can talk about your assignment some other time if you want."

Mayra shrugged. "You asked, Mom. I was just making conversation—you know, like you and Dad say we have to. See what happens? Hank acts like a jerk, and Nora—"

Roger put his fork down with a clatter. "That's enough, Mayra. Eat your dinner."

Annie pried Nora's fingers from around her thumb and smoothed her baby-fine blond hair back from her forehead, tucking a lock behind her ear. "Drink up, honey." She set a small glass of milk in front of Nora.

Nora's fingers trembled as she took the glass, her wide, unblinking gaze fastened on Annie's.

Her little girl shouldn't look like that. Annie leaned over and wiped a trickle of milk escaping down her chin, thinking Nora would probably have another nightmare tonight.

She'd been having them off and on for a few weeks, her piercing screams wrenching Annie awake and sending her flying down the hall to the room Nora shared with Kimmie. Something about her bed being covered in "buzzies"—Nora's word for flies. Nora hated any flying bug. She could pick up a snail or a lizard, even a mouse, but if the creature had wings, she'd scream and run.

Annie suspected Hank had been egging it on, chasing her with dragonflies or bees clutched by the wings. She'd caught him at it before.

"Feel better, honey?"

Nora nodded and picked up a blob of mashed potatoes with her hand.

"Use your fork, sweetie."

The child picked up her fork and smeared potatoes all over the handle.

Annie cleaned the fork and handed it back to her.

To Annie's relief, the meal progressed as usual after that—she and Roger breaking up arguments, wiping noses and mouths, and reminding them to eat their vegetables.

After they finished, Roger excused them to the living room to play before bedtime, then went to the kitchen to refill his teacup, bringing more hot water for Annie.

She appreciated the gesture but fervently hoped he wouldn't try to get her to talk about what had happened at dinner. It was over as far she was concerned.

Settling himself, he frowned at her. "Are you okay?"

"Yes, I'm okay." She knew she sounded irritated. "Why do you keep asking?"

He shrugged and looked away. "I don't know. I saw your hand shaking."

Hank's voice blared from the living room "Hey, thief! That's my card. Give it back."

"No, it's not—" Nora's volume matched Hank's.

Roger slapped a palm on the table, rose, and headed for the living room.

Annie stopped him with a hand on his arm. "Let them figure it out. We can't always be there to mediate their squabbles."

He sat again. "You're right. Habit, I guess." He listened a moment longer, then grinned at her. "Guess it's over."

He moved to the chair next to her. "I was wondering. How would you answer Mayra's essay question?"

His question thudded between them. Why did he keep asking, and why did it disturb her so? It wasn't as if she'd never experienced the death of family or friends before. She'd even wondered sometimes how she would spend her last months if she knew she was dying. For some reason, on this night, the question caused turmoil in her soul, her past rising up to haunt her.

Because it was Thursday? Some kind of portent, an omen? She didn't believe in such things.

"Annie?" His voice sounded harsh, but his eyes were mild as they peered over his teacup.

"I have no idea, Roger. I'd have to think about it. Besides, we used to tell each other we'd be together forever. Remember?"

Roger looked over her head at the photos of their parents and the empty space between.

"Yeah, I remember. But forever isn't as long as it used to be." He covered her hand with his. "Right?"

Annie removed her hand and frowned. "Nice sentiment. You could be a little more cheerful." She sipped her tea, now cold.

"And you didn't answer my question."

"Yes, I did."

She stood. "I know it's my turn, but would you mind putting them to bed? I'll clear the table and load the dishwasher. And maybe you could see what's wrong with the clock—"

He looked at it. "The clock?"

Annie glanced at the corner where the antique timepiece— inherited from Roger's great-grandfather—had stood for twenty years. "Yeah, it—"

But the delicately carved second hand ticked away against the silver-backed gold numbers. She checked her watch. It had the correct time.

How could it have the correct time after having stopped? The niggle of fear burrowed itself deeper in her brain.

Annie twisted her ponytail around her index finger, a nervous habit since childhood, to clear her mind. "Oh, never mind."

He stared, one finger tapping the table. "Okay."

She couldn't hold his gaze, picking up her plate and silverware with jerky movements. "Well?"

His face softened. "It's just an essay question, hon."

She tightened her fingers on her plate. "Then stop bugging me about it, okay?"

He stood and touched his lips with his napkin, then reached for her, enclosing her, plate and all, in his arms. He gave her a peck on the cheek.

"Relax. You look tense."

"I have four kids. Who wouldn't be tense?"

"We—*we* have four kids."

The walls closed in on her again, or was it his arms? She looked at him and tried to smile. His warm dark eyes looked into hers, melting some of the tension.

"Right. I've had a long day. I'm sorry I've been so touchy. I think I need a walk."

"In the rain?"

"It stopped."

He searched her face, nodded, and headed for the living room.

Annie put her plate down and followed him to the archway between the dining room and the spacious living room.

Her cell phone rested in the wide bowl on the credenza, where all cell phones were muted and dumped during dinner—another of Annie's strict rules to maintain her own sanity. No phone calls, texting, or games during family time. As she passed the bowl, she saw she'd missed a call from Ellen, her best friend.

She reached for the phone, her finger hovering over Ellen's number.

Never mind. Tomorrow was Friday, and they'd see each other in the morning.

She stuck the phone in her jeans pocket—she'd need it for her walk—and followed Roger into the living room.

4

The three younger kids played a card game on the floor, sitting knee to knee in a small circle. Mayra sat curled up in her favorite place on the sofa, eyes glued to her tablet.

They entered quietly—as always, wanting to see what they were up to—just in time to hear Hank's latest one-liner. In addition to bedeviling his sisters, he loved making them laugh.

"Hey, Mayra, do you know what a day without sunshine is?"

She laid her tablet facedown on her chest. "No, Hank. What *is* a day without sunshine?"

"A day without sunshine is . . . wait for it . . . wait for it . . . night!" Hank slapped his knee.

"Ha-ha. Now be quiet." She picked up her tablet and turned away, her fingers tapping at a furious rate.

Kimmie laughed so hard she fell over backward. "Hank, you're so funny. You should have your own YouTube channel. I bet you'd have a million hits." For a child of seven, she was quite tech savvy.

She'd even taught Annie a thing or two about her phone.

Mayra lowered her tablet again. "It wasn't that funny, Kimster. You're too easy to please."

Hank gave a sidelong glance at Roger, who gave him a victory sign.

"Think whatcha like, Mayra." He leaned over and tapped Kimmie's leg. "I think you're right. I can see it all now—crowds of people subscribing to my channel. I could call it Hank the Hilarious. And maybe I could even get a TV contract—"

Roger clapped his hands, causing Mayra to jump. Her iPad slipped to the floor.

"Geez, Dad—"

"Fun's over."

"This isn't fun. It's boring."

"Are you reading or texting?" Annie knew it was the latter.

She sat up with a pout. "It's no big deal, Mom. I'm just talking to Cassie on Messenger."

"It's a big deal when it's homework time." Annie held her hand out for the tablet.

Mayra glared at her.

"You know the rule. No phones or tablets upstairs during homework time or bedtime. Hand it over."

Roger stepped to the sofa. "Mayra, do what you're told, now."

She did, clearly recognizing defeat.

Annie laid the tablet down and pointed upstairs.

"Betcha I know what you and Cassie were talking about," Hank teased.

Mayra bristled. "Put a sock in it, Hank. It's so none of your business—"

"Never mind that now. Come on, kiddos. Time for baths, showers, and bed. Everyone upstairs." Roger picked Nora up, scattering the cards in her hand.

"Daddy—"

"Game over, sweetheart."

She clasped him around the neck and put her soft baby lips to his ear. "Story?"

"Done."

Mayra stood and stretched. "Dad, I've got tons of homework." She started across the room, pausing to thump Hank the Hilarious on the head.

"Get at it, then. Lights out for you at ten. It's 7:23 now. You've got"—he looked at his watch—"exactly two hours and thirty-seven minutes. Don't waste time."

She groaned like a theater diva.

Annie and Roger exchanged looks, clearly communicating *shall it be me or you this time?*

Annie lost. "Don't be a drama queen," she said, hands on her hips.

Mayra stopped halfway up the stairs and spun. "Like you *weren't* a drama queen at dinner? Unfortunately, I'm a chip off that old block, Mom." She ran up to the landing and turned the corner before Annie could reply.

Roger threw up his hands and turned to Hank. "That was a good joke, Hankster the Prankster. And good delivery. You're getting better. Now, do you have homework?"

"Nah. Finished it."

Too quick, slick . . .

Roger was on it. "I'll take a look at it, then, after I get Kimmie and Nora down."

Hank threw up his hands at Roger's parental diligence, stomped toward the stairs, pivoting in a last-ditch effort. "Dad—"

Roger cut him off. "You're first in the shower. You can use ours while I give the girls a bath."

"But—"

"This is not a democracy, Hank. It's not up for a vote. Come on. Everyone upstairs, on the double!"

Roger stood back and let Hank and Kimmie precede him up the stairs. He gave Annie a victory sign and salute before following them up.

Halfway up he stopped and turned. "Great dinner tonight, hon."

He winked, then nuzzled Nora's face as he started up the stairs again. "Come on, sweetie. Your princess story awaits."

Nora's bright-blue eyes were the last thing Annie saw, peering over Roger's shoulder.

Annie stood a moment longer, focused on the childish cacophony upstairs.

"Hey, I was first. You have to wait."

"Get out of my way."

"Dad said—"

"No he didn't."

"Yes he did. You weren't listening."

Then Roger's voice rising above the fray, telling them to stop all this nonsense.

Annie listened and grinned, glad it was Roger refereeing. The earlier tension had been replaced by the every-night bedtime shenanigans. Sometimes the noisy routine produced a headache, but not tonight. Tonight it was a welcome diversion to the usual Thursday weirdness.

Back in the dining room, she looked down the long table, littered with dirty plates and crumbs and half-filled water glasses, detritus of another family meal. Overhead she heard the giggles and thumps of bedtime—daddy-style—as Roger settled them down.

What if?

Mayra's essay question loomed in Annie's mind. *If I knew I would die tomorrow . . .*

Annie stepped into the adjoining family room, filled with family pictures and child-made knickknacks, evidence of fifteen years of parenting in this house.

And butterflies. Everywhere.

Ever since grade school, Annie had been fascinated with butterflies and had collected photographs, books, and small figurines, which were now scattered throughout the Lee home. She even had a set of silver-trimmed red, green, and blue butterfly Christmas-tree ornaments, usually a big hit with friends and family during the holidays.

When she was old enough—in her early high school years—her parents had bought her a camera, and she'd started taking photos of butterflies. She had albums filled with colorful varieties, and her passion for the winged creatures had resulted in a few school essays that had wowed her teachers.

Roger had asked her once, when they'd first started dating, why she liked butterflies. She'd had trouble coming up with an answer then, but she knew what it was now. Butterflies escape from their ugly, wormlike existence to become gorgeous winged creatures capable of flying away as high as they wanted, escaping the confines of gravity.

She picked up one of her favorites now and turned it over in her hand—a monarch with vivid orange wings, long antennae, and colorful markings on the tail. She'd found this one in an antique store nearby, and in spite of it being overpriced, she'd bought it. Poised for flight on a small ceramic-leaved branch, wings stretched, the insect looked as regal as its name.

Butterflies were the only winged insect Nora wasn't afraid of, and this particular one was also Nora's favorite. She'd once asked Annie if it could fly all the way up to heaven. Of course, Annie had told her it could.

Nora's face had lit up. She'd run around the living room flapping her butterfly wings, shrieking that she was in heaven, and "Come with me, Mommy!"

Annie recalled grasping Nora by a wing and telling her to settle down, that it wasn't time to be in heaven just yet. Nora had pouted and said, "How do you know, Mommy?"

Annie replaced the figurine, thinking that if she had to be anything else in the universe but human—if a genie suddenly appeared out of one of her flower vases and made her choose—she'd become a monarch butterfly. After the four stages of growth, clinging to the underside of a milkweed plant, she'd grow beautiful wings and fly away from all the sadness in the world. And as an extra bonus, she'd only have to exist for five to six weeks at the most. Not decades and decades of turmoil and tragedy and fear, as was the lot of humanity.

She'd never have to build another fence to keep the bad out of their yard or drive by Kimmie's school at recess time to make sure she was there—on the swings or the merry-go-round. She wouldn't have to log in to the high school app on her phone to confirm Mayra was there, evidenced by turned-in homework from the night before. Never have to count her migraine tablets or Roger's pills for back-pain flare-ups, to quell the fear that one of the kids was taking them or, God forbid, selling them.

And she'd never have to look over her shoulder again at the park or the grocery store or even the church parking lot, wondering if someone was there, stalking her or leering at tiny Nora gripping her hand.

Yes, if she could choose, she'd be a butterfly, here now and gone in a blink.

5

Annie retraced her steps into the dining room. Two large, elegantly wood-framed pictures graced the center of the pale-yellow wall, beckoning her closer. They hung, lined up perfectly, over the antique buffet cabinet inherited from her great-grandmother. A small, empty rectangular space divided the two pictures, just big enough for a five by seven. Annie lingered over it for just a second.

Mayra's essay echoing in her brain, she caressed the space with her index finger. *No. Not now.* She couldn't think about that right now, just before bed time. If she did, she knew she wouldn't sleep.

She focused on the larger frames. Roger's parents and her own smiled at her from the two pictures. All four had died before Mayra was born—Roger's parents first, in a car accident, and her own a year later in a freak boating accident. Their parents had never met their only grandchildren—neither she nor Roger had siblings.

She remembered the day the two of them had hung these photos like it was yesterday.

He'd said, "Here? Right in here where we eat every day? It'll be like my parents are spying on us." That'd been twenty years ago, when they'd first moved in.

She'd laughed. "Yeah, that's true. But you wanna know what's worse? *My* dad will be watching you." The look on his face had been priceless, like on their first date when Roger and her father shook hands for the first time. Roger froze, like a rabbit in the headlights.

Their fathers had been best friends and had married best friends, having met in boot camp. After the years of moving around, then mustering out, Annie's parents had finally settled close to their roots in Washington State when Annie was ten, while Roger's folks had lived in Germany for a few years, then settled on the East Coast. The friends had kept in touch though, and Roger's parents eventually moved to Washington. Annie and Roger were the same age and had met for the first time as seniors in high school.

Annie loved these two pictures. Her father had sandy-brown hair, and her father-in-law's was jet black. Both men wore formal naval dinner dress uniforms, their bars making a colorful splash on their black jackets topped with stiff white bow ties.

Two sets of deep-brown eyes stared out of the pictures, focused on something beyond her. She'd always had the curious sensation that their fathers were sizing up some unknown enemy lurking behind her. She stopped herself now from turning and looking, as she'd often done before. There'd never been anything there. They'd both spent time deployed overseas on foreign coastlines, protecting US forces and evacuating women and children. She guessed their eyes had always focused on hidden dangers, ready to protect their own families at the merest hint.

Their mothers wore formal attire also, complete with corsages. Roger's mother wore pale blue, and Annie's wore regal red. Worry lines crinkled around their eyes, like so many women whose husbands wore uniforms. Thankfully, Roger had never had to wear one. She knew that sometimes he wished he'd had that honor. He had the greatest admiration for both their fathers, but she was grateful she'd never had to say goodbye to him in that way.

Annie roused herself. If she wanted a walk, she'd better get busy.

She cleared the table, put the leftover food in the fridge, and loaded the dishwasher.

As she worked, she thought about Mayra's essay question. It seemed like such a macabre subject for a tenth grader—and the question weighed on her.

How *would* she answer?

What would it be like to know for sure? To know she'd die the next day?

She shook her head. Seemed to her like one of those questions no one could answer.

Tying up the trash, Annie stepped out the back door and toward the street. She dropped the trash bag into the small wheeled dumpster at the edge of the driveway, breathing deeply of the cleansed, damp air of mid-February.

The sounds of their small neighborhood, muted by heavy fog, seeped into her ears—a garage door closed somewhere, a woman laughed, a car door slammed. The neighbors at the corner had twin Great Danes that behaved like a hired security team, barking ferociously at any sound. They woofed a duet now as Annie dropped the dumpster lid with a crash.

Comforting, familiar sounds. Across the street to the south, their elderly neighbors, John and Eleanor Baxter, sat close together on folding chairs on their enclosed front porch. Annie knew it was a nightly ritual for them. They were always together, always holding hands.

John and Eleanor were a staple of familiarity in the small neighborhood. They knew everyone's names and delighted in the children who sometimes played in the street. Eleanor, never without her flowered apron, always had brownies or chocolate chip cookies to pass around.

Annie had enjoyed some conversations with Eleanor over the years. Her favorite goodbye phrase was, "See you tomorrow . . . maybe. Never know."

Once Annie had asked her why she always said that. Eleanor had smiled and said, "Isn't it the truth?"

"Well, yeah, but it seems so depressing," Annie had replied.

"Depressing? What's depressing about leaving this depressing world? And, my dear, since when is the truth depressing?" She'd patted Annie's hand and told her someday she'd understand. Someday when she was older.

I'm not older yet, Eleanor.

Annie saw Eleanor lift a hand in greeting. She waved back, smiled, then turned to go back in the house.

Something in her side vision caught her eye.

Annie swiveled back toward the street. She saw it again, in the glow of the streetlamp. Walking across the damp grass, she reached the waist-high white picket fence Roger had built three or so years ago. It ringed their front yard on three sides, following the sides of the house and meeting the high board fence that enclosed the backyard.

Roger had argued—they didn't need a fence around both front and back yards. His justification was the safety and security of this neighborhood. The neighbors always watched out for each other, he'd said. And they had gotten along without a front yard fence for a while, so why now?

Nora, Annie had answered. And that was the end of the discussion. He'd built it over the next three weekends, with help from John Baxter, still strong and healthy in his eighties. And Hank—

but at only ten years old, Hank mostly slowed them down. Roger was so patient with him, though, that Hank still talked about "the time I helped Dad build the fence."

She stepped to the driveway edge, to the corner where Hank's soccer ball had kissed the fence last spring. One picket had come loose and now leaned sideways. Bending low, she saw that Roger still hadn't fixed it. She'd have to get after him again. In the daylight, everyone on the block could see the crooked board. He'd promised to fix it but never seemed to have the time. Maybe she'd do it herself.

Annie moved the offending picket back into line with the rest of the fence, then stepped back to check it. She adjusted it another millimeter, then nodded.

Fences were important.

She entered the back door and stepped into the kitchen. All was quiet upstairs. Roger was probably reading the promised story to Kimmie and Nora.

Annie grabbed her jacket off the hook in the back hallway, stepped back into the dining room, and stopped at the pictures of their parents again. Their solemn eyes bored into hers. An uncanny feeling swamped her, like they were trying to tell her something. Something vital. She searched their faces for a clue, but there was nothing.

A shimmer caught her eye from the center of her parents' photo. Her mother clutched her father's arm tightly, the fingers of her right hand exposed. The shimmer emanated from the ring her mother wore, identical to the one on her mother-in-law's hand. According to the story, Roger's and Annie's fathers had given their young wives the rings just prior to their first deployment to southeast Asia toward the end of the Vietnam War, before Annie and Roger were born. The two mothers always said they would never part with them—the rings were a promise from their husbands that they would come back. They'd kept that promise, only to die stateside with their wives years later.

Annie shook her head. Such needless tragedy.

She leaned in close and could barely make out the detail— ornate silver band and a gleaming thread of pale turquoise. Both rings were heavy, with large, flat milky-white stones in the centers. Roger and Annie always wondered what had happened to the rings after their parents had died. They'd disappeared mysteriously, without a trace.

She focused on the center of the white stone on her mother's ring, then jerked back from the picture.

What was this?

Pain shot into her neck. Rubbing it, she leaned forward again.

Strange. She must be seeing things—the stone was different. Were those words?

Her gaze darted to the other picture. Transfixed, Annie saw that the ring on her mother-in-law's hand also looked different. But . . . how could that be?

She stepped even closer, her knees bent in order to get as near to the pictures as possible.

Tiny words were etched on the stones of both rings. Words she'd never noticed before, neither in these pictures nor on the rings themselves when their mothers had worn them.

Annie shuffled back, reached behind her, and grabbed for the edge of the dining room table. She leaned back on it, breathing heavily. Her mouth felt dry, like the sagebrush-littered hills surrounding their town.

What was happening to her? She rubbed her eyes and looked again. Leaning toward the photos, she reached and touched her mother's ring, rubbing her index finger over it.

Where had these words come from?

The photographs had hung in this dining room for twenty

years. She could swear these words had never been part of these rings until this very moment.

Annie looked from one ring to the other, squinting at the twin phrases. She couldn't make out the words. She jerked open the top drawer of the buffet and rummaged through little-used serving utensils, Christmas napkins, and other odds and ends.

She spied what she wanted—Roger's tiny magnifying glass.

She slid it out of its case and placed it over both rings in turn, moving it until she could decipher what the markings were. Snakelike letters came into focus.

Just two words.

No tomorrows.

Annie dropped the magnifying glass back into the open drawer and slammed it shut.

Her head jerked upward as a gleeful shriek from Nora wafted downstairs. Bedtime with Daddy was rarely quiet for long.

She leaned forward again and looked into her mother's eyes, then down at the ring again.

She thought she knew what her mother was trying to say, but Annie didn't want to hear it.

Backing away, Annie Lee threw her jacket around her shoulders and fled out the front door.

6

Annie's sandals squished on the wet pavement. She should have changed to sneakers but hadn't wanted to take the time. She had to escape the house. She had to stop this madness.

Escape? Madness? Those were curious words for a married forty-something, churchgoing mother of four to think.

They scared her. Those words didn't fit into her ordered universe. But that ordered universe she'd created for herself was never more than one moment of inattention away. She knew that. She thought she'd prepared for that, but after tonight, she wasn't so sure.

The fog had closed in again after the late-afternoon pounding rain. It eddied around her, shrouding her in cold white anonymity as she walked away from the house.

She zipped her jacket and flipped her hood up over her head. It felt good to be walking somewhere, anywhere. She looked up into the fog and determined to find *as usual* again.

As Annie left the porch and gained the sidewalk, her phone

vibrated in the pocket of her jeans, startling her. She'd forgotten it was there.

Pulling it out, she saw it was Ellen. She smiled when her friend's assigned photo came up on the caller ID—the little redheaded girl from the Charlie Brown cartoons. Ellen's flaming-red hair hadn't dimmed one iota over the thirty-odd years they'd known each other.

Ellen was likely disgruntled that Annie hadn't return her call from earlier this evening. She'd just have to get over it. Ellen knew that Annie had strict rules about phone calls during family time.

"Hi, Ellen. What's up?"

"You busy?"

"Just out walking."

"At this hour?"

"It's barely eight o'clock. You're making us sound like geriatrics, for crying out loud."

"Yeah, but aren't you usually hunkered down at home about now? Homework, bedtime? All the usual stuff?"

"Roger's putting the kids down. I needed some air. Now, what's up? For the second time."

"You coming tomorrow?"

"Of course."

"Bringing Nora?"

"Don't I usually?"

"Usually. Your favorite word."

"What's that supposed to mean? I don't have a favorite word."

"Chocolate?"

"There's that."

"I just meant that you like to have a plan and work the plan. And the plan never varies."

"Hey . . . my plans vary sometimes."

"Not since high school."

"Don't be ridiculous." Annie stopped walking to concentrate on where in the world Ellen was going with this jumbled conversation.

"Let's see. It's Thursday. Pork chops and mashed potatoes for dinner?"

Annie broke out in a sweat. "Well . . ."

"You did, didn't you? And you made those cheesy mashed potatoes—"

"Yeah, but I didn't put onion salt in them this time—"

"Big deal. It's Thursday, and I know exactly what you made for dinner."

"So what? The kids love my pork chops. They expect it. If I didn't—"

"What, the world would end? There wouldn't be a tomorrow?"

Annie gripped the phone tighter. "Ellen, what's going on in that head of yours?"

"Let's see . . ." Ellen continued. "You still fold your dirty laundry before putting it in the hamper?"

Should she tell Ellen what she'd dreamed about last night? Where she'd stood on shore and watched the speedboat careen toward her parents? No, Ellen would just demand all the details and analyze it to death. Dreams meant nothing, after all.

"Get over it. I can fit more in the hamper that way."

"Right. You know that's not why. So tell me about a variation to your routine. Right now. Betcha can't."

The rings?

"Hmm. Well . . . I'll get back to you on that."

"Thought so. Did you think of Abby today? Or butterflies? You always do on Thursdays. It was on a Thursday that—"

"Stop being so snarky." Annie gripped the hem of her jacket. "Why did you call? Just to find out if I'll be there tomorrow? You've never done that before. Or to find out if I still fold my dirty laundry? Or made pork chops for dinner?"

"Not usual, huh? You rattled?"

"Come on, Ellen. What gives?"

"You *are* rattled, I can tell. You get this little squeak at the end of your sentences."

"I don't squeak—"

"Have you told the kids yet about Abby? That they had . . . you had—"

"Mind your own business, Ellen."

"I thought not."

"Ellen, for crying out loud, what does it matter now that I had a sister—what?—forty years ago? A sister I never even met. It'd mean nothing to them."

"Says you."

Annie dropped the phone to her side and tilted her head to the sky. Ellen was *so* exasperating sometimes. Always poking around, trying to get her to loosen up, to break her own rules.

Ellen's voice, pressed into Annie's thigh, sounded frantic now. Annie put the phone back to her ear.

"Ellen."

"Thank God. Where'd you go?"

"Ellen, why did you call?"

"Just wanted to hear your voice, I guess. Been hearing it since fifth grade. Remember the day we met?"

"Of course. Pink sneakers. We finished each other's sentences that day for the first time. I can still hear the other kids laughing at us."

Ellen didn't answer right away. Annie waited. Two cats squared off on Annie's left, growling and yowling at each other in turn.

"Annie?"

"What?"

"Don't ever forget me."

"What're you talking about? Why would I? We see each other at least three times a week—"

"Usually. But usually doesn't last forever, you know. It always ends at some point."

"You're talking crazy."

"If ever you wake up and I'm not here, you know where I'll be. Just don't forget me. I couldn't stand it if you forgot me. I mean, I'd want you to move on, make new friends, but . . ."

Annie couldn't think of a thing to say. What'd gotten into Ellen? Her best friend since fifth grade had been replaced by a stranger, like some sci-fi movie.

"Annie?"

"Fine. I won't forget you."

"Thanks."

"And by the way, I've had some weirdness of my own today—"

"Gotta run. See you tomorrow."

"But—"

Click.

1

Annie stared at her phone, then shoved it back into her pocket. Ellen, as much as she loved her, had always been a little off the rails.

She stood on the cold, drizzled sidewalk, remembering Ellen in grade school. Such a clown, always making the kids laugh with her antics. And she wasn't above playing tricks on the teachers too—which had often landed her in the principal's office.

Annie had tried to squelch Ellen's enthusiasm for hijinks, worried about the trouble she always seemed to attract, but Ellen wouldn't have any of it and told her to lighten up. Still told her. But the truth was, Ellen had been right, just now on the phone. Annie needed the rules, the boundaries, and the fences to feel safe. Ellen never cared about feeling safe. Her mantra was that life wasn't about being safe—it was about pushing back.

Annie sighed and started walking again. She knew she'd never change, and neither would Ellen. They were stuck with each other, she guessed, and the pinky-swear promises they'd made on the playground made them best friends forever.

Annie walked to the end of the street, where a path veered to the right. The play area where she and Roger had often enjoyed hide-and-seek, tag, and catch with the children over the years was just a few steps down the path that wound through the park.

She swerved onto the path. It was dark, but the trail was lit by ground-level lanterns and overhead by bright decorative lamps, and she didn't plan to go far.

Just back about forty years, I guess. Back to Abby . . .

The air smelled fresh and clean. She glanced back and saw nothing but whiteness behind her. It reminded her of the rings—it was almost like she was inside the rings.

What a fanciful thought . . .

She brushed damp hair out of her eyes. She could just make out the swing set a few yards in front of her. She smiled as she recalled countless hours of happy laughter playing on these swings with her children—and even before that. She and Roger used to come here before Mayra was born and push each other, ride the merry-go-round, play with frisbees. They'd been so young when they'd married, just out of high school and still children themselves. They'd decided to wait at least three years before having kids.

Then the three years became five while they grieved for their parents. Images, some indistinct, some wretchedly vivid now, coursed through her brain cells.

The wrecked, burned-out car resting at the bottom of the canyon where Roger's parents had breathed their last. When their corpses were recovered, they were still holding hands. Seeing that, it was the only time Roger had broken down and wept.

Annie shook her head at the memory of her strong, capable, optimistic husband weeping over the bodies of his parents. He couldn't touch them, hold them, even get within ten yards of them because of the barriers erected by state troopers.

Weeks of meetings with attorneys followed as they'd gone through every minute detail of their lives, searching for anything that would help the case against the drunk driver who'd struck them head on. One attorney had told Roger that anything that would make his dad and mom look good—like heroes—would result in a bigger financial settlement and a longer prison sentence for the other driver. As if it was about money. And of course, one was criminal and the other civil. But still.

It had been an excruciating time for Roger. Every memory they'd dug up prolonged the agony of losing them. Once, in one of those meetings, he'd had a meltdown and yelled at the tribunal of experts and attorneys at the other end of the ornate conference table.

His usually calm, polite demeanor had exploded like a bomb. He'd jumped up and rounded the table in front of the others, shaking his fist in their faces. "They *are* heroes—you trying to scrape all this stuff out of me doesn't make them any more heroic."

And her own parents, barely a year later. Her father, a decorated naval officer, *drowns*? Her mother's body was all but cut in half when the speedboat hit their jet ski at forty miles an hour. More meetings with attorneys, as if all the money in the world would make the pain stop, buy them an escape from feeling like orphans, or provide their future children with loving grandparents. Absurd.

Somehow during that five years of grief recovery, they'd both gotten their college degrees, he in finance and she in literature.

And then the world righted itself in the form of children born to them. Children who'd never have grandparents.

Annie stepped off the path to the wet grass, again wishing she'd changed from sandals to sneakers—now her toes were wet and cold.

Shadows enclosed her. Annie was glad the swings weren't near the trees and shrubs lining the perimeter of the play area. She didn't fancy having her back to them. Just last year, there was a story in the news about two young girls who'd encountered a too-friendly man in this very park. Luckily, their moms were vigilant that day and nothing happened. Even in a small town, you had to be careful.

She sat on one of the swings, feeling the icy puddle of water on her backside. No matter. Annie didn't much care at this point. She needed to think. She looked at her watch in the lamplight. She'd only been gone twenty minutes—Roger was probably still reading to the kids. She hoped he'd chosen an uplifting story and had not been swayed by Hank's usual picks—anything involving swords, knives, and bad guys. He was certainly all boy.

Roger had been that way when they'd first met in high school. He'd mimicked the strong protector, boasting how his uncle had taught him to hunt, fish, and target shoot. Her face softened as she thought of the stories he'd told her of hiking to the old quarry with his uncle and shooting at soup cans, balloons, and plastic jugs filled with colored water. He bragged about how he could shoot better than his uncle. He was still her protector. Always would be.

Her brain returned to the puzzle.

Annie didn't feel up to tackling the mystery of the rings yet, so she focused on Mayra's essay first. It seemed more of a straight-forward problem than mysterious words appearing on rings where they'd never been before.

What *would* she do tomorrow if she found out—for sure— she'd die the next day? Forget trying to figure out *how* she would know for sure. Just assume that somehow she knew.

So what would I do?

Go to the church and talk to their pastor? She imagined presenting herself to him and saying, "Good morning, Pastor Mike. God told me I would die tomorrow, so I thought I'd come and talk it over with you. Are there any verses in the Bible that cover this?"

She visualized his concerned face. He'd probably get right on the phone and call a meeting of the church leaders to pray over her mental state.

"Annie Lee requests prayer because she thinks she is going to die tomorrow."

It'd go out on the prayer chain, then people's tongues would start wagging.

She smiled and shook her head. *No.*

She dug her sandals in and pushed herself. As she glided back and forth, she wrestled with the answer. It wasn't an unfamiliar question—humankind had batted it around for millennia.

She'd just never faced it at the dinner table, in front of her children, for God's sake.

What was that teacher thinking anyway, assigning an essay like that to a group of fifteen-year-olds? Maybe she should call the principal of the high school tomorrow.

Maybe, if the day after tomorrow was to be the day of her passing, she'd go see Ellen. At least they could cry together and she could ask Ellen to be there for her kids. She knew Ellen would. She was always the brains of the outfit—if a bit quirky—ever since they'd met. Ellen would figure something out, maybe have a wise answer for her. At least Annie knew Ellen would make her laugh over it. Would tell her not to take herself so seriously.

Or maybe she wouldn't go see anyone. She'd just get in her car and drive somewhere. Maybe it would be better to be alone and talk to God. Dying was a solitary thing—even if you died in a plane crash with hundreds of other people, you still had to do your own death alone.

Annie dragged her foot on the ground to stop swinging.

How could you plan tomorrow if you knew there wouldn't be a tomorrow after it?

Annie shook her head at the knotty question. The curious thing was, she wasn't afraid to think about it anymore. Something had changed. She now considered the question logically, dispassionately—unlike at dinner, when she'd had to hide under the table to stop her fingers from shaking.

That's probably because I'm not convinced. I don't really believe I'll die the day after tomorrow. It's not real. If it were . . .

If it were, she wouldn't be sitting here in the park, alone, after dark. She'd be with Roger—

"Something to think about, isn't it, Annie?"

The warm, deep voice sliced the fog behind her, shattering the stillness of the black night.

8

nnie leaped off the swing. Her feet tangled, and she fell, landing in a sandy mud puddle. Scrambling up, she gripped the swing's chain, chest heaving. Eyes darting this way and that, she saw nothing. She let go of the swing, rotated, and strode back toward the street and home. She must hurry. Her foot left the damp sand of the play area and touched the grass.

A chuckle stopped her. Annie whipped around, one hand to her throat, the other flung out in front of her.

He sat on the swing she'd just fallen out of.

She backed up, tripped over a discarded rubber ball, and almost fell again.

"Now, Annie, you must be more careful. You've got a big day tomorrow—"

Annie blustered, frightened out of her wits. "Who are you? I've never seen you around here before."

"There are many things you've never seen before."

Her lungs emptied. The heavy fog suffocated her—she breathed it, choked on its milkiness like she was drowning in it. All she could think of was the usual end of a situation like this—a woman alone in the dark with a strange man who seemed unhinged.

Or am I the one unhinged?

Scenes from dark, nasty movies—movies she shouldn't have watched—careened through her mind.

"What . . . what do you want?"

The man's eyes shone in the moonlight. But there was no moon—the fog and clouds covered it.

Annie's gaze darted upward, looking for the source of the light. It couldn't be the park lights above—they were behind him. And there were no foot-level lanterns around the play area.

Her head rotated back by inches until she faced him again. The skin on her face felt tight, stretched to the breaking point. Fear was now an ocean she swam in.

Her hand closed around the small container of pepper spray she always carried in her pocket.

"What do I want? Why, nothing, Annie. It's what *you* want that's important."

"I . . . I don't want anything from you. Except for you to get away from me and leave me alone."

"Come now. I'm not going to hurt you. If that was my intent, I would've already done it."

She thought she saw a twinkle in his left eye.

"Then why are you here? What do you want? And how do you know my name?" The questions shot out of her mouth like bullets from a rifle on full automatic.

He stood. His head swiveled first right, then left, as if making sure they were alone.

He lowered his voice, silky and comforting. "I'm here to help you answer the question. And I know your name because I've always known your name, Annie." He gestured toward her with both palms up, as if inviting her to come closer.

In spite of herself, there was something about him that intrigued her. He was so *ordinary*.

Yet, he'd *always known her*? Definitely not ordinary . . .

She wiped her trembling hands on her jacket and pushed her hood back from her face, still clutching the pepper spray.

Annie couldn't help herself—she had to know. She took a hesitant step toward him, feet on the sand again. But no closer.

She knew this was foolhardy. One side of her brain argued with the other, telling her to leave . . . *now*. The foolhardy side won the debate.

The fog lifted for a moment, and she saw his face clearly.

"You know my name. What's yours? And why did you say I have a big day tomorrow—what can you possibly know about tomorrow?"

"Joshua. You can call me Josh though."

He didn't elaborate, didn't answer her question. Just stood there with his thumbs hooked in his jeans pockets.

"I'm not going to call you anything. I'm leaving."

He shrugged.

Annie scrutinized his features, thinking she might have to describe him to the police. He had kind brown eyes and a gentle mouth. His longish black hair curled around his leather coat collar, open to reveal a blue Seattle Seahawks sweatshirt. She judged him to be in his thirties, maybe forties. Muscular, but not overly so. A normal-looking man who'd fit in anywhere, even in the park at twilight.

Then *normal* vanished into the fog.

Joshua reached into his inside coat pocket, pulled out a small square box—shiny black—and held it out to her.

"This is for you, Annie. It'll help you think."

She froze. It looked like—exactly like—a ring box.

"You should wear it tomorrow."

Her eyes darted right and left. The large, rambling park squeezed and contracted until the boundaries were no bigger than the sandy play area on which they stood—about twenty square yards. The fog walled them in, making it feel like they were the only two people on the planet. Annie couldn't see the grass or trees beyond the sand, as if the rest of the park had vanished into thin air.

"Go ahead, take it. Go back home to your family. But don't forget to wear it tomorrow."

Annie couldn't take her eyes off the box. Unable to breathe, hands clutching the hem of her jacket, her knees buckled. She sank to the wet grass, her legs folded under her.

Tearing her eyes away from the box, she stared at his face. Moisture dripped off the tip of her nose.

He exhaled and stepped toward her, his gaze never leaving her face.

"You're scared. I'm sorry."

Annie opened her mouth. She wanted to scream at him, to call for Roger, for help from anywhere. But she couldn't force enough air into her lungs to make a sound.

Joshua squatted, six feet away, his gentle eyes locked on hers.

"Your mother was scared too. When your father put the ring on her finger, her first reaction was fear. But then she learned the lesson of the ring—although it took her a while. You will too, Annie."

Annie shrank back in terror, one hand clutching her middle and the other covering her mouth. Her stomach churned with vomit.

She wretched out the words surging up from her gut. "What do you know about my mother? She has nothing to do with you. If you don't get away from me, I swear I'll scream at the top of my lungs. Then you'll wish you'd never come here—"

He stood, stepped a pace back, and stretched an open palm toward her. "Okay, my dear."

"Don't you dare call me that."

"Okay, Annie. I'm leaving now. But first, promise me you'll take the box."

"I'll do no such thing."

Shrugging, he set the box on the seat of the swing, then turned his back on her, shuffling across the grass, in the opposite direction from the neighborhood.

He stopped a few feet away and swiveled in slow motion to face her. "Take the box, Annie. We'll talk again . . . soon."

Her heart seized, then beat again. "Wait—"

Wait? What was she saying? She wanted him to leave . . .

Then he was gone, swallowed by the fog as if he'd never been. He disappeared in pieces—first his arms, then his back, then his left foot. His right foot was the last to go.

Annie sat motionless for several moments, her mind emptied of coherent thought, her vision ending where she'd last seen the thick tread on the bottom of his right hiking boot.

She stared at the spot, thinking he'd pop out of the fog and say that one of her friends—Ellen, maybe—had put him up to it. He'd introduce himself, they'd laugh, and she'd plot her revenge. But . . .

Of course he's not coming back. He's not real. He can't be real.

But if he wasn't real, then what was he? What did that say about her mental condition? That she'd just spent the last thirty minutes talking to a figment of her imagination?

He had to be real though, because his footprint lay right there in the sand next to the swing. Figments didn't make footprints, right?

She peered at it, remembering the tread on his right boot.

It was the same.

Annie sat unmoving. She couldn't move if she'd wanted to. Her knees locked, her hands gripped the edging surrounding the play area, and her mind froze. The cold sank into her bones, but sweat dripped on her forehead and leaked between her shoulder blades.

Somewhere in the distance a motorcycle revved to life. His? His jacket looked like one a biker would wear. She hadn't seen a helmet though . . .

She shook her head and wiped her hands across her face. *Who cares about his clothes?*

She couldn't stay here. She had to get out of here, get back home to her family. Annie heaved herself up, hearing her knees creak as they unlocked.

She rotated and stumbled back onto the grass as a thought forced itself into the forefront of her brain.

She couldn't leave it here.

Annie tottered to the swing, grabbing at the chain. It creaked, deafening in the misty silence. Looking around, seeing nothing and no one, she picked up the box. She half expected a bolt of lightning to strike her when she touched it, but the night shadows only cozied around her. Lifting the lid, she saw what she expected to see.

A ring, heavy silver setting, with tiny letters etched in the white stone.

A twig crackled behind her.

She whirled, holding her arms out in front of her.

A long-haired white cat jumped the high board fence directly across from her, then hopped down and disappeared into the yard on the other side, no doubt on its way home.

Annie settled her nerves again and held the ring up to the glow of the lamplight, reading the words.

No tomorrows.

Her throat constricted. It didn't matter that she'd expected to see those words.

Annie clamped the lid down on the box and drew her arm back like she had when she'd pitched on her high school softball team. She flung it as hard as she could. It bounced, then rolled end over end toward the massive oak tree on the edge of the play area.

Good. She didn't need this weirdness.

Annie jerked around and strode to the path out of the park.

But as she put her left foot down on the paved pathway, she stopped and looked up over the roofs of the houses ringing the park, vaguely aware that all the normal night sounds—owls hooting, dogs barking, traffic—faded as she stared into the foggy darkness. The night covered her like a weighted blanket, heavy and still.

What she saw made her rub her eyes and hope it was a dream.

It was not.

It hung over the nearest house for a moment, huge and shimmering. Then it floated to her on the fog like an alien spaceship.

The framed picture of her parents—the one she'd left securely fastened to the pale-yellow wall in her dining room—hovered just over the tree nearest the play area. It spun around, the back of the frame showing for a moment, then spun again, her parents facing her. The frame grew until it obliterated the neighborhood beyond. When it stopped growing, it was so close Annie could reach out and touch her mother.

When she did, her finger went through her mother's shoulder. She panicked and snatched it back, shoving a fist into her mouth to stop the scream rushing from her toes.

God, what is happening? her mind shrieked. *Why are you doing this to me?*

She wanted to run, but her feet had taken root in the grass. She tried to close her eyes, but they wouldn't obey. She had no choice but to watch.

Annie saw the frame constrict and the human likenesses become more distinct, like a photo editor sharpening details of a fuzzy image. Then the frame disappeared.

Her father faded away pixel by pixel, like an unseen hand using a digital eraser. She stretched out her hand, as if to prevent him leaving.

No! Don't go, Daddy . . .

Then her mother disappeared in the same way until only her eyes remained, the corners downturned, moisture threatening to spill to her cheeks. Her mother stared out of the misty darkness.

What? What are you saying to me, Mom?

The misery in her mother's eyes drew her in, threatened to drown her. Annie waited for an answer. But there wasn't one. All rational thought fled.

What? Is it me, Mom? Have I done something to disappoint you? Or . . . is it Abby?

Annie remembered stamping her foot when she was a child and didn't get her way. Her right foot now itched, but she held it firmly in place. She wasn't a child anymore, and she was past disappointing her mother.

She backed away, but the eyes followed her.

"Stop it." Annie felt foolish yelling to the sky. But evidently her yell of frustration worked.

Her mother's eyes narrowed to slits and became a horizontal line. The line shrank to a dot, then a pinprick, and disappeared, like punching the Off button on her grandparents' old picture-tube television.

So that's how it's going to be. Fine.

Annie retraced her steps back to the grass. She kicked leaves and branches aside and found the box where it had fetched up under the tree. She shoved it deep into her pocket, then turned to head for home and safety.

As she passed the swing again, she stopped at the offending footprint. Something broke in her mind. Angry, she obliterated the tread with her sandaled foot, flinging sand between her toes. She didn't care.

Home. I have to get home.

Annie turned and fled, not stopping until she stood on her porch.

9

She let herself in, then turned the deadbolt. Upstairs, silence reigned. The hands on the living room clock told her she'd been gone about forty minutes—it was closing in on 9:00 p.m. She expected Roger to be reading in bed, where he usually was at this time. At least she hoped so. She'd had just about enough of this night.

Annie tiptoed into the kitchen to get a glass of water, stopping at the stairs to pick up Hank's soccer shoes, one resting on the bottom step and the other two steps up. She put them in the Upstairs Box sitting conveniently to the side of the stairs—the box the children were to pile their belongings in until they went up to their rooms the next time. Hank's rarely made it into the box. It'd become a family joke. If Hank couldn't find something, someone would snicker and say "Goooo toward the box, Hank" in an eerie-sounding voice.

Annie brought her ice-cold water back into the living room and chugged it as she gazed out the window into the darkness. Across the street, the neighbors' porch light was still on. That was odd. They never left it on this late. She stared at the light, feeling a stab of fear. Maybe something was wrong over there. Maybe she should go check—

Why was everything scaring her? She'd had a weird evening. So what? Maybe it was something she'd eaten at dinner or the phone call from Ellen. That was it—she'd blame Ellen. She'd tell her about all of it tomorrow, and Ellen would laugh at her and tell her not to be such a silly goose.

As Annie climbed the stairs, she remembered what had started the weird. Tomorrow might be her last day. She'd come full circle and once again felt the brush of buzzards' wings as they wheeled overhead, waiting.

She pushed the bedroom door open a crack. Roger seemed to be asleep, his head lolled to the side, book splayed open on his chest.

Good. He'd just ask her stuff she didn't want to deal with.

She tiptoed toward their bathroom.

His garbled words, spoken through a wide yawn, stopped her in her tracks. "Hey. Did you have a good walk?"

She stepped through the bathroom door. "Yes. I'll be out in a minute."

"Okay." He snapped his book shut.

Annie brushed her teeth and her hair, lathered her face with lotion, and couldn't think of anything else to prolong the inevitable. After slipping into her nightgown, she opened the bathroom door.

Roger stood in front of the window overlooking their front yard.

He spoke without turning around. "The fog lifted." Then, "The Baxters' porch light is still on. That's odd, don't you think?"

Here it went—she must nip it in the bud. "Maybe they forgot.

They're allowed."

He shrugged. "Don't recall it ever happening before, that's all." He stepped back to the bed and slid in, plumping his pillows. He looked up at her.

She'd stopped halfway from the bathroom to the bed.

He patted the quilt next to him. "Aren't you coming to bed?"

Her feet wouldn't move.

"Honey, what's wrong?" He sat up and threw back the covers on her side. "Come on. You need some sleep. I know you were a little tense earlier, but I thought your walk helped."

If he only knew.

"Do you want to talk about it?"

Maybe I should tell him.

She relaxed her hands, slid in, and covered her bare feet. "I've just had the most frightening thoughts flying around my head. I can't seem to relax."

She stopped short of telling him what had happened in the park, knowing what he'd do next—fling his clothes on and charge out to look for the guy. But he'd never find him. He was part of the fog now, swirling over the neighborhood. Had he ever been real? Did it really happen? That was why she couldn't tell him. Then it'd have to be real. Or he'd think she was losing it.

Roger took her hand. "What kind of thoughts?"

"I've been thinking of things. Abby."

His eyes widened. "Oh."

"Yeah."

"But, Annie—"

"It was never resolved, remember? They never caught the guy. Even though it was almost forty years ago—"

"You're thinking he may still be out there? After all this time? Honey, that's crazy."

"Of course I'm thinking that. Always have, since we had Mayra.

Look, if he was young, a teenager, when he . . . did that to Abby
. . . he might only be in his sixties or seventies. Even if he's in his
eighties, he might still be alive and—"

Roger's face paled, going from incredulous to concerned.

Annie decided she'd better back off before he called someone.
"But . . . chances are he's dead by now, right?"

"Chances are—"

"But maybe not. And Nora—"

"What about Nora? What's she got to do with this?"

She lowered her face and focused on the muted tan and black
of their bedspread.

"Annie, you've got to stop this."

"I can't. Don't you sit there and tell me you've never thought—"

Roger squeezed her hand so hard she cried out. "I'm sorry. But
you have to stop thinking like that. What? You think he might be
stalking *us* now? That he . . . did that to Abby, and now he's after
Nora?" His voice turned harsh, shrill. "Listen to yourself. You've
been watching too many movies. Nothing's going to happen to
Nora, ya hear? We won't let it—there's five of us who won't let it."

Part of her resented his aggressive tone, but she knew it
stemmed from his protective nature. And it reassured her, just a
bit, that he would stand between his children and anything that
tried to break through the fence.

Annie gulped. "I know. I shouldn't imagine things, but I can't
help it. Nora's my—" She broke off, not daring to say what was
on her mind, or it'd be real. She leaned her head on his shoulder and snuggled down under the covers. "Will you promise me
something?"

"Annie—"

"Please."

"Okay, what?" He put his arm over her shoulders and pulled
her in.

"Promise me that if I only have tomorrow left, you'll take care of the kids and protect them and—"

"Annie, stop it, please—"

"I'm serious."

"So am I."

"Just promise me. Then I'll go to sleep. Scout's honor."

He put his head back on his pillow and crossed his arms.

She pressed against him and slipped her hand under his fingers. She felt him inhale.

"Please?"

He turned and leaned over her. "I promise."

Kissing the top of her head, he said, "Now, go to sleep. That's an order." He switched off the bedside lamp and settled down, back turned away from her.

Annie pulled the covers up to her chin and closed her eyes. After a few minutes, Roger was asleep. Usually his snoring didn't bother Annie, but tonight was different.

She rolled over, facing the partially open bedroom door. A small night light plugged into a wall outlet across the hall sent a slivered beam across the floor.

She stared at it. Her eyes closed again. She forced herself to think of cheerful images, like family trips and celebrations. She thought of their last anniversary, when Roger had surprised her with a trip to Yellowstone. As she let the memories wash over her, she felt herself relax.

She opened one eye to check the time. Ten forty-five. Morning came early, she thought. Must get some sleep.

Annie closed her eyes again, willing the memories of their life together to continue, to lull her to sleep. They obeyed, and she drifted off. Her last thought was of the night when Roger had proposed. It was the night before their high school graduation. She fell asleep to the image of him holding out an engagement ring to her, a scared look on his face, afraid she'd say no.

Of course she hadn't.

But she'd teased him a bit, making him plead. Then she'd laughed at him and told him of course she'd marry him. Wild horses couldn't keep her away from him.

"Wild horses," he'd said, "but what about your father?"

Annie had giggled and told him to let her handle her father.

Then he'd taken her in his arms and kissed her for the first time. It was Annie's first real kiss. They had been so young and so much in love.

Annie wanted to stay forever in this memory. She rolled over, sure she'd chased away the fear, the tension, the weirdness of tonight, and she'd be able to sleep now.

Until a scream shattered the night.

10

Roger didn't stir.

His rhythmic snores followed Annie as she slipped out of bed, saw by the red glow of the digital clock that barely thirty minutes had passed, and rushed down the hall to Nora and Kimmie's room.

She saw Nora's empty bed, then turned and met Kimmie's wide eyes shining in a patch of moonlight.

Kimmie said nothing, just pointed at the window in slow motion.

Annie jerked her head the other way. "Nora? Honey?"

Nora stood in front of the window, palms flat against the glass. She whimpered, not turning around.

Annie picked the child up. It was like lifting a wooden doll.

Nora's body was rigid, her eyelids pinched tight. She held her stiff arms out in front of her, palms out, as if she brought the window glass with her.

Annie's mom radar told her what had happened. Nora had dreamed of flies covering her bed again.

Once she had her laid down, Annie stepped to Kimmie's side and gently patted her face. "Go back to sleep. It was just a nightmare."

"Okay, Mommy." She turned her face to the wall and closed her eyes.

Annie heard a gasp from Nora's bed, and swiveled.

"Mommy. You woke up."

The child sat up, her chubby fingers fluttering over the blankets as if sweeping something away.

"Honey, was it the flies again?"

"Y . . . yes, Mommy. They were so big. And the man said to open the window and they would fly away. So I was trying—"

"What man?" Nora had never mentioned a man in any of her dreams.

"He was nice. He knew my name."

A shrill bell went off in Annie's head as she smoothed the child's hair. She ignored it, thinking the dream must've been one of the bad ones—the kind where she'd have to crawl into bed with Nora so they'd both be able to sleep.

Thanks, Hank . . .

"What did he look like, sweetheart?"

Nora scrunched her face up. "He had black hair, and he had a shiny coat . . . and . . . and, Mommy, he had Hank's sweatshirt on."

Annie frowned. "Hank's sweatshirt?"

"You know. That blue one. It has a bird with a big beak on it. He says it's his favorite."

Annie dropped to the edge of the bed and grabbed the collar of her nightgown, twisting it tight against her neck. Hank's Seahawks sweatshirt—had to be.

The man in the park—Joshua—had visited Nora's nightmare and told her how to get rid of the flies?

Her thoughts swirled and refused to land. She must pull herself together. It wouldn't do to let the child see her terror.

Annie gathered Nora to her chest and kissed the top of her head. She rocked back and forth and hummed a soft tune, one of Nora's favorites.

When she felt the child relax, she settled her against the pillows and pulled the covers up.

"Okay, honey. Do you think you can go back to sleep now?"

"Can you leave the light on?"

Annie reached for the small bedside lamp, Disney characters dancing around the shade. She switched it on, and a soft glow filled the room. "Will that help?"

Nora nodded, one arm tight around her favorite stuffed animal, Mr. Bear, and her other hand clutching her favorite blanket.

Annie tiptoed out, leaving the door open, and made her way down the hall.

Hank's door was open and his light still on.

She detoured and stuck her head in. He was fast asleep, both arms outstretched above his head. It was funny how children slept differently. Some rolled up in a ball, while others splayed out sideways on the bed. Kimmie and Hank were splay sleepers—Annie constantly had to adjust them and cover them back up.

Before turning off Hank's light, she peeked into his closet, where he kept his truck collection. Being almost a teenager, he didn't play with them much anymore, but he still wanted to keep them. Annie suspected he rolled them around his bedroom when no one was looking.

She noticed a big yellow dump truck wasn't lined up with the tractor-trailer rig next to it, so she moved them with her toe until they were perfect. When Hank was little, she'd tried to teach him to park his trucks in a straight line, but he'd never mastered it nor wanted to. So Annie had taken over that duty for him.

She turned off his light and pulled the door almost shut, then continued down the hall.

She arranged the covers, trying not to awaken Roger. He had to get up so early for work—she always felt bad if he was disturbed. She could at least take a nap during the day with Nora, but Roger had no such luxury.

She knew she'd be awake a long time, so she didn't even try closing her eyes.

She lay on her side facing the door, waiting for another scream, hoping for none.

11

Annie waited, watching the numbers flip on the clock. When nothing else happened, she rolled toward Roger. Her nose touching his T-shirt, curled in a fetal position with her hands folded against her chest, she finally closed her eyes.

Try as she might, though, sleep wouldn't come. The grim specters from her and Abby's childhood flowed into her brain to their usual spots, taking up residence and pointing their bony fingers at her. Nora was there too. She peeked out from behind the ghosts, her childish voice reminding Annie that bad things could happen to her, too, if Mommy wasn't watching. And if Daddy didn't fix the fence.

Roger was right. Imagination was always scarier at night.

After an hour of fighting off the ghosts, Annie finally gave up, slipped out of bed, and shuffled down the hall. She looked in on each of the children. They slept like the dead—even Nora.

She straightened covers and plucked books and toys off blankets.

She went into Mayra's room last. Nothing ever needed straightening in here—Mayra was almost as manic as Annie about tidiness. Mayra and Kimmie—total opposites—had shared a room when they were younger, but their sisterly relationship had suffered. They'd had to be separated just to preserve the peace.

She turned to go, but stopped and stared at the corner of Mayra's pillow. The side of a slim red notebook stuck out from under it. *What was she hiding?*

She stepped closer and tugged the notebook out an inch at a time, but then it stuck.

Mayra rolled over and groaned but didn't wake up.

Annie pulled the notebook out.

She carried it down the hall, turning it over in her hands. She saw nothing on the front or back that would identify what was inside. A moment of guilt gave her pause. She was sure Mayra would consider this an invasion of her privacy. Annie promised herself she would just look at it to make sure Mayra wasn't into anything harmful. After all, she was only fifteen.

Annie entered a small spare room where random, unneeded household items, books, toys, and clothes were organized in the closet and on shelves and tables.

There was an old overstuffed sofa—brought from her parents' home—where Annie, and sometimes Mayra, liked to curl up with a book. Some of Annie's favorite childhood memories involved this very sofa and the hours spent on it watching movies with Mom or adventuring with a novel.

Annie had placed the sofa facing the floor-to-ceiling window, which gave a splendid view of the mountains beyond their little cul-de-sac. The best season to be in this room was spring, when the scent of freshly mown grass and newly budded flowers wafted through the window, which could be opened at the bottom.

Annie stood before the sofa and looked out the window. She

took in the vista of the snowy mountain range glistening in the moonlight. The mist might have lifted outside, but the fogginess in her brain she'd slogged through since dinner still remained. Now that Nora was safely asleep, her mind and emotions were full of Abby, and she knew what she longed to do.

But first the notebook. She sat, switched on a small lamp on a nearby table, and opened it, realizing in an instant it wasn't a journal. She read through the first two pages in Mayra's neat handwriting.

Two pages was all Annie could handle. Gripping it tightly, she stopped and flipped through the rest of the eight pages.

She closed the notebook and held it to her chest, holding back an avalanche of tears.

Ellen . . . why had Mayra—Annie couldn't grasp what she'd just read.

I can't deal with this now.

Annie loosened her grip on the notebook and set it aside.

She stepped to the closet and reached up to a shelf, grasping a medium-sized brown cardboard box crammed full of pictures from the past. She tugged it off the shelf, almost dropping it.

This was why she was here.

Carrying it to the sofa, she placed it on the floor, then crouched next to it.

Annie ran her thumb over the edges of the lid, smoothing the places where the cardboard had frayed over the decades. She picked a piece of lint off the top, leaned over, and smelled the mustiness of time.

Annie knew she was procrastinating. She wanted to open it but knew it'd release Pandora all over again.

She'd rummaged through it exactly three times before—the first when she'd brought it from her parents' house after their deaths—thinking it'd help her to know Abby. That she could somehow embed in her memory details of the sister she'd never known. Maybe create a new memory out of the void that she could hang on to.

But, as in the myth of Pandora, opening the box had been more of a curse than a blessing. It had opened a wound that had festered before her own birth, somehow attaching itself to her through her mother's bloodstream.

After the last time she'd opened it—three years ago—she hadn't touched it again.

Her heart had hurt so hard, shredded with fear because every photo of the sister she'd never known now had Nora's face on it where Abby's had been, and that Annie could not endure.

But maybe this time. Maybe it wouldn't peel back the edges of the gaping wound, wouldn't cause more unanswerable questions in her mind.

Maybe if she looked and found exactly the right photo, she could figure out how to tell the kids about their aunt Abby. Ellen would be pleased about that.

And maybe she would find out something about those infernal rings.

She opened the box and breathed in the scent of her mother, the lavender lotion she'd loved. Annie closed her eyes at the delicate scent, carrying her back in time to a childhood curiously blended with security and fear, joy and tragedy.

She opened her eyes. Abby's christening photos stared up at her. A small group surrounded her parents in the dimly lit church, Abby dressed in a lacy white gown and wrapped in her mother's arms. Daddy stood close by, one hand on Mom's shoulder, the other resting on Abby's tiny feet. Mom and Dad looked so joyful, so young and carefree.

Annie had no memory of this joy. There'd always been a somberness about their expressions—from the time her memories started—until this moment. As if taking care of her, Annie, was a fearful duty, one they'd rather not have. Mom and Dad were always afraid, always hovering, the umbilical cord never quite cut. Those were the faces Annie remembered.

She dug down, pulling up loose pictures at random. Abby's first birthday party, attended by friends of her parents, most of the men wearing uniforms. She looked closely at the room in which everyone posed with plates of cake, Abby taking center stage—cake and frosting plastered on her face, her hair, even her bare feet. The look of the room indicated base housing. The same kind of room she herself had grown up in.

Annie snagged another photo, of three-year-old Abby riding her trike down a cracked and potholed sidewalk. In the background, she saw Daddy waiting up ahead, arms out to catch Abby, eyes alight, with his face split in a wide grin that'd bring the sun right up from the eastern horizon. A grin Annie had never once seen on his face when he'd looked at *her*. Even at her wedding, Daddy's face held a grimness Annie couldn't fathom.

She looked again at his face, eagerly waiting to catch Abby sailing down the sidewalk. About six months before she was taken, Annie judged. No shadow of apprehension on his face.

Two hours later, Annie couldn't look anymore. She threw the mound of jumbled pictures back into the box, jammed the top on, and pushed it back on the shelf. As she did, a sealed envelope fell out of the box and landed at her feet.

She picked the envelope up, turned it over, and stared in shock.

Her own name in her mother's handwriting. She'd never seen this envelope in the box the three other times she'd rummaged through it.

Annie stared. Turned it over and started to slit it with her fingernail. Then clasped it to her chest.

Not now, Mom.

She put the still-sealed envelope on the shelf next to the box, picked up Mayra's notebook, then crept out of the room. She took the notebook back to Mayra's room and managed to stuff it back under her pillow without waking her up.

Then she retreated to her room and lay down next to Roger.

She stared at the ceiling, watching the elegant white fan go round and round. The air felt good on her cheeks, cooling the sweat collected there.

Annie let her eyes close, hoping . . .

She stood in the park, the fog swirling around her feet.

Looking down, she watched the ring rise up from her feet and hang in the air in front of her face. The words glowed in the lamplight.

Annie's eyes blinked open.

Lying rigid, she watched the clock flip to 3:00 a.m. Annie closed her eyes again, her mind pleading for sleep.

But it was Thursday, and she knew the night wasn't finished with her yet.

Where would it take her next? She knew she couldn't fight it. She'd learned to just ride along with it, her fear in the passenger seat.

Tonight would be no different.

12

A sudden creak of the bathroom door caused her eyes to flick open almost as soon as she'd closed them.

But what was this? Where was the fan?

She bolted straight up in bed—a narrow twin bed in a room not her own. But it *was* her room. Moonlight streamed through a window that was not where it should be. It lit up some areas but cast the rest in lumpy shadows.

Annie's gaze traveled the room, steeling herself against the shock of what she saw.

Small desk in one corner, her oversized high school backpack resting on top.

Closet door hanging open, a jumble of clothes visible inside, shoes littering the floor.

A sparkly blue dress wadded up and flung into one corner. Matching high-heeled shoes—one heel missing—rested on top of the gown.

Nausea rose like a tidal wave and threatened to spew over

Annie's pale-blue pajamas. She stared down at those pajamas, a death grip on her blankets.

She knew this night.

This can't be happening. Roger! Her mind screamed his name.

But Roger wasn't here. He wouldn't enter her life until next year.

Annie swung her feet over the side of the bed and immediately felt the pain between her legs. She collapsed into herself, fell back on the handmade quilt, and curled into a fetal position. Her heart screamed for God to make the throbbing pain stop, the shame of it, the ugliness.

The room spun. She gasped as a kaleidoscope of dizzy colors whirled in front of her eyes.

She squeezed her eyes shut, hoping against hope that when she opened them, she wouldn't be *here*, in this place and time—junior prom night when she was sixteen.

She willed herself to keep her eyes shut, but a scraping sound close by forced them open.

She knew what she'd see.

The shadow of the high school gym loomed ahead, faint music floating on the air.

He rose to his feet next to her, zipped up his black pants, and tucked in his white shirt, straightening the stiff bow tie against his neck.

Annie raised her head, feeling the cool grass under her back. Trying to get her bearings, she saw her feet stretched out, touching asphalt. One foot was bare. She moved it, feeling small pebbles roll under it.

She looked down the length of her body, saw the prettiest dress she'd ever owned bunched up around her waist, both straps torn and lying across her exposed bosom. One new shoe lay next to her, the slender heel broken off.

Her chest hurt where he'd strongarmed her, holding her down. A trickle of blood showed on her breast where his fingernail had scraped.

She gripped the torn material and covered herself as best she could.

Annie finally braved a look at his face.

David grinned and gave her an air high five. "Thanks, Annie. That was fun. See ya around."

He bent and picked up his tuxedo jacket and threw it over his shoulder, then turned his back on her and sauntered away, disappearing inside the back door of the gym.

Annie strapped her broken shoe back on and limped home, a mere three houses down the street.

Before she let herself in, she glanced behind her at the school and saw a shadowy figure on the sidewalk, looking in her direction. She stared, then hurried in, locked the dead bolt, and tiptoed up the stairs.

She stopped in the bathroom first, not daring to turn on the light. She washed him off as best she could in the dark, and thought furiously. *Daddy must never know. He'd probably kill David.*

She entered her bedroom and stripped out of her dress, her nose wrinkling. It smelled of his cologne . . . and a pungent odor unfamiliar to her. She wadded it up and threw it in a corner of the closet.

No one must know. She couldn't bear anyone to know. It was too . . . hideous.

Annie crawled into bed and wrapped her arms around her middle, finally letting loose into her pillow the tears of her stolen childhood and girlish dreams of a perfect night with a perfect boy. Dreams that now lay in broken shards around her feet.

She woke up hours later, feeling drugged with pain, her mind sluggish as she looked at her bedside clock. Three in the morning.

It reminded her of something, or someone. That was odd . . . *Ellen?* But whatever it was drifted away before she could capture it.

What had awakened her? Then, as the dull pain crept from her toes to her waist again, she remembered. She rolled over, facing the unshaded window and stared at the butterfly figurines scattered on her window sill, backlit in the moonlight.

If only.

If only she could emerge from this harsh ugliness, grow beautiful wings, and flutter away.

If only she could leave this life, like butterflies did, after only six weeks . . . instead of six or more decades of pain and misery.

But there were other ways.

Annie sat up. She knew where Daddy's revolver was. She muscled through the wretched thought until it no longer scared her.

She lay down again, thinking, discarding plan after plan until she hit on the best one.

After deciding exactly when and where, with a lighter heart she rose from her bed and stepped to the closet. She picked up the dress and shoes, stuffed them into a plastic bag, and put the bag into her backpack. It wouldn't do for Mom and Dad to see the dress and shoes. She'd throw them in the dumpster at school tomorrow.

Then Annie tackled the rest of the room.

When her clothes hung straight in the closet, none touching each other, and her shoes were lined up on the floor according to color, she closed the closet door. She tidied the rest of the room, putting away pencils and papers, lining up skewed pictures on her wall, and putting away jewelry she'd left strewn on her dresser.

Then she scrutinized her small laundry hamper in the corner by her bedroom doorway. She dumped out the clothes, folded them neatly, then stacked them in the hamper, reducing the jumbled pile by a third.

Perfect. Annie wasn't a slob, but her room had never been this orderly before. Looking at it now, bathed in the moonlight, it soothed her nerves and lessened her pain.

Annie remade the bed. Military corners, just the way Daddy had taught her. She was sure a quarter would bounce high if she took the time to find one.

She paused for a heart-wrenching moment, staring wide eyed at her journal.

No, she mustn't. No one could know.

Then she lay down and tugged the bedclothes up tight and straight over her body, feeling the unwrinkled smoothness of the sheets and reveling in the weight of the heavy quilt, pulled cocoon-like up to her chin.

She closed her eyes and thought of tomorrow.

She'd go to school, of course. She'd check in, then sneak out and come home. Daddy would be at the base, and Mom had already told her she planned to go to a friend's house and help her with a project and wouldn't be home when Annie arrived from school. Annie was to do her chores, then start on her homework. She grinned, thinking she'd already finished her last homework assignment ever.

She hoped she wouldn't see David before she managed to leave the school. Or Ellen.

Ellen. Red-haired, freckle-faced Ellen—the best friend ever.

How could she do this to Ellen? For the first time since hatching this plan, Annie stalled.

But what else could she do? Ellen would understand. Of course she would—Ellen the rule breaker always understood. Annie relaxed again and went over the plan one more time.

She glanced at the clock again. Three forty-five. Seeing the glow of the numbers, emptiness swamped her. She had the feeling again that she was missing something, something she didn't understand.

Something connected with the time.

Annie rolled over, facing the window where her butterflies danced in the moonlit darkness.

Tomorrow, she told herself, the pain would be gone. She'd never have to face it . . . or him . . . again.

13

Annie stretched in the early morning light, basking in the delicious sensation that always accompanied waking up on Friday mornings. In spite of little sleep last night, she felt refreshed. Yesterday was over. Tomorrow was here. Almost the weekend.

Weekends at the Lee house were always busy. Shopping, sometimes day trips with the kids, Hank's soccer and baseball games, dance lessons for Kimmie and Nora, and church on Sundays. Annie kept a schedule posted on the refrigerator of everyone's activities, including Roger's twice-a-month golf games. That way everyone knew what everyone was doing. Annie was a strong believer in schedules, especially sticking to them, and she hoped to instill that discipline in her children.

But this was still Friday, a school day. She sat up on the edge of the bed and stretched again. Steam floated through the half-closed bathroom door—Roger was up. She heard Mayra downstairs. Her bossy big-sister voice drifted up the stairs, admonishing someone to turn off the television. No TV on school mornings had always been an inviolable house rule. And being Mayra, she took it upon herself to enforce the rules—unless, of course, she was the one breaking them.

Annie stood. What crazy dreams she'd had. A jumble of impressions was all that was left in her memory. Had she actually met that strange man in the park last night? Her glance darted to her bedside table. No shiny black box.

There was something else trying to surface in her mind, some other dream, but it wouldn't come. She looked out the window and saw it would be a sunny day—after the fog last night, that'd be nice.

A butterfly floated past the window and then was gone. In February? Odd.

She shook her head and reached for her clothes on the end of the bed. No time to puzzle it out now. She'd better get downstairs and organize breakfast for everyone. She remembered Roger had mentioned an early meeting, and the older three needed to get to school.

She looked at herself in the mirror over her dresser. Definite under-eye shadows.

Annie heard the shower shut off. The door creaked open. Roger hummed to himself.

Dear Roger. He'd tried to comfort her last night—as he usually did when her emotions got the best of her. Her wild ramblings and fears never seemed to throw him. He always knew what to say, had always been a rock to lean on, her protector. She only wished . . . what? That he understood why she was afraid? But how could she make him understand when she herself didn't? Maybe fear was genetic and she'd inherited it from her parents. If that was so, it didn't bode well for their four kiddos.

Glancing at the clock, Annie clapped her hand to her forehead.

Good heavens. I don't have time for all this introspection. Gotta get going.

She stood and smoothed the bed covers, pulling the sheets tight and squaring the corners, then plumped the pillows.

She and Nora had a moms and toddlers meeting at the church at ten. She always looked forward to it. It was the best part of Friday mornings. Maybe she'd even share her bizarre dream with the other women. She would tell her strange story, and everyone would laugh and tell her not to be such a worrywart. She imagined Ellen's know-it-all smirk.

Annie smiled at her sudden optimism. The strangeness of last night faded.

She planned her day while she stepped into jeans and threw on her favorite pink sweatshirt. She'd have time to shower later, after she dropped the kids off at school.

Grabbing her purse, Annie hustled down to the kitchen. She set cereal bowls, cups, and four different kinds of cereal on the breakfast bar, along with orange juice, milk, and bananas.

The kids tromped in from the living room and surrounded her, pushing and shoving to get on their stools.

"Good morning, kiddos. Clean hands?"

They showed their palms.

Annie pretended to inspect them, then gave a nod of mom approval.

She served them quickly, then poured herself a cup of coffee. Roger always brewed the coffee in the mornings.

Stepping to the kitchen window, Annie looked out at the early morning sun. The weather had been mild so far for February. No snow on the ground since December. She hoped it would continue.

She heard Roger come down the stairs and open the front door, like he'd done every morning for the last twenty years, rain or shine. He said he liked to greet the day while it was still young and shiny and innocent, untainted by worry and problems.

He entered the kitchen, tousled four heads, and grabbed his briefcase and jacket.

"Gotta go, hon. That meeting with clients from Seattle is today. Oh, and lunch with Harv. Where's my cup?"

She found his insulated cup, filled it with coffee, and handed it to him.

He took it from her, scanning her face. "You good? Did you sleep okay?"

"No, had a hard time sleeping, but yes, I'm good." She patted his hand. "If it's a partnership discussion with Harv, don't be a wallflower, okay? You've done good work for him over the last ten years, and he should reward you, don't you think?"

"Yeah. Maybe. Wouldn't that be something after all these years? My name on the company sign, with *Partner* after it." He struck a theatrical pose. "It does kinda have a ring to it."

She stood on her tiptoes and kissed his chin. "It does. You just remember to speak up for yourself. And don't let 'em give you any grief."

"Nope! See ya tonight, kids. Be good. Have fun. Stay safe." His usual exit line.

Halfway through the back door, he slewed around. "Hey, did you hear sirens last night? Sounded close."

"N-no." She wondered why she hadn't heard them, since she'd been awake half the night. "Do you know if it was on our street?"

"Couldn't tell. I was mostly out of it." He lifted his shoulders. "Maybe I dreamed it. Oh well—if it was about anyone we know, it'll make the neighborhood gossip grapevine soon enough. Gotta go."

He waved and hurried out the back door.

Annie stood on the back porch until the four-year-old silver Jeep Grand Cherokee rumbled out of the detached double garage and continued on down the driveway. Roger waved at her again as the garage door came down. She stepped back and closed the door behind her, turning to find the children watching her.

Hank slurped the last of the milk out of his cereal bowl and wiped his mouth with the back of his hand. "What was Dad talking about—sirens? I didn't hear anything."

Mayra threw her brother a scathing glance. "Yeah, like you would—the whole world could be burning down around you and you wouldn't wake up. And stop being such a slob—"

Annie clapped her hands. "Never mind that now. Get upstairs and brush your teeth. Are your backpacks ready to go?"

She herded the older kids from the kitchen. Passing Nora teetering on her stool, Annie reached and grabbed her around the waist before the toddler crashed to the floor.

"Come on, baby. Let's go get you dressed. It's Friday—you get to play with your friends at the church today while I have my mommy meeting. Won't that be fun?"

"Yes, Mommy. I bring Mr. Bear?"

"Of course, sweetheart."

Annie was glad the child hadn't seemed any worse for wear after her bad dream last night—she'd even played a guessing game with Kimmie during breakfast.

She fervently hoped Nora wouldn't remember the dream at all, especially the part about the man in the Seahawks sweatshirt.

Annie knew *she* wouldn't forget it.

14

Ten minutes later, Annie loaded kids, lunches, and backpacks into her white minivan and backed out of the garage.

Three kids and three different schools later, she pulled into a coffee drive-up five blocks from home and bought Nora a hot chocolate and herself a muffin—the usual Friday ritual. Even the barista who served her was the same vivacious young girl she saw each week. She and Annie were now on a first-name basis, and Hailey never forgot to greet Nora and Mr. Bear. Except today.

Hailey came to the window. "The usual?" She wouldn't meet Annie's eyes.

"Yes please." She watched Hailey put a small cup under the hot chocolate machine, turn it on, then reach for the muffin plate. Her hand caught the cup of chocolate and swept it to the floor.

Hailey let out a yell as the hot liquid splashed on her forearm.

"Oh, are you okay? You'd better put some ice on—"

"I'm fine." Hailey grabbed a nearby towel and cleaned up the mess.

She handed the wrapped muffin to Annie, then a fresh cup of chocolate for Nora.

Annie handed her card to Hailey, noting her eyes shiny with tears.

"What's wrong, Hailey? Does your arm hurt? Is it burned, or is it something else?"

Hailey turned her back, shoulders shaking. "It's . . . it's my dad." She faced the window again. "He left last week. Just packed up and left while I was at class. Didn't even say goodbye to me—"

She covered her face with her hands. "How could he do that to us? And Mom—"

Annie handed her a tissue from her purse. "Oh, honey, I can imagine how hard this must be for both of you."

"That's not all though." Hailey handed Annie's card back to her. "Mom told me yesterday she just found out she has lung cancer. She's never even smoked! She said they were waiting to tell me until they had more information. And she said that's why Dad left. Said he couldn't handle it."

Annie's heart hurt watching Hailey's face contort with pain, then anger.

"Ah, sweetie, I'm so sorry. What can I do?"

"Dad's a wimp. 'Couldn't handle it'? Mom's the one who has to go through chemo . . . and . . . all that other stuff. She's the one who might die—"

"Now, don't let your thoughts go there. Most of what we're afraid will happen never does. Listen, there's a line behind me and I have to go, but let me give you my phone number. Call me anytime, okay? If you need to talk, or if you need a ride anywhere, or . . . whatever. Okay?" She handed Hailey a hastily scribbled note.

"Okay." She dabbed the corner of her eye with the tissue. "Thanks, Annie. Sorry to unload on you at the drive-up. I guess that wasn't what you came by for, huh?"

"No worries. Call me if you need to." She put the van in gear.

Poor kid, she thought as she tucked the sack down into the console between the seats. That was too much for someone so young to handle.

Annie's earlier optimism took a hit as she pulled away from the Coffee Shack and drove slowly through the parking lot.

"Mommy, why was that girl crying?" Nora's shrill voice broke into Annie's thoughts.

Another land mine to negotiate, trying not to scare Nora.

"Oh, she's just going through kind of a hard time. Sometimes crying's the only thing we can do. Understand?"

"Yes, Mommy." With no pause, Nora continued. "Jesus, that girl back there who's crying, can you help her not to be sad anymore?"

Annie watched Nora in the mirror as she whispered her innocent prayer, her face buried in Mr. Bear's fur. She wished there could be a Nora in every family in the world.

Nora's head popped up. "Mommy? Jesus said okay."

The simple faith of a child. If only she still had that, but it had died a long time ago. Having faith seemed so complicated now. Her schedules and her fences gave her more comfort than prayer these days.

Her mind drifted back to Mayra's essay question and what Annie had read in Mayra's notebook last night.

But no one's going to die tomorrow. Not if she could help it.

Annie steered the van forward and took the first right turn, heading toward their neighborhood.

Five minutes later she pulled into the dimness of the garage and switched off the ignition, staring through the windshield at Roger's tools hanging neatly on a large pegboard on the garage wall.

She sat in the dark stillness, focused straight ahead, and tried to calm her jangled nerves.

It isn't every day you think you'll die tomorrow, she said to Roger's tools.

He'd arranged them by size, smallest to largest, and in categories. Wrenches here, power tools there, screws and nails and bolts collected in mason jars, their lids attached to a specially built metal strip—to open one, he only needed to unscrew the jar while the lid remained on the strip. The bench under the pegboard was pristine, nothing haphazard about it. Every drawer and cupboard labeled. She was positive there wasn't a scrap of metal or a wood shaving to be found anywhere.

Hank sometimes used a tool without replacing it correctly, which resulted in a stern lecture about discipline . . . and a day in the garage with Roger, cleaning it from top to bottom.

Annie, soothed by the familiar order, drew a shaky hand through her hair. Life should be like Roger's tools. Neatly arranged with predictable outcomes. Square corners, no rumples, no dirty spaces, and, most important . . . no surprises.

In the dim quiet, the tick of the cooling engine reminded her of the tick of the dining room clock last night. Her mind raced again, reviewing the entire evening along with this morning. Once again she was under the table, hands trembling. Then the strange conversations with Ellen and the man in the park. Nora's dream. Her own, rising up from two decades ago, weaving itself almost seamlessly into the first moment the fear had returned and slithered up the table leg last night.

Annie jammed her fists against her temples as she tried to make sense of it all. She'd awakened this morning thinking it was a dream, all of it. *It must be,* she thought now. It had to be.

"Mommy, aren't we getting out? I have to go potty," Nora whined.

Annie jumped. "Okay, honey. Let's go in."

After helping her in the bathroom, Annie settled Nora in the upstairs playroom with her dolls, then headed to the shower.

She relaxed as the warm water washed the tension out of her neck and shoulder muscles.

But when she closed her eyes against the dripping soap, the image of the man in the park passed her field of vision in slow motion.

Annie gasped and opened her eyes, wincing as soap slid into the corners and stung. She rubbed and splashed water in them, then placed her palms flat against the shower wall and leaned her cheek against the warm wet tile.

The man in the park, the ring. It wasn't a dream—it was real?

Annie stepped out of the shower and wrapped herself in an oversized bath towel. What nonsense—of course it wasn't real. *Get a grip. Move on.*

It was a dream. No other explanation was plausible, she told herself as she hastily dried off and threw her clothes on.

Running a comb through her hair, Annie set aside her depressing thoughts. Somehow she must regain her optimism, or this day would devolve into a repeat of last night.

She peeked into the playroom at Nora, who sat on the rug with her back to the doorway, engrossed in her favorite doll. She whispered in the doll's ear, then used her hand to nod the doll's head. Annie wondered what Nora had whispered. She must remember to ask her. Sometimes Nora's imagination rivaled Hollywood's.

She turned and ran lightly down the stairs to the kitchen and poured herself another cup of coffee. Roger made the best coffee and had always refused to share his secret.

This part of the day was the best—just her and Nora—and she enjoyed having the kitchen to herself.

Annie gulped her coffee, then poured another cup. She and Nora had about forty-five minutes before they had to leave for the meeting at the church.

She turned on the small TV next to the coffeepot, selecting

a morning news program, the kind where people yammered on about this and that but never solved anything. Roger always called it *The Morning Gossip Program.*

She turned up the volume, then retrieved bread and butter from the refrigerator. She grabbed cinnamon out of the cupboard—Nora loved cinnamon toast.

The loaf of bread, cinnamon, and glass butter dish balanced precariously in her hands, Annie elbowed the refrigerator door closed and pivoted back to the counter.

She stepped toward the counter, but then halted in her tracks, focused on the TV screen.

"There are no guarantees for a tomorrow, are there?" the news commentator said to the co-anchor sitting next to him.

The young blonde agreed with a dramatic toss of her head. "I guess we never know, do we?"

Annie gasped and stood rooted to the kitchen floor, waiting for her heart to start again, feeling the blood drain from her face. The next beat of her heart thumped hard and painful.

She felt her knees give way as she grabbed for her chest without thinking.

15

nnie dropped the butter dish. It shattered. She looked down at a blob of butter on her toe, the dish now in three pieces.

"Mommy, what's wrong?" Nora's voice bombarded Annie from the doorway.

She jumped, staring at the screen, and waved Nora to silence. "Shh. I need to hear this."

The commentator looked directly at her. It was the man in the park—no, no, it couldn't be! That was crazy . . . She leaned down and looked closer. No, this man's eyes were . . . No, they weren't brown. They were a brilliant green, and he was older.

They aren't brown—they're green. It's not the same man.

Annie put her hand to her chest again and turned, leaning on the counter, her back to the TV.

"Mommy, it's the man in my dream." Nora pointed at the screen.

"Annie, are you wearing it?" the voice said from last night.

Annie stiffened, then whirled. The news show had now been

replaced by a commercial advertising a toothpaste that would cure all dental ills. She slammed her palm down on the top of the TV.

What did she hope to accomplish—to bring the man from the park back to the screen and demand he explain why he was doing this to her?

"No, it's not, Nora." She didn't mean to sound so harsh, but she couldn't help it.

She stepped back and punched the Power button, then watched the screen wink off. The last to go was the gleaming white teeth of the actress in the toothpaste ad.

"Mommy, what's this?" Nora's chirpy voice made her jump.

Annie inhaled sharply, tension radiating to both shoulder blades.

Nora held a tiny black box in one chubby hand, the lid in her other.

Annie staggered back against the counter again, one foot landing in butter and sliding out from under her. As she went down, she grabbed at the counter, missed, and ended up with the wrong end of the open bread package in her grip. Bread slices rained down to the floor. She came to a stop on her seat, the back of her head thumping against the cabinet.

The cinnamon fell with the bread, the lid popping off as it landed beside her, spraying its contents over her jeans.

Annie closed her eyes and waited to make sure there was no pain screaming anywhere in her body. Nothing seemed to be broken except the butter dish. She opened her eyes and looked at the mess on the floor, seeing a yellow spot on the back of her leg—butter smeared on her jeans all the way to her thigh and across the floor. Cinnamon sticking to the butter. Bread slices lay around her—on the floor, on her lap, and one teetering on her shoulder.

Oh Lord, what a mess.

She felt a sting in her right palm and plucked out a tiny shard of glass from the butter dish.

Her cell phone—stuck in her back pocket—vibrated.

Of course. Never fails.

She plucked it out, punched the button to send it to voicemail, then reached up behind her and laid it on the counter.

Annie looked up and found she was now eye level with Nora.

Wide eyed, the toddler stood motionless, except for the thumb sneaking up toward her mouth.

"Mommy?"

Annie's mouth twitched. A chuckle escaped without warning.

Nora giggled, then leaped into Annie's lap. They laughed and laughed until the tears ran.

Annie stopped when she heard her own voice take on a maniacal sound. Gulping, she leaned her head back on the cabinet, hugging Nora to her chest.

Nora pulled back, trying to unwind Annie's arms from around her.

"Mommy, you're squeezing me too hard. Why did you throw the butter on the floor?" She leaned down and trailed her pudgy finger through the cinnamon and butter on Annie's jeans, then put her finger in her mouth and sucked it off.

Annie loosened her grip and carefully picked up Nora's bare feet and put them in her lap. She put her hands on Nora's tiny shoulders and looked her over from head to toe. No scrapes or cuts.

"I dropped the dish, then I slipped in the butter, silly. You saw, didn't you? And I'm squeezing you because I love you so much. Here, honey, there's glass on the floor. Let me carry you back to the dining room." She tried to gather her legs under her while hanging on to Nora.

"But *why* did you drop the butter, Mommy?"

Annie collapsed back to her seat.

Of course, the box.

Still gripping Nora to her chest, Annie examined the floor for the black box. She didn't see it. Where had it gone?

She cupped Nora's cherubic face in her hands. "Honey, where is the little box you had in your hand?"

Nora frowned and put her hands out, palms up, and gazed at them, forehead and nose scrunched up.

If Annie hadn't been so rattled, she would've laughed.

Nora's blond curls bounced as she shook her head. "I don't know, Mommy."

"You had it right over there in the doorway, remember? I saw you holding it."

Nora's eyes lit up. "I found it on the floor. But now it's gone." She pursed her lips in a pout. "It had a pretty ring in it."

"I know. I . . . I saw it before. But the box was on the floor? Where?"

Annie distinctly remembered putting it in her jacket pocket last night at the park.

"Your coat was on the floor, and—"

She never left her coat on the floor, not since she'd been a child Nora's age. Her mother had been very strict about that.

"My coat was on the floor?"

She knew her voice was too loud and accusing. She saw Nora's eyes widen again, her little mouth downturned. Annie gulped and calmed her voice. "What are you talking about? Honey, tell me the truth. My coat wasn't on the floor, was it?"

Nora's eyes leaked tears. "It was, Mommy . . . it was. Right by the Upstairs Box. I promise."

"I've never left my coat on the floor, honey."

"But you did, Mommy. You did. I picked it up for you, and the box fell out of the pocket."

Why am I making such an issue out of this? Annie knew. It was because if she'd left her coat on the floor, one more piece of her fence cracked and toppled.

Annie lifted her head and stared through the kitchen doorway into the living room and knew Nora was telling the truth. Now she remembered coming in from her walk last night and dropping her jacket by the box when she picked up Hank's shoes.

She should have known Nora wouldn't lie—it wasn't in her. Most of the time, the child was painfully honest.

She lowered her head and kissed Nora's hair. "I'm sorry, Nora. I guess I did leave it on the floor. I just this minute remembered. But I wonder where that box got to—I'd like to look at the pretty ring again—"

"We can look for it. I'll find it for you, Mommy." She wiped her eyes with the back of her plump hand and jumped off Annie's lap.

"Nora, the glass—"

But the toddler was gone before she could latch on to her.

Annie stood with some difficulty. Her left knee hurt and felt swollen. She flexed it gingerly. Just jarred, she guessed.

She remembered her phone vibrating. Her phone log said it'd been Margo, a friend in her moms' group at church. She hoped they didn't need more snacks made for this morning—Annie was in no mood, and she was out of time.

She shoved her phone back into her pocket. She'd call her back later—right now there was a floor to clean up.

Surveying the mess, she thought how funny Ellen would find this. There'd be a high five in it for her, she was sure, because this morning was definitely *not usual*. Ellen would approve.

Annie cleaned up the bread, butter, cinnamon, and pieces of glass. After sweeping up the last piece, she took the trash bag out to the dumpster.

She stood breathing the fresh air, settling herself before going back in.

What a morning! Something to laugh at with the other moms.

Reentering the kitchen, she heard Nora's bare feet speeding around the living room, then thumping up the stairs and running through rooms overhead. Three-year-olds had boundless energy.

Spying another small glass shard under the cabinet against the baseboard, she grabbed the broom again. As she swept the glass out and picked it up, a fleck of shiny black caught her eye. She shoved the broom under the cabinet again and flung the box out of its hiding place, along with the lid.

She stared, then picked it up gingerly with thumb and index finger and stumbled over to the table, dropping into a chair. She placed the box and lid side by side in front of her.

No tomorrows.

Hands clasped in her lap, Annie squeezed her eyes shut—so hard she saw stars.

How can this be?

The dream from last night—the man, the swing, the ring box—came rushing back. Only now she knew for sure it wasn't a dream.

A loud thump above her head made her jump. She looked up at the ceiling, hearing Nora dragging something across the floor of the playroom, directly over the dining room.

Annie rose and shuffled to the bottom of the stairs.

Massaging her stiff knee, she called to Nora. "Honey, I found the box. You can stop looking."

"What box, Mommy? I'm playing with my dollhouse."

She'd already forgotten. Annie exhaled. At least Nora wasn't there to see her hands shaking again.

"Okay, honey. You just play up there until it's time to go. I'll call you when I'm ready."

She wiped sweat off her face, stepped back to the table, and stared down at the ring. What should she do with it? The man in the park, Joshua, said to put it on and wear it today. Then what?

And why should she do what some stranger told her to do?

Oh, this is just ridiculous!

She glanced behind her at the pictures of their parents again, both rings winking at her, lit up by the morning sun streaming through the dining room window.

Annie stared at the box again, wishing she'd never gone for that walk last night.

This is absurd.

Why was she so afraid of it? It was just a ring—it wasn't as if she'd be whisked off to some fearful dimension if she touched it.

The ring willed her to pick it up. She reached for it. Her fingers touched the edge of the box just as her cell vibrated.

Jerking her hand back, she tugged her phone out of her back pocket before it went to voicemail. Her nervous fingers lost their grip, and it clattered to the floor. She bent—wincing as her knee resisted—grabbed it, and answered just in time.

"Annie? Margo here. I tried calling you earlier, but you didn't pick up."

"Yeah, sorry about that. I was . . . never mind. Long story. What do you—"

"I'm calling to let you know the meeting this morning has been canceled."

"Oh. Why—"

"—and . . . and I have bad news. You should sit down, Annie."

16

Annie clutched her phone with slick fingers. She'd heard those words over the phone only two times before—spoken by a state trooper to Roger when his parents were killed, and again a year later when her own parents died.

"What?"

One of the kids? Roger? But why would Margo be calling—

She heard Margo struggle for words, gagging with the effort to speak.

"Margo . . . what is it?"

"Ellen . . . Ellen Jarvis died last night."

Unreality swirled, grabbing Annie by the hands. Faster and faster, spinning around, then everything caved in around her, sucking her into its vortex. The pale-yellow paint cracked as the dining room walls closed in and threatened to crush her like a twig. The ticking of the clock was a raucous sound in the silence. She heard Margo's voice as if coming from far away, from the past, or from the tunnel stretching above her.

"Annie? Are you still there?"

Annie pushed upward in her mind, surfacing again in her dining room.

"What . . . what did you say?"

Ellen, her friend. Ellen, the leader of the moms' group and the mother of three lively boys. One was Hank's age—they were best friends.

"We heard they think it was an aneurysm in her brain. Mark said she'd had a headache for a couple of days, then she just didn't get up this morning. Her oldest boy found her after Mark had already gone to work."

Nausea spread through Annie's belly. She bent over, supporting herself with one palm on the table.

Her eyes strayed to the ring, still nestled in the box. She hadn't even had to slip it on her finger to be whisked away to an unknown, frightful dimension.

No tomorrows. It was for Ellen?

For the second time that day, Annie stifled a scream.

"Annie? You okay? No, I guess not . . . Stupid question. I know this is sudden, and I hate to be the one to tell you. I know you and Ellen were close."

Annie gulped, trying to get her unruly stomach under control.

"Yes, I'm here, Margo. And yes . . . we have . . . had been friends since middle school."

Ellen? Past tense?

A lifetime ago. Fifth grade, Miss Palmer, Annie and Ellen showing up on the first day of school—the day they'd met for the first time—wearing identical outfits. Ellen, with the unruly flaming-red hair and uncountable freckles. Gangly arms and legs that never seemed to obey what her brain told them to do. Ellen—the best friend ever. Giggling sleepovers, high fives when their soccer teams won, secrets spilled in the middle of the night. First ear piercings, first hormones, first dances, first crushes, first dates. So many firsts.

Ellen, her life-saver after that disastrous night outside the high school gym, the night when Annie almost decided to quit life for good. It was Ellen who'd helped her breathe again, live again, see the sun again. And to see herself as more than some boy's plaything.

Annie hadn't been able to hide it from her that next day when she went to school. As usual, they'd met at their lockers first thing, before English class. Annie had tried to appear nonchalant, but Ellen hadn't been fooled. Hands on her hips, she'd demanded to know what was up, why Annie's makeup was running, and why she had two different shoes on.

Annie had looked down and burst into tears.

Ellen threw her books into her locker, grabbed her bag and Annie's arm, leading her out.

They ended up ditching the rest of their classes and going to the park, spending hours on a bench talking it through.

Ellen had even pried it out of Annie what she'd planned to do. To her credit, Ellen hadn't been angry at her. She'd gripped her hand and told her, promised her, she'd never let her do that to herself.

She'd let Annie bawl on her shoulder and had shooed away a woman who'd stopped and asked if everything was all right.

And it was Ellen, her fierce friend, who'd cornered the boy the next week and threatened to tell the school authorities, and Annie's father, if he ever so much as breathed in Annie's direction. Because of Ellen, Annie had had a tomorrow.

Senior year. Ellen hovering in the background the day Annie Walters met Roger Lee. Ellen smirked like an imp when Roger knelt in front of Annie in the cafeteria, in front of the whole school, to wipe mashed potatoes and gravy off her new shoes—where they'd spilled when she'd dropped her tray at her first close encounter with the handsome basketball star.

And later that day, giggling at their side-by-side lockers, they watched Roger approach with a group of his friends. His eyes met Annie's, and his face turned scarlet. That was when Annie knew.

But she hadn't been able to admit it to herself.

It was Ellen who told her—during a shopping excursion to buy senior prom dresses—that of course Roger was in love with her and that Annie should marry him. She could still hear Ellen whisper, "Any guy who kneels at your feet and wipes food off your shoes is a keeper."

Graduation, marriage, college, kids. Annie and Ellen.

They'd been there for each other through it all. Now they attended the same church, and their kids played together.

Ellen Jarvis.

Mark's wife.

Shane, Sam, and Steven's mom.

Everyone's friend and prayer warrior. Annie's soul sister.

Yesterday there'd been a tomorrow for her. Today there wasn't.

Annie closed her eyes and gripped the phone so hard she felt a fingernail snap.

"Annie?"

She shuddered as a cold shadow drifted over her.

Ellen was Mayra's second mom. Mayra—the page in her notebook Annie had read last night—

But how . . .

Her throat thickened with mucous she couldn't choke down.

"Margo, I've got to go. Please . . . please let me know if there's anything I can do. Maybe meals for Mark and the boys—or something . . ." Annie trailed off as she floundered and sank into a whirling cesspool of emotion. The stink of death filled her nostrils, clung to her clothes. She was well acquainted with the rancid odor.

"Yes, of course. Take care, Annie. We'll talk later."

Click.

A dog barked outside. A neighbor gunned his engine. Someone laughed.

Everyday sounds in their neighborhood.

And upstairs, Nora giggled—something that usually brought a smile to Annie's lips.

She waited for normal to come back, but it didn't. It couldn't. Normal was a hollow, meaningless word without Ellen. She wouldn't be surprised to look outside and see every vestige of color removed from the landscape, a gray world with no Ellen of the fiery-red hair.

Roger. She had to hear his voice.

Touching his contact on her phone, she let her eyes stray to the small photo on the other side of the dining room. Herself and Ellen arm in arm on graduation night, Roger lurking in the background. He stood just a pace or two behind them, as if he knew nothing could ever separate them, not even himself.

Nothing? A lie.

She realized she'd been listening to Roger's *Sorry to miss your call. Please leave your name and number* message. Annie had no idea what message to leave, what to say.

She touched End and laid her phone gently on the table next to the box. She reached for the ring, put her finger on the letters etched in the stone, felt a jolt travel up her arm, and jerked her hand away.

She picked up the lid, clapped it on the box, and shoved the box behind the TV on the counter. Gripping the edge of the sink, she leaned over and spit death out, then washed it down the drain. Done.

Annie wandered into the living room and dropped into her special chair placed near the front window, where it soaked up the morning sun most days. She always had a stack of books next to it.

She stared at the family pictures across the room. One was crooked.

She looked away. Looked back at it. Felt the reflex in her hand.

Striding to the wall, Annie straightened the picture. Then lined up another one.

She backed away, scrutinized the photo grouping, and sat in her chair again. But still, it didn't help the way it always had before. Why should it? Lined-up pictures didn't mean a lined-up life. A tidy, calm schedule, each item ticked off when done, didn't mean her fences were mended and nothing monstrous could break through. Last night and this morning were proof enough of that.

Annie leaned back in her chair and drew a calming breath from somewhere deep. Yes, the pictures were perfect. Hank's trucks were perfect. Her laundry basket was perfect.

But life? Not so much.

Ellen. Gone for good. It sounded like a bad lyric in a bad cowboy song.

Oh, God—why? Why?

Silence . . . but what did she expect? God didn't owe her an explanation, did he?

Without warning, the torrent of grief surged from the deep, slamming into her chest. She screamed silently into her palms. She mustn't let Nora hear. Bent double in her chair, fingernails digging into her cheeks, thirty-odd years of friendship dissolved around her, spilling through her hands and splashing on her lap. Behind her eyelids she watched Ellen's face go last of all. Her dear freckled face.

She heaved a breath and sat up, collapsing against the cushion of the wing-back chair. *Ellen, dead?*

Annie couldn't wrap her brain around it.

They'd just spoken—twice—yesterday. She'd promised to bring Annie a recipe for her special cornbread today—to the moms' meeting at the church. She hadn't said anything about a headache. Ellen wasn't supposed to die like this—so young and vibrant with life, love, and young children—after she'd promised to bring you a cornbread recipe.

And then the other call last night, the one Annie still couldn't make head or tails of. It was like Ellen had known.

Annie stayed in her chair, willing her mind to come up with a reasonable explanation for the last thirty minutes. Something that would make sense. There was none.

Roger. Roger would know. She dragged her phone out and tapped it again. Got his message again. She tapped End and let it drop in her lap.

Nora's question of last night popped into her brain. "What's *die* mean, Mommy?"

Annie had an explanation last night. Today it belonged in the drawer of no answers.

Outside, the planet spun and people lived their lives. Inside, Annie's orderly existence, the one she'd created for herself when she was sixteen, had blown up in her face and lay in shambles at her feet.

She leaned back in her chair and closed her eyes. Her tortured mind conjured up pearly whiteness and tiny etched letters on thousands of rings floating in a sea of darkness.

She jerked to her feet, swaying slightly, then hurried to the kitchen, snatched the box, and ripped the lid off. She grasped the ring and lifted it out—dropping the box and lid into the trash—and held the ring in her palm. Carrying it into the dining room, Annie held the ring close to the picture, placing it side by side with the ring in the photo.

Identical.

Her eyes found her mother's.

In slow motion, her gaze never leaving her mother's, Annie slid the ring onto the fourth finger of her right hand, exactly as her mother wore it in the picture. It fit perfectly.

Fine. Now what?

She leaned toward her mother's face. No more sadness in her eyes—only encouragement. Her eyes shifted to the space between the two large pictures of their parents—to the empty space that once held another photo, faintly outlined where the edges of the frame had marred the paint.

After removing the frame years ago, she didn't have the heart to clean the wall or reposition the other two pictures. The emptiness on the wall was important to her.

She wondered again, staring at the marks on the wall and the uninhabited space within, what it would have been like to grow up with a sister.

She always wished she'd known Abby. Ellen was the closest thing to a sister she'd ever had.

Was. Had.

She remembered the times she'd begged Mom and Dad for information about Abby. When in high school, she'd badgered them constantly. It was her right, she'd said.

Now it made her cringe, her arrogance and snarky harassment of two people who'd lived through a grief no parent should ever have to endure—an understanding that only came to Annie with her own children's births, particularly Nora's.

She'd found out about Abby by accident when she was seven. Snooping in some albums hidden away in a closet, she'd come across pictures of a baby wearing a pink dress. She knew it wasn't herself. She'd seen her baby pictures, and this baby looked different. Annie couldn't figure out why her mother was cuddling this baby and why Daddy was leaning over kissing her cheek.

She'd carefully carried the album to the kitchen table, where her parents sat having their Saturday morning coffee. She put it in front of them and asked who it was.

Her father got up without a word and left the room. Her

mother followed him out, plucking at his sleeve. But he shook her off, and she returned to the kitchen and sat. They heard him gun the engine of his pickup and peel out of the driveway.

Annie remembered the hot glare from her mother as she snatched the album and shut it with an audible *snap!*

"Look what you've done, you little snoop—he probably won't be back tonight."

She sent Annie to her room. When she started to argue, her mother pointed at the kitchen doorway and said, "Just go, Annie. I'll be up in a little while."

Her father had not come home that night, and her mother had not come upstairs.

The next day, her mother gave a few more details, but her parents never did get beyond telling her that her older sister by four years had gone away one day and not returned.

What that meant she'd had to piece together herself years later—the subject was forbidden territory, and her questions as she'd grown older were usually met with frosty stares and turned backs.

It was Ellen who'd encouraged her to ferret out the wretched story. It wasn't until Annie was pregnant with Mayra that she and Roger finally learned the truth of what had happened to Abby. The gruesome details still haunted her. That was why the emptiness on the wall must remain.

And now Ellen lived in that emptiness with Abby.

Whatever would she do without Ellen? Tears threatened again, but she refused to give in to them. She'd cried enough. It was one more thing to set aside, to steel herself against.

She checked her phone to see if she'd missed a call or a text from Roger, but there was nothing. Then she remembered he'd mentioned meetings today.

Annie ran lightly up the stairs, feeling the weight of the ring on her finger. Oval whiteness danced on the walls as light from the skylight in the upstairs hall caught the stone and created dozens, hundreds of reflections.

She stopped and moved her hand back and forth, watching the tiny glowing orbs move from walls to ceiling in a spectacular light show.

Nora stood in the doorway of her room. "Pretty, Mommy! Pretty—"

Annie knelt and hugged her tight. She'd decided what she must do. "Come on, honey. Let's get ready to go."

"Where are we going?"

"It's Friday—we're going to the church, remember? Where's your shoes?"

Nora fetched her sparkly high-top sneakers from under her bed and sat on the floor to put them on. Annie had bought them because of the small butterflies perched on the uppers.

Nora scrunched her face in a frown. "Mommy, they don't look right."

Annie helped her put them on the right feet and tie the laces, rethinking her decision to go to the church and talk to the pastor. How would she possibly make him understand?

It might come to nothing, but she had to go. *Maybe he'll have some answers.*

17

Annie pulled into the church parking lot ten minutes later. She noticed several cars in the lot, and her hopes rose that there might be someone available who could watch Nora while she talked with Pastor Mike.

She'd called him before leaving home, and he'd said, "Of course, come by. I'll be here for a while yet. What's on your mind?"

Annie told him she preferred to tell him face to face. She wanted to see his eyes as she told her story. To see him discount it as some weird chain of circumstances—anything but real. *Anything but . . .* She couldn't yet put her fear into words.

She sat in her car, scanning the front of the church she and Roger had called home for several years. It wasn't a megachurch by any means, but it was large by neighborhood standards, and well kept.

Orderly was a good word for it. Unchanging. It'd been part of the neighborhood for decades and would likely go on for decades more. Annie felt comforted by that thought, that something in life would remain exactly as it'd been for so long. Solid, unshakable, fitting into her *as usual* box.

Annie immediately thought of Ellen and winced.

The church boasted a twenty-foot spire crowned by a cross handcrafted by a local artisan. Tall stained-glass windows paraded across the front, and a newer wing housing the children's department completed the L-shaped building. Finished in sand-colored stucco, the grounds professionally landscaped with local tree varieties, colorful flowers, and even cactus beds, it held an elegant appeal for Annie.

But the truth of the attraction was that she'd never encountered any surprises within, from the templated worship services to the many potlucks and other activities. She always knew exactly what to expect when they entered on Sundays. Not that there weren't a few ongoing changes. Last year, for instance, the men had constructed a gurgling water fountain to enhance the front.

Annie liked the soothing sound of the water bubbling up from the rock-faced fountain, then flowing into a miniature creek bed. The entire project was enclosed by a short fence to discourage children from playing in the creek. Roger had lent his help during the project, and Annie remembered the first time she'd laid eyes on it, approving heartily of the beauty and peace it added to the front of the building. People driving by would be attracted to it, she'd thought.

She and Roger were proud of their church and the impact it'd had on their town over the decades. The congregation had doubled in just ten years—and the church's reputation for compassion and helpfulness had drawn them in the first time they'd attended.

That compassion and helpfulness was what she counted on today of all days.

She carried Nora and Mr. Bear across the parking lot and entered the cool, dark interior.

Annie looked across the wide foyer and caught sight of a teenage girl who attended the youth group. She had her back turned as Annie approached. Her long, straight black hair hung down her back in a thick braid, topped by a ball cap.

Cassie was a friend of Mayra's and the daughter of the youth pastor. She was homeschooled, as were many children in the church. Mayra had often begged to be homeschooled when she was younger, but now she was entrenched with her friends and the routine of attending public school and didn't want to change.

Annie was glad about that—she knew her own limits.

She walked up behind Cassie, her feet making no sound on the thick carpet. The slender young girl knelt in front of a small pamphlet and book display in the corner of the spacious foyer.

"Cassie, are you busy right now?"

Cassie jumped up and turned, face crimson, her purse falling off her shoulder in her haste. She dropped the pamphlet she'd been holding, then picked it up, wadding it before she shoved it back on the shelf behind her.

"No, Mrs. Lee. I'm . . . I'm just hanging out here until my mom's done in the children's department. She's putting up some pictures to use on Sunday." She grimaced. "I have a dentist's appointment. I hate going to the dentist."

Annie commiserated with her. "So do I. But a necessary evil, I guess."

Cassie's eyes looked everywhere but at Annie's face.

"Are you okay, Cassie? Homeschooling going okay?"

"Yeah, I guess. Sometimes I wish I could be with my friends more."

"I'm sure you do. Maybe you can spend the weekend with Mayra soon. Would you like that?"

Cassie's eyes brightened. "That sounds like fun, Mrs. Lee. I'll ask my mom."

"Okay, just have her call me, and we'll work something out. Right now, I have a favor to ask of you."

Annie gestured to Nora. "Would you mind watching Nora for a few minutes while I talk to Pastor Mike? I won't be long. If I'm not done when you have to leave for your appointment, just bring her into his office. I wouldn't want to hold you up."

"Yeah, I can do that."

She held her hand out to Nora. "Do you want to go play in the Toddler Time room with me?"

Nora looked up at Annie. "Can I, Mommy?"

"Go ahead, honey. I'll be in to get you after a while. And thanks, Cassie. I appreciate it."

Cassie took Nora's hand and headed to the children's wing.

Annie stepped to the shelf and smoothed out the wrinkled pamphlet Cassie had tossed there. It was produced by the local crisis pregnancy center.

Annie looked in surprise at Cassie, disappearing down the hall. *Oh my. I hope . . .*

She and Roger had discussed the possibility of facing something like this with Mayra, hoping against hope they'd never have to deal with it. They'd watched other families go through the rough road of a teenage pregnancy, some making decisions they now regretted.

Annie wondered if Mayra knew what was going on with her friend. The two girls had known each other since first grade and were like two peas in a pod. Annie decided she'd ask Mayra about it. She didn't have any illusions about Mayra telling her the truth though. She and Ellen wouldn't have snitched on each other about anything.

Annie drew a breath, thinking how difficult life was sometimes, how much more complicated things became each day. She wished her children wouldn't have to confront such things, but the days of childhood innocence that she had enjoyed—at least for a time—were over.

Annie moved to the adjacent wall, where several memorial plaques hung, knowing she was procrastinating. She looked at some of the names of parishioners who'd passed away over the years. Each person's name was engraved in silver, with an epitaph written underneath.

Always cared

Mother, teacher, friend

He gave his life for his country

Prayer warrior

Annie wondered what would be written on hers. *She built her fences well?*

She stepped back hastily and made her way through the ornate double doors into the sanctuary.

She'd decided before she heard the news about Ellen that talking to the pastor about the rings was a stupid idea. What would he be able to tell her about the bizarre events of last night and this morning? She could see him reaching for his phone, calling Roger to tell him that his wife seemed to have gone off the deep end.

But now there was Ellen, and it seemed like talking to Pastor Mike was the next logical step. Pastors know things about death and dying—and didn't they have a hot line to God? She knew how to pray, but sometimes it seemed that God took his own sweet time with answers. Annie hated feeling rebellious, but she needed answers—today. Maybe Pastor Mike could connect her to that hot line.

Because tomorrow . . .

She couldn't finish the thought.

The hush of the empty sanctuary washed over her. She and Roger had attended Garden Street Chapel since Mayra was three years old. She loved the history they had here. Most of their close friendships were here. It was where they'd put down roots, where they'd connected with like-minded young parents. Their children were growing up here—they would call this their home church someday, and maybe their own children would too. Several families boasted three or four generations who attended.

She stopped halfway down the center aisle. Her gaze traveled to the front, where a large handmade cross hung directly behind the choir loft. It'd been made by a parishioner—long since passed away—and donated to the church by his widow some sixty years ago.

Annie had always felt unnerved by that rough-hewn cross—there wasn't a straight edge or perfect corner anywhere on it. It even hung slightly askew—not that you could easily tell, but to Annie, its crookedness was like a beacon.

The first time they'd seen it, Roger had said he felt drawn to its simplicity, its honesty.

Imperfect, rough, crooked. Just like life, he'd said.

Annie couldn't look at it without wanting to fix it.

The one-hundred-year-old sanctuary had recently been updated with new carpet, chairs, and altar rails. New windows had been installed, as well as new light fixtures. The walls were now a sedate off white instead of covered in old-fashioned cheap paneling. The upgrade had definitely improved the look and feel—she'd heard many of their friends say how much they liked it.

She stopped and glanced at the row they always sat in. At first they'd thought it was funny that parishioners sat in the same places every week. Now, *their* pew felt comfortable, like coming home. Pastor Mike sometimes joked that if someone sat in the wrong seat, he wouldn't recognize the person.

The morning light streamed in through the tall narrow windows, shafts stabbing the floor in front of her, laying out a path to the cross. Although she attended the mom meetings every Friday—held in the large fellowship hall—she rarely stepped into the sanctuary except on Sundays.

Her feet made no noise as she continued through a small door into the pastors' wing. Inside was a short hallway leading to Pastor Mike's office, and in the other direction, the youth pastor's office. They had one secretary between them, whose desk sat in a small alcove between the two private offices.

The U-shaped desk filled the space, with tall file cabinets behind. Two monitors and a small laptop sat in front of Jenny, the secretary. Fragrant coffee perked on a corner table, and across the open hallway from the desk was a long work table spread with programs for the coming Sunday service.

Jenny looked up as Annie approached, and smiled a greeting. "Hi, Annie. He's waiting for you." She squinted, giving Annie another look. "Did you cut your hair?"

"Yes, a couple of weeks ago. It was getting shaggy."

"Looks nice. Shorter hair suits you, and you can still put it in a ponytail."

"Thank you. How are you? I was sorry to hear about your dad."

"I'm doing okay. Thanks for asking. He was sick a long time, and now he's out of all that pain." Jenny looked at her for a long moment.

"I heard about Ellen. I'm so sorry—"

Annie looked away, hand tightening on her bag. She managed a "thank you" and then fell silent. The tick of the clock on the wall behind Jenny filled the space between them.

"Is everything else okay, Annie? Kids doing well? And how's Roger?"

"Everything's fine. Kids are . . . well, they're kids—what can I say? And Roger's fine. He likes his job—"

"That's not what I meant. You look . . . a bit hassled. Are you sure you're all right?"

"I have four kids and a husband. What's not to be all right? Of course I'm hassled—I have four kids and a husband, not to mention a large dog named Max, who thinks he's human."

Jennie's face flamed, and she looked down at her keyboard.

Four kids and a husband. Annie wished she could snatch those words back. And good grief, why did she have to say them twice? She was usually more careful of how she spoke.

Jenny was alone now that both her parents had passed away. Her sister lived on the East Coast, and they weren't close. There'd been some scandal attached to her. Annie had never heard the details, and Jenny had never offered.

And Jenny was a much-too-young widow. Her husband had died several years ago in Iraq. Annie recalled that he'd been a civilian contractor who'd been in the wrong place at the wrong time when a roadside bomb blew up. They'd never had children.

Ashamed of herself, Annie touched Jenny's arm. "Look, I didn't mean to be sharp with you. I'm so sorry. It's just that I need to talk to Pastor Mike, and I'm a bit short on time. I can go in now?"

"Of course, Annie. And I didn't mean to pry. Go ahead and go in."

"You weren't prying. I just need to relax, I guess. Your day going okay?"

"Yes. Got the bulletins done for Sunday and the lessons printed for the youth group."

"You're good for this church, Jenny. You work so hard. It's like you're always on call for the whole church. The congregation appreciates what you do—I've heard it more than once."

Jenny beamed from ear to ear. "Thank you. It's nice to hear."

Annie smiled and stepped to the pastor's closed door and knocked lightly.

"Come in!"

18

Pastor Mike stood—towering over her, as he did most of his flock—ambled around his desk, and gave her a quick hug.

"Annie, good to see you." His deep James Earl Jones voice filled the room.

He gestured to the chair on the other side of his desk, taking the one next to Annie instead of sitting across the desk from her. Mike always said he didn't want folks to feel like they were in the principal's office.

"Now, what can I do for you? You mentioned some confusing things had happened. And, Ellen, I don't know what to say except that I'm profoundly sorry."

"Get right to it—no bland small talk this morning, huh? Are you pressed for time? If you are, we don't have to do this now—"

His voice was gentle and as smooth as expensive chocolate. "No, I don't have any other appointments this morning. I just figured you—a busy mom—would be on a tight schedule and you'd like to skip right to the point. Was I wrong?"

Annie glanced down. Why was she so caustic with Pastor Mike? After all, she was the one who'd called this meeting. She set her purse down on the floor next to her chair and shifted to face him directly. "No. You're not wrong. I do have things to do today."

"Okay then. I'm all ears, and I can take as much or as little time as you have."

His desk phone rang. He twisted around in his chair and called out to Jenny to please answer it. Then he waited, big hands folded in his lap, alert eyes focused on hers.

Now that she was faced with explaining herself, Annie didn't know where to start.

She looked away, out the window to the parking lot, hearing Jenny's soft voice telling the caller that Pastor Mike was in a "session" and would get back to him or her.

That's what this is . . . a session?

So formal. It made her feel like a specimen or a patient. She almost wished she hadn't come. What could Mike possibly say to her? But here she was.

"Annie, I know there's a big hole in your life now—"

"Pastor Mike, please let me say this my own way. I do want to talk about Ellen, but I always have to do things in order, you know? So I need to start at the beginning, which wasn't Ellen." Annie found she couldn't speak her friend's name without choking on the gravel in her throat.

"Okay, take your time. Sorry if I jumped the gun."

Annie relaxed her hands. "I don't know how it all started. I guess at dinner last night, and then the last thing happened just now right outside your office. I was rude to sweet little Jenny, and I don't know why. It was when she asked me if I'm all right—Roger asked me the same thing last night, twice. Guess I'm getting tired of telling people I'm just fine, thank you very much."

"I won't ask you then," he said with a wink. His warm dark

eyes swam in a sea of brown skin, smooth and unlined. A faint scar snaked down his forehead, crossing his left eyebrow—a souvenir of his past life, an African-American kid who grew up on the streets of Chicago, barely managing to stay out of the gangs.

Pastor Mike was young to be a senior pastor—younger than she and Roger by a few years, married to a schoolteacher, and had one five-year-old son, with another on the way. He was a mountain of a man who'd started his ministry life as a youth pastor, then was ordained and installed at Garden Street as the senior pastor after the previous minister retired.

Annie and Roger had liked his style of preaching from the start. He used plain, sometimes brusque language and never tried to sugarcoat anything. He always said it came from pastoring young people—you had to tell them the unvarnished truth about the world and themselves without pandering to their delicate, over-done feelings.

Some of that unvarnished truth had led to people leaving the church in a huff, but even so, the growing number of attenders more than made up for it. Mike's rough past was no secret, and he often said it enabled him see through his parishioners' occasional dissembling in counseling sessions.

"Why don't you just start at the beginning, Annie—at dinner last night. What happened?"

"It started with Hank asking us if we knew what would happen if the earth suddenly stopped rotating. Can you believe such a question coming from a twelve-year-old?"

"Intriguing. What did he say was the answer?"

"Something about thousand-mile-per-hour winds, ocean waves a hundred miles tall—you know, the usual complete global devastation and end of life as we know it. And you know what he said after that?"

"I can't imagine. Or maybe I can."

"He said it'd be 'cool.'"

Mike shook his head and grinned. "Kids."

Annie twisted her hands together in her lap. "Then there's this essay Mayra has to write."

"Essay?"

Annie led him through the conversation they'd had on the topic of Mayra's essay.

"Hmm. New take on a centuries-old question. Although I'm not sure it's appropriate for a tenth grader."

He looked away from her and gazed out the window. "Kids are forced to tackle adult subjects much too young these days, don't you think?"

"I was just thinking that this morning when Cassie—" She stopped herself from giving away a confidence.

"When Cassie what?"

She grimaced. "Oh, never mind that. It has nothing to do with what we're talking about anyway." She thought for a moment. What to say? "Mayra didn't seem too upset by the essay question. Maybe it's not as big a deal as we think it is."

Mike chuckled. "Yeah, she was probably putting on a brave front. Kids do that sometimes, in my experience. Especially in front of their parents." He spread his hands. "Adults, too, I'm afraid. It's better than being vulnerable." His sharp-eyed gaze pierced her own.

"Roger asked me how I'd answer it, and I'm still trying to figure it out."

She paused, then went on with her story—recounting to him the details of the rings in the photos, the man in the park and his gift of the black ring box, which had mysteriously disappeared this morning, hers and Nora's dreams, Mayra's notebook, and ending with the news announcer.

The more she talked, the more irrational her words sounded to her ears. She couldn't bring herself to tell him all of it—like seeing her dead mother in the park last night and the unopened letter she'd found in the box.

Pastor Mike didn't help either. He listened to her without asking any questions—and other than the one statement, an occasional "uh-huh" was his only comment.

She wished he would stop her and tell her something, *anything*. Even if he called her weird or silly, at least it would be something.

He laughed out loud when she got to the part about the butter. "I bet that was a funny sight. What'd Nora have to say?"

Annie allowed the corners of her mouth to lift in spite of how foolish she felt. "She jumped into my lap, and we laughed until we cried. It was pretty funny, I suppose. Mommy sitting on the floor looking like a giant piece of cinnamon toast in sweatshirt and jeans."

An awkward silence followed. Annie wasn't used to baring her soul like this to anyone but Roger. She didn't have any girl-friends—now—with whom she was close enough to let her hair down. And besides, Mike was a man. He was bound to look at things differently—analytically, she supposed, like Roger. It was such a farfetched chain of events. He was probably thinking right now of doctors he should connect her to. The kind who made a business of tackling other people's weirdness.

"Is that all? I mean, were you finished?"

Annie shook her head and gripped the arms of her chair like it was a car on a roller coaster.

19

"No. There's more." She forced herself to loosen her grip and put her hands in her lap.

"After I cleaned up the mess in the kitchen, I found the box under the cabinet. The ring was there, and it *is* identical to the ones our moms are wearing in the pictures. The same words are on it. Can you believe that? And I didn't tell you before, but the man in the park told me to wear it today. I was afraid . . . Don't know why. Maybe *Lord of the Rings* stuff, like if I put it on, I'd vanish into another dimension or something."

Annie stopped again, unable to go on. She stared out at the traffic whizzing by, the sunshine, heard the faint sound of the babbling fountain.

Mike didn't interrupt her thoughts, just sat waiting for her to go on.

She dug her fingernails into her palm. The physical pain pushed her next words into the room. "Then I got the call about Ellen."

His eyes turned bleak as he nodded, eyebrows raised to his

hairline. "Ahh. May I say again how sorry I am? I know it doesn't help much, but—"

"She called me last night and as much as told me she wouldn't be around today. It was the most bizarre conversation I've ever had with her—and she's done plenty of bizarre over the decades we've been friends. Now, what do you think about that? Anything in your *pastorese* to explain that?"

Annie was surprised he wasn't put off by her tone, but his expression didn't change.

He picked up a pen from his desk, twirling it. "If you've got a hammer, everything looks like a nail," he murmured to himself.

Annie barely caught his words. "What did you say?"

He put the pen down and looked at her, brows pushed together. "Oh, just something my dad used to say. Mostly to my mom. Meaning, sometimes when something weird happens and then another thing happens, we connect dots that aren't really there. We make everything seem like a dot."

"That's what you think I'm doing?"

"I have no idea."

"You have no idea? Just what *do* you have an idea about?"

He sat up straighter. "Apparently not much. About Ellen—I know you two were friends for a long time." He paused. "I can see how this is all piling up on you. Is that how you feel?"

"That's one way to put it." *Like dirt piled on a grave.*

"I'm going over to visit Mark later today. Would you like to tag along? Maybe it'd help." He broke off, staring at her face. "I'm sorry, Annie."

Words exploded out of her mouth without thought. "You're sorry? About what? The man in the park? The essay question? Or this ring nonsense? Ellen? Just who or what *exactly* are you sorry about, Pastor Mike?"

That got his attention—he looked like he'd been slapped.

She berated herself again. "I'm sorry. I shouldn't have said that." She wanted to add, "You're just a man," but stopped herself in time.

He crossed his muscular arms in front of him, a tattoo peeking out from under his shirtsleeve. "I was going to say, I'm sorry that this is one of those times when I have no answers for someone I care about."

Annie was thunderstruck. Her good manners took a backseat again, but she was tired of the pretense. She needed to make rational out of irrational.

"That's it—no answers? Aren't you a pastor? Don't you shepherd your flock? I'm one of the sheep, Mike, and I need to know what's going on. That's why I came to *you* today. This is all just so . . . so crazy! I don't believe in crazy stuff like this. I never played with a Ouija board when I was a kid, never smoked pot, never liked horror movies. This is just too scary—"

She broke off, trying to get herself under control before she lost it completely.

"Mike, I'm—"

Jenny's voice in the doorway interrupted her. "Can I get you guys anything? Water or—"

She broke off and looked down at her feet. "Sorry to interrupt."

Mike twisted around in his chair. "No, thank you, Jenny. Please close the door."

Out of her side view, Annie noted Jenny's disturbed expression, but there was nothing she could do about that. She hoped Jenny wouldn't gossip—

Annie decided she shouldn't have come. She should be at home with Nora, not sitting here spilling her guts to a busy pastor, interrupting his day with her problems. Whatever possessed her to think that he or anyone else would be able to make sense out of her nonsense?

The silence stretched on, and Pastor Mike seemed in no hurry to fill it.

She raised her head and looked at him, her eyes now swimming in tears. "Mike, I'm sorry. Maybe I shouldn't have burdened you with this."

He waved a hand, dismissing her apology. "I have a question for you, Annie. First, though, you and Roger have been members here for how long?"

She shrugged. "What's that got to do with anything?"

"Just humor me, okay? I have a reason for asking."

She had to think a moment. "About twelve years, I guess. I think Mayra was three when our other church ran into that bit of trouble and we started looking for a new place to attend."

"Hmm, twelve years. And I've been here about six. Time flies."

"Why are you asking?"

"Just getting my bearings with you. Your family has been to dinner with us once, and you attend regularly, but I don't recall either of you coming to my office for any help or counseling. We've had no in-depth conversations that I remember. Can I ask you something personal?"

She managed a weak chuckle at the irony of his question.

"Pastor Mike, I just unburdened myself to you—told you a crazy story. Unzipped my fly, the way Roger would say it. Personal? Of course."

"Do you believe in God?"

Now it was her turn to feel slapped.

"Of . . . of course I believe in God. How can you even ask?" Her voice squeaked on the last word. She remembered Ellen telling her last night that her voice always squeaked when she was rattled. Why was Ellen always right about her?

The silence stretched, punctuated by the creak of Jenny's chair in the outer office.

Annie pulled at her next breath and pressed her hands together in front of her. "Do you . . . do you think this has something to do with God?"

She couldn't bring herself to say what she really wanted to, that maybe God was trying to tell her something.

"Life usually does, Annie," he said with a wry grin. "Have something to do with God, I mean. No, I just wanted to know your perspective. I assumed you believe in God, but if there's one thing I've learned being a pastor—especially a pastor to kids—it's never to assume anything."

He tapped his pen on his chair arm, clearly giving his words time to sink in.

Annie, though, had lost the train of words flowing from her pastor's mouth. She was stuck on the thought that God might really be telling her something. Would God tell her ahead of time?

She gulped. "So you think God's trying to tell me something? God doesn't do this kind of thing, does he? Make words appear where they've never been before, men appearing and disappearing in the fog. Mike, this sounds like a Stephen King novel, not God. I refuse to believe that . . . that—"

"That what? That God can speak to us any way he chooses?"

"I guess."

"I can assure you from personal experience that God knows exactly how to get my attention—and yours."

"I suppose."

"No supposing about it. And as far as words appearing where they've never been before, just ask old King Belshazzar. Ya know—from Daniel 5—the writing on the wall? I can assure you, when that disembodied hand appeared, the heads wagged and the Babylon mainstream media started their spin."

Annie didn't know what to say. She'd expected her pastor to say it was just coincidence, her imagination on overdrive, or some bad food. She thought he'd pat her on the head and tell her to go home and read her Bible, pray—and all the other pastor counseling she'd heard before. She hadn't expected him to take this craziness seriously.

Mike took a sip of water from the bottle on his desk and wiped his mouth.

Annie studied his face. Was he was trying to decide what to say next and how to say it? Like a doctor with bad news? She steeled herself.

20

"Annie, I can tell you're surprised. It's just that I've seen some things. Things that defy explanation. Things even more weird than this. I'm no stranger to death, as you know. You've heard my story, right? How I grew up in Chicago?"

Thank goodness! Let's get off the Annie train . . .

She nodded. "Some of it. Your dad was a cop, and you had a brother who was killed. That's pretty much what I know."

"Yes. Dad and Mom did their best to protect us from gang activity, even moved us to three different neighborhoods over the years we were growing up. And we stayed out, thanks to them. My bro, Lenny, and I were tight. At least, until he was gunned down on a Saturday night outside the minimart where Mom sent him to buy milk. He went to buy milk, and they killed him because he refused to join them. Then they came after me."

Annie shivered. She'd heard some of this over the years but had always found it hard to believe that this humble, compassionate, gifted pastor could have had beginnings like this. "What did you do?"

"Almost gave in. Almost. I was scared. I didn't want to die, but I didn't want to disappoint my parents either. There was a guy I met one night. Name was Shake, on account of he was good at what he did—shakin' the locals down for money and favors. He was the man with the plan, the one who promised to take care of me, the one who ran the drugs and the girls. Shake was finally payin' attention to *me*, the kid. If I joined, my street cred would go through the roof. That is, if I played my cards right, played it cool, acted like I didn't care if I impressed him or not. Shake didn't like groupies and fanboys, always begging for attention."

His eyes had a faraway look in them, like he was back in Chicago, on the sweltering streets he'd been rescued from.

Annie had trouble following the street jargon Mike had lapsed into, but she didn't want to interrupt him. The way he talked reminded her of cop movies she and Roger had watched when they were younger, before kids.

"Was Lenny older or younger than you?"

Her question brought him back from whatever mean street he'd been on. He focused on her. "I was the youngest—just seventeen at the time. But I was also the biggest and strongest."

"Seventeen? So young—" She thought of Mayra and Hank.

Mike's gaze sank to his shoes then. "And then Lenny was killed. I wondered at the time if Shake had anything to do with it. That was the last time I ever even thought about joining a gang."

Mike looked up at Annie, eyes like liquid pools of memory. Some of those memories slipped down his cheeks.

"I don't think I can make you understand . . ." His voice trailed away. Then came back.

"Anyway, the way it happened was Lenny walked out of the minimart and stopped on the sidewalk to smoke. Witnesses said a car came screaming around the corner, three short-barreled shotguns poked out the windows. Lenny had just lit up and turned his head away a split second too long. He didn't have a chance."

"Did he die right there?"

"No. He lived for three weeks—a vegetable—before he finally died. That's what did it for me, and it just about killed my dad."

She pushed the words out. "You didn't know his tomorrows were used up that night."

"Nope." He paused and stared over her head at his bookshelves.

"They never solved the case. No one ever paid."

"That doesn't seem right—"

"Street justice—"

"But it still isn't right."

"Dad agreed. He worked the case on his own time for years. Got fired over it."

Annie winced at the harshness of it. How had Mike survived?

"Where was your mom in all this, Mike? Didn't she try? Didn't she care?"

Mike looked down at the floor, clearly struggling with his answer.

Maybe she'd run off with another man. Maybe she was still alive somewhere, in a home or in jail. Maybe she shouldn't have asked, but it was too late now.

"Mom gave up on life years before Lenny was murdered. She couldn't deal with Dad's job anymore—and the struggle. Dad found her one morning in the garage with the car running. There was a bottle of whiskey on the floor under her feet and the empty pill bottle—antidepressants. I was ten."

Annie gripped the chair arms until her knuckles whitened. Tears slid out between her closed eyelids. She opened her eyes and stared at her hands. Her troubles didn't compare with what he'd been dealt. She felt a red tinge of shame creep up her neck. "However did you survive? It must've seemed so hopeless to your parents."

"That's true, Annie. But not if God steps in."

"Did he?"

"Big time. In the form of a friend of my dad's, who took me under his wing and saw to it that I went to college and made something of myself. And here I sit. I'll never be able to repay that man. He did what my dad was unable to do. That's why I became a youth pastor—to give back just a tiny bit of what I was given."

"Is your dad still . . . around?"

"Nah, he died about eight years ago. Cancer."

Annie met his eyes, then looked away. So much suffering. She supposed it was why Mike was able to empathize with people. He'd always been compassionate to hurting folks .

Mike tapped his fingers on the arm of his chair. He had a faraway look in his eyes, and Annie got the idea he was about to say something hard to her, words she wouldn't want to hear.

She was right.

21

"So," he began, "as I said, I'm not unacquainted with death. And neither are you, as I recall. Your parents, Roger's parents. And Abby, although I never heard the details—"

"Don't go there."

"Okay. Just saying. Listening to you, I can see this has made you think. Annie, it's not a bad thing to think about that essay question of Mayra's. For any of us. Maybe it would change how we do life, how we treat others, how we plan for the future. Maybe if we'd thought about it when we were kids, we'd have done things differently. Maybe I'd still have a brother and parents. Who knows?"

"Are you telling me you think your story is like mine? Because it's not."

"Not in the least. But in some ways, all human stories are alike."

"What do you mean? I've never come close to being in a gang—" Annie rubbed her hand over her forehead. "Sorry, Mike. I didn't mean that the way it sounded."

"How did you mean it?"

"I meant you can't compare your story with mine, unless I'm missing something."

"You are. Think about it."

"What if I don't want to think about it? I'm tired of trying to understand what's happening to me. Maybe I *am* just going crazy."

"Don't think so. Annie, our stories are alike in one way. We're both created by a loving God who wants us to know him. He knows exactly how to speak to each of his creations, whether it's a human, a kangaroo, or a spider."

"Mike, you never cease to amaze me. I had no idea God talked to spiders."

He grinned. "Why not? He thought them up. Annie, maybe it's time to consider the possibility that you might have something to learn."

"Well, what do you suggest I do? Accept that tomorrow is my day to die? Be more like Ellen? Get my affairs in order? Eat chocolate all day? What?"

He smiled and lifted his shoulders. "I have no idea, Annie. But chocolate might help."

She slumped against the back of her chair. The shame she'd felt over her harsh words to him eased into profound disappointment. She'd come here—to her pastor—looking for answers, and there were none. She turned an accusing eye on him. But she didn't have the heart to say what she wanted to say. That coming here was wasted time, time she could've spent . . . *doing what?*

"I'm sorry. I guess I should have answers for you." He leaned over and patted her arm.

She jerked away from him, her arms tight around her middle.

He retreated, leaning back in his chair.

"I assume you've told Roger about . . . all of this?"

"I thought you never assumed."

"Hardly ever—"

"And no, I haven't."

"May I ask why? Would he laugh or think you're crazy?"

Annie couldn't answer. In her mind's eye, she saw Roger's face. She couldn't read what was there. "He didn't answer his phone this morning. And anyway, I have no idea what he'd think. So I guess you and I are rowing the same canoe."

Pastor Mike dropped the question. Instead, his gaze drifted down to her hand. "Is that it?" he asked, pointing. "The ring?"

Annie lifted her hand and spread her fingers. "The same as in the photos of our parents—and I'm positive I've never seen these words before." She sucked in a breath and clenched her fists. "Mike, it's beyond weird, isn't it? How can this possibly be God?" Her voice was too loud, but she didn't care. "Do you think it could be . . . well, the opposite? A demon or something? I've heard of such things."

He shrugged. She was glad he didn't answer—she was afraid of what he might say. She saw herself strapped down on a bed while Pastor Mike leaned over her chanting Scripture at the demon, like in the movies. She shuddered.

Mike took her slim hand gingerly in his own massive black one and gazed down at the ring, the stone flashing in the overhead lights. He rubbed his thumb over it.

"Can you see the words?" she asked.

"Yeah. And you've never seen these words before last night?"

"No, I swear. I'd remember, don't you think?" She slapped a palm to her forehead. "What am I going to do?"

He let go of her hand and sat back in his chair again. After a moment, he spread his hands and said the reassuring words she'd come to hear.

"Some people might say it's a demon. I'm not one of them. But if it's not God, then who? I don't believe in people talking to us from the grave."

That question got her. Indeed, who? And if it was God, then why was she so afraid? Didn't she believe he loved her?

"Annie, have you *asked* God if it's him talking to you?

"No."

"Why not?"

"Because if I do, it'll be real." She shrugged. "I don't want this to be real."

Pastor Mike didn't make a move to comfort her. She was glad—she didn't want to be comforted. She needed the truth, no matter how frightening it was.

"Mike, I don't think this could possibly be God. Why would he talk to me this way?"

"I'm sure a guy named Balaam thought the same thing. But it *was* God—talking out of a donkey's mouth."

"Guess I should be glad I don't have a donkey—" She put her face in her hands.

Pastor Mike stood and walked around behind his desk and sat, all business now. "Annie, I would encourage you to ask God if it's him talking to you. Just ask him. He won't think you're silly. You do understand that he knew all of this was going to happen anyway, don't you? He knows each moment of our lives before the moment comes. He knew my life from my beginnings on the streets of Chicago to where I ended up today—the pastor of a church in Washington State. He went ahead of both you and me and was waiting for us to arrive. Do you believe that? Really believe it?"

"I guess. I just didn't think God did weird stuff like this. I thought God was logical."

Mike grinned. "C. S. Lewis would disagree."

She raised her eyebrows.

"'He's not a tame lion'. Aslan . . . you know, *The Chronicles of Narnia*?"

"Yeah, I know. Always the kids' favorite storybooks." She stood and shouldered her purse. "I guess I should be going. I've taken up enough of your time."

"Not at all. Anytime—and remember, Annie, God's thoughts are not ours. His logic isn't ours either." He grinned. "That was a Pastor Mike paraphrase."

She reached for her keys in the side pocket of her bag.

"Pastor?"

"Yes?"

"Do *you* think I might . . . I might . . . die tomorrow?"

There. It was out. The question she needed answered. Annie couldn't meet his eyes. She folded her hands together, gripping her keys between her palms, and felt the hardness of the ring's stone against her fingers.

He pushed his chair back and stood, his six feet six inches dwarfing Annie. His frown deepened as he ran a hand through his curly black hair, streaked here and there with gray, then locked eyes with her.

"I don't know, Annie," he whispered in that silky smooth voice, the same voice he used when he presided over a funeral. "But here's the thing. Death doesn't end life. Never has."

22

Annie felt at loose ends as she strapped Nora into her car seat. It was only a little after 11:00 a.m., and she had until 3:30 before the after-school kid roundup began. On any other Friday, she'd be with the other moms until after lunch, then would go home and put Nora down for a nap.

She didn't want to go home yet. She thought about going to the park, but the thought of Nora sitting on the swings where Joshua—if that was really his name—sat last night made her stomach heave.

She stopped at the entrance to the church parking lot, now empty save the pastor's vehicle, indecision making her stomach do flip-flops. Annie knew what was wrong. She usually planned her day and knew exactly how it would progress, but between last night and this morning, *usually* had become meaningless, a foreign word.

She lowered her head to the steering wheel, closed her eyes, and rested her forehead on her fingers. The ring pressed into her skin.

She opened her right eye. There, on the console between the seats was the answer—her hastily scribbled grocery list. They did indeed need a few things. She sat up, put the van back in gear, and turned left instead of right out of the parking lot.

"Nora, we're going to the grocery store before we head for home. Okay, baby?"

"Will you buy me something?"

Why do they always want something? Human nature, she supposed.

"What do you want?" Annie asked as she braked at the four way stop sign at the next block. She wondered if Roger needed anything. She decided to call him when they arrived.

"M&M's for me and Mr. Bear?"

"Well, I'll think about it. Maybe something healthier, okay?" Even as Annie gave her auto-mom answer, she thought how good M&M's would taste right now. Maybe her favorite, the ones with peanut butter instead of chocolate. *Maybe I should buy a case. After all, today might be my last day.*

Carefully looking both ways, she put her foot on the gas pedal and started through the intersection. Out of nowhere, a late-model gray Mercedes ran the stop sign and screamed through in front of her, missing her front bumper by mere inches.

Annie jammed her foot on the brake and lay on the horn while pounding the steering wheel and yelling at the inattentive driver, who didn't even slow down. She glanced to see if anyone was bearing down on her from behind, unable to stop. Luckily, there wasn't. It'd happened so fast, she doubted if a serious accident could have been avoided. She didn't fancy being the middle of a vehicle sandwich.

As the Mercedes peeled out past her hood, the driver turned a white face to her and gave her the one-finger salute. Really? Annie had the impression he was an older man, probably not fit to be driving a car. She noticed a dent in the rear fender of the Mercedes. Not surprising.

"Mommy! What happened?" Nora squealed.

Annie turned and reached back, patting a butterfly on Nora's sneakered toes. "It's okay, honey. Just a stupid driver running a stop sign. I'm sorry I stopped so fast and yelled, but he almost hit us. You okay?"

Nora nodded, her eyes wide and moist. She clutched her blanket to her cheek and put her thumb in her mouth.

Annie stopped herself from saying *thumb out*. She didn't have the heart for it right now.

A horn blew behind her, three loud blasts in quick succession. Putting the van in gear, she muttered, "Okay, okay. Keep your shirt on back there."

Annie's heart still raced from the near miss as she found a spot in the grocery store parking lot. She grabbed her purse and helped Nora out of her car seat, then found a cart nearby and lifted Nora into it.

"Can I take my bear, Mommy? He wants to come."

Annie picked the bear up off the car seat and handed it to her. "Sure you can, honey. But you're in charge of him. Just like I'm in charge of you. Make sure he doesn't wander off."

Nora clutched it to her neck, eyes wide. "Just like me?"

She cupped the child's face between her hands and kissed her forehead. "Yeah, baby. Just like I'll make sure *you* won't get lost."

Not like some mothers, she thought, then shoved the harsh thought away. She wasn't like some mothers.

Annie pushed the cart through the parking lot. Near the front doors, she stopped, staring.

The Mercedes—the one that almost hit them—was parked on the sidewalk at a crazy angle, right in front of the store's automatic doors, blocking one side.

What in the world?

She was sure it was the same car because of the dent in the rear fender. Did the man think he owned the world, parking like that? Annie maneuvered carefully around the car and continued through the entrance.

Maybe someone would key his fancy car. It would serve him right.

"Mommy, you have your frowny face on again," Nora chirped.

"I'm sorry, sweetie." Annie gave her a goofy grin. "How's that?"

"Better, Mommy. Mr. Bear likes it." Nora dangled the stuffed animal in front of her face. One eye had fallen off last year, and Annie had found a large green button to stitch in its place. Nora loved it and said Mr. Bear could see better with the button than with his real eye.

Annie leaned over and kissed the tip of Nora's nose and then planted one on Mr. Bear's droopy ear. "Thank you, Mr. Bear." She drew back and took Nora's chubby hands in her own. "And now, Miss Nora, we need to get our shopping done."

Annie, watching Nora, made a sudden decision. "How about we get it done fast, drop it off at home, then go to the park for a playdate? Just you and me."

Nora's stare lasered her with warrior fierceness. "And Mr. Bear?"

Annie smiled. "Yes, and Mr. Bear too, if he wants to come."

She'd decided it was foolish to avoid the park today—such a nice day—just because of what happened last night. She knew how quickly time passed—it wouldn't be long before Nora would be in school, and the days of playing in the park with her would be gone.

"Would you like to take a picnic lunch to the park?"

After an enthusiastic nod from Nora and Mr. Bear, they were off. She sped around the store, adding picnic supplies—and M&M's—to her list.

As she exited, she noticed the Mercedes still parked in front of the store. Annie wheeled her cart around it. The driver who'd flipped her off in the intersection stood next to it, arguing with the manager of the store. The manager finally flung his hands up and retreated back inside.

Annie shook her head and loaded Nora and the groceries into the car.

"Mommy, why were those men yelling at each other?"

"I'm not sure, but maybe it's because the man's car was on the sidewalk blocking the door. That's my guess. He didn't seem to care that people had to go around his car to get inside."

Annie locked the last strap of the car seat in place, but before she could close the door, Nora patted her hand.

"Mommy, maybe something's wrong with him—his face was frowny just like yours."

She held Mr. Bear's mouth close to her ear. "What did you say?"

Nora nodded and looked up at Annie. "Mr. Bear said we should pray for him."

Annie drew a deep breath. "He's probably right, honey. We should always pray instead of getting mad." *Out of the mouths of babes . . . and their bears.* "Okay, honey, let's get going."

She remembered she hadn't called Roger to see if he needed anything, but his usual answer to that question was, "All I need is you, babe."

Smiling, Annie put the car in gear, glad to be heading home.

23

fter arriving home and putting the groceries away, Annie sent Nora upstairs to change into her play-in-the-park clothes while she made their favorite picnic food—PB&J sandwiches, cut into bite-sized squares. She packed a small cooler with fruit, a thermos of milk, and two bottles of water. After adding small plates and napkins, she snapped the lid shut and plunked down on a kitchen stool, thinking over the last what . . . six hours? And that on top of last night. How had so much happened in such a short amount of time?

Annie rubbed her eyes, suddenly realizing how emotionally drained she was. Her chest felt tight, and she felt exhaustion in every bone. She decided she couldn't do the park today. She was worn to a frazzle, and the day wasn't even half over. She'd tell Nora they could spread a blanket in the living room and pretend they were at the park. Annie hoped she wouldn't be too disappointed. Of all her children, Nora was the scrappiest and would probably put up a fight over it.

She tiptoed upstairs to find Nora. Peeking into her room, Annie heard Nora talking to herself, huddled on the floor at the foot of her bed with Mr. Bear on her lap. Annie sidled closer to the door to listen.

"Mr. Bear, we're going to the park to have a picnic. I'll push you on the swing like Mommy pushes me."

Annie slumped against the doorframe. Guilt washed over her for wanting to cancel after she'd promised, but she didn't have the energy. She could always take her to the park another day.

"What did you say, Mr. Bear?"

Annie managed a weak smile. She'd always thought the best part of parenting was to stand back and let your children be who they were . . . and this was all Nora. She was truly her own little person. Her imagination knew no bounds, and for a three-year-old she had an astonishing vocabulary. Annie and Roger had always insisted on no baby talk with her. Even the other three kids were diligent about that.

She peeked into the room again.

At first she didn't see her. Then she realized Nora had moved. Her voice now came from the far side of her bed, under the window. Annie stood on her tiptoes and saw the top of her head.

Nora sat cross-legged on the floor with her back to Annie, the bear facing her on her lap. She answered the stuffed animal with all the intensity of a three-year-old in a make-believe world. "Mr. Bear, speak up. I still can't hear you. Stop *mubbling*."

Nora's version of *mumbling*, Annie guessed. They'd have to work on that word with her.

"There, that's better. Of course you can go—Mommy said. The park will be fun for Mommy too. She had her frowny face on today, so we have to take her to the park so she'll feel better. Get it?"

Mr. Bear evidently got it, because Nora jumped up and laid

him on her bed. "You sit here while I put my play jeans on, okay? You already have yours on."

She went to her dresser and pawed through her clothes.

Annie barely had time to escape from the doorway without being seen. She made her way downstairs.

By the time she reached the bottom, she'd changed her mind again—Nora was wise beyond her years. They both needed a playdate.

She heard Nora start down the stairs. "Mommy, are we going now?"

"In a few minutes, honey. I'll be ready soon. Just play in your room until I call you."

"Okay, Mommy." Nora's feet tromped back down the upstairs hall.

Annie closed the drapes and blinds in the living room, then went to the kitchen and made sure the back door was locked. With the cooler and their backpacks on her arm, she opened the front door and set them on the porch.

She heard a rustle of paper and looked up. The Baxters' newspaper lay in the middle of the cul-de-sac, blowing in the breeze.

She stepped off the porch, walked into the street, and picked up the scattered newspaper. The Baxters' house looked quiet and deserted. She thought about knocking on the door, but finally decided to put the paper in their mailbox. Studying the front of the house, she wondered again about the sirens Roger had mentioned this morning. She hadn't heard them. It was unnerving to think she'd been awake until the wee hours and hadn't heard sirens in their small cul-de-sac. How could that be?

And at this time of day Eleanor Baxter could usually be seen puttering in her flowers, raking dead leaves and getting her garden ready for spring. But nothing stirred across the street. Even the tall windows on either side of the Baxters' front door looked blank, empty, like the life inside had emptied overnight.

Annie shook herself and realized she stood in the middle of the street, staring at her neighbor's house. Maybe someone was watching her and wondering what she was doing. She strode back to her own yard.

Annie entered the house again, intending to call Nora and get going, but instead found herself wandering to the dining room and leaning breathlessly against the credenza.

The two pictures had always brought a measure of peace and security to Annie's soul, but not today. Instead of a symbol of family heritage and stability, they mocked her. Why?

She locked eyes with her mother, twisting the ring round and round on her finger. She was certain her mother was trying to say something. Something Annie couldn't quite hear—something important. She leaned forward until her hair brushed the frame, so close she smelled the paint on the wall. Annie blinked, not believing what she saw. Her mother's lips were moving?

Impossible—

She took a sharp breath and focused on her mother's eyes. But her mother's eyes had disappeared, sunk into her head. Shocked, Annie realized the photo had changed—her parents were gone, and now she saw a tree-lined street. The branches of the trees moved in a slight breeze, some fluttering to the ground while she watched.

It was happening again . . . would this never stop?

Leaning close again, Annie smelled damp leaves instead of the paint on her walls. Her hair stirred and brushed against the picture frame. She felt a light touch on her back, pushing her ever so softly. Panic surged upward from her toes to her chest as she death-gripped the edge of the credenza.

24

nnie tried to step back, but her feet were leaden, as if they were magnetized on a metal floor. She couldn't stop herself from being pulled, or pushed, into the frame. From somewhere above and off to her right, she heard Nora giggle, then Ellen's voice saying, "Annie, just go with it. Don't fight it."

She loosened her grip on the edge of the credenza, letting her hands drift to her sides. The edge of the picture frame brushed her hair, and Annie forced herself to relax as she floated in.

She glanced backward at her shrinking dining room, fading and becoming smaller and smaller. The tick of the grandfather clock grew faint, then disappeared as she left her home behind. Annie faced forward again, just as she felt rough concrete under her feet.

She found herself on a pitted, chipped sidewalk covered with red and golden leaves. The slight breeze stirred them into little eddies, and a hint of chill in the air pricked the skin on her arms.

Annie judged it was early fall here, wherever here was. Eyes wide, taking in the scene, she thought it a pleasant place, but something wasn't right. The light around her was shinier, brighter than wherever she'd come from. And the trees were taller. Sounds were . . . louder. It was as if her vision and hearing were somehow . . . *younger.*

And what's this? She looked down and gasped at how close to the ground she was. Then she caught sight of her feet. She knew those shoes. They were the first pair she'd been allowed to pick out all by herself, when she was ten years old.

She put a hand to her hair and felt the ribbon. She never wore ribbons in her hair now. . . that was a Daddy's-girl thing. Annie's heart pounded as looked down at her body, no bigger than Kimmie's.

She ran her hand over her pink T-shirt and lightweight jacket, noticing her smaller hand and lack of rings.

A car moved slowly past her on the street. She didn't know cars very well—not like Hank and Roger—but she knew this model had to be at least thirty years old, though it looked brand new.

Annie let her eyes drift over the neighborhood. Worn, pot-holed sidewalk. Small, neat clapboard homes with faded paint. Trees dotting the grassy strips on both sides of the narrow roadway. Cars parked in driveways, on lawns, and in the roadway, some with their hoods up.

Children's voices carried on the breeze. Two teenaged boys rode by on bikes too small for them, weaving on and off the sidewalk and between parked cars.

Likely a community of young families, she thought.

Annie turned her attention to the yard she stood closest to, stomach churning. The house was painted a pale green with white trim. A dented blue Chevy pickup sat in the driveway. An impossibly long white four-door sedan occupied the driveway space in front of the truck.

She stared at the pickup. One fender—the front driver's side—was painted black, and she knew why. Her father had hit a power pole one day trying to avoid hitting the neighbor's cat. He hadn't wanted to pay someone to fix and repaint, so he'd done it himself.

She stared at the green house again. A wind chime hung to the right of the front door. She'd made that wind chime for her mother last year . . . no, no . . . at least three decades ago.

Three decades ago.

Annie couldn't escape it now—this was the home and neighborhood she'd lived in when Mom and Dad had finally settled down. She'd been ten, just started fifth grade, and had just met Ellen. Somehow, the picture of her parents had drawn her into her past.

She looked across the street to where her best friend lived . . . used to live. Becky and her family had moved last month, just before school started, leaving Annie with no one to play with. Being an only child sucked. But then she'd met Ellen, who'd moved in the day before school started.

She looked down at her watch to see how much time had passed and how long she'd left Nora alone in the house. But of course her watch was no longer there. Her mouth tasted bitter fear, like the strong acidic coffee her father had preferred.

She must find a way to get back to Nora. She looked behind her again, but of course the picture frame had disappeared.

Annie heard a screen door slam, and she whirled to see her mother marching toward her, a sweater around her shoulders and her floppy gardening hat shoved over her old-fashioned bun.

Annie wanted to ask why she was here, why she was a child again, but those weren't the words that shot out of her mouth.

She looked *up* at her mother's angry face. "Isn't Daddy coming?" Her voice sounded whiny and demanding, reminding her of Mayra.

Daddy?

Annie breathed in short gulps as realization crept in. She knew this day. She'd lived it before.

Her mother's pained expression made her take a step back. "No, he's not—"

Annie was surprised to feel her heart plummet to her feet.

"But why, Mommy?"

She felt like a curious mixture of grown woman and little girl, able to think adult thoughts while in a child's body.

Maybe that's how we always are, the grown-up Annie said to the little-girl Annie.

"I don't know. We'll just have to go by ourselves again." Her mother turned at the sudden slam of the screen door.

Annie found herself darting around her mother. She leaped into her father's strong arms. "Daddy! Are you coming?"

"Yes, Angel, I'm coming." He put her down and reached for Mommy's hand.

Her mother clasped it with both of hers. "What changed your mind?"

"You."

"Because I got mad at you?"

Annie listened to this surreal exchange between her parents, able to understand with the grown-up part of her brain but somehow experiencing—at the same time—the raging emotions of a ten-year-old witnessing her parents argue.

"No, not because you got angry at me. Because I agree with you. Most of the time, I don't give you enough credit. But you *are* usually right when it comes to family stuff—when it comes to her. I know I don't say that enough." He looked down at Annie, touching the top of her head with his large hand.

Annie closed her eyes, reveling in his warm touch.

"You're right. She won't be ten forever, and I don't really *have*

160

to go to work on a Saturday. The base can get along without me today. I called in and told the boys to carry on today without me. They can handle things, and they can always call if they need me."

Joy blew through Annie's little-girl-grown-woman soul like a fresh evening breeze after a scorching-hot day. Seeing her parents smile at each other was all it took to make it a special day.

She reached for their hands, feeling the graceful, long-fingered softness of her mother's and the calloused hardness of her father's—and the empty space where his index finger should be.

He'd lost it in an accident a long time ago when he was on a ship somewhere far away. That was as much as he would ever say about it. That, and, "I'm lucky it wasn't my whole hand." He'd laughed when Annie kissed it. He told her if she kissed it enough, maybe it'd grow back.

"Where are we going, Daddy?"

"Ask your mother. She's the boss today."

"Let's go to the park."

Daddy looked surprised. "Are you sure?"

"I said it, didn't I?"

"To the park we go, then."

As they started down the sidewalk, Daddy was the first to kick leaves, and soon all three kicked, a competition to see how high they could make them fly. And from time to time as they strolled along, they lifted Annie and swung her between them. Her joyous cries and the raucous Mommy and Daddy laughter echoed up and down the street, causing neighbors to stop and stare.

They walked to the park and played under the bright autumn sky, then stopped and bought ice cream cones on the way home— the special kind with sprinkles, for this extra-special day, Daddy said.

Annie slurped her cone, some of it landing on her T-shirt. She looked down and wiped it off, but it smeared. She cast a worried look at her mother.

Mommy patted her head. "It's okay, Anna Banana. It'll come out in the wash."

Annie started to take another lick but was distracted by a butterfly dancing on the breeze in front of her face. Mesmerized, she reached for it with an ice-cream-smeared hand.

"Daddy, look! A butterfly. Can I catch it?"

"Ah, Annie, don't try. Sometimes when butterflies are caught, the magic dust gets wiped off their wings. Then they can't fly. Do you want to do that to her?"

"She's a lady butterfly? How do you know?"

"Because she's as pretty as Mommy."

Mommy gave him a little push. "Don't be ridiculous. I don't even have wings."

Daddy smirked at her. "Yet. Someday, when—"

Annie looked from one to the other, her child-self seeing in their expressions something she didn't understand, but her grown-woman-self comprehending perfectly.

Annie turned away from them, watching the butterfly dance higher and higher, finally disappearing over the trees. "Bye, Mrs. Butterfly. I hope you come back and see me some day."

It was a magical day. They ordered a gooey pizza for dinner, a treat not often indulged in, topped off by chocolate chip cookies for dessert. And they ate in front of the TV so Annie could watch her favorite programs, another rare treat.

Daddy even read her favorite story to her after dinner while Mommy cleaned up the kitchen. Annie sat on his lap, listening to his deep voice take the parts of Christopher Robin, Piglet, Tigger, and Pooh, laughing when he'd forget which part he was reading.

That night she'd buried herself under her warm covers and dreamed of golden leaves and holding hands with Mommy and Daddy. It was a day to remember—one of the few days she could recall her father's stern face ever laughing with such glee and her parents holding hands with each other.

But it was their smiles she'd remember forever.

Hiding under her covers, waiting for them to come and tuck her in, she saw those smiles again and hoped they were for her, Annie, this time.

Her grown-up self knew why their smiles had vanished underground and only occasionally made an appearance, but the little girl inside had never understood.

After they'd come, smoothed her covers, kissed her, and Daddy had checked her room for the monsters, her child eyes closed.

Just as they reached the doorway, she opened her eyes. "Daddy?"

"Yeah, baby?"

"Will you teach me more about butterflies?"

He walked back to the bed and laid his hand on her head. "Sure, honey. We'll go to the library and check out a book on butterflies."

Annie smiled and closed her eyes. She fell asleep still feeling the touch of Daddy's hand on her head.

When next she opened them, she found herself back on the sidewalk outside the house. It was as if no time had passed. It wasn't dark, and the street looked just like it had when she'd arrived.

Annie looked down at herself. She was still ten years old, but she knew what'd happened, because somewhere inside her was her grown-up self.

And there behind her hung the picture frame, the dining room visible on the other side. She strained to hear—yes, she heard Nora's giggle drift out of the frame. She turned and gazed one more time at the house and saw Mommy and Daddy waving goodbye to her from the big living room window. She waved back, wishing with all her heart they could meet Nora.

Then the pretty leaves swirled around ten-year-old Annie's

head as she rose and floated backward into the frame, out of the past and into the present.

Grown-up Annie felt her feet touch down on the solid wood of her dining room floor.

She stood for a moment, willing it not to end. She leaned closer to her mother's eyes and saw the beautiful lady butterfly dancing there on the breeze. Her father's large hand still warmed the top of her head, and her mother's eyes held hers.

The vision of the old neighborhood shrank into her mother's pupils, and she heard the ticking of the clock in the corner of her own family room—faint at first—then growing louder in her consciousness, like turning up the sound on the radio.

She was glad now she'd changed her mind about going to the park.

Staring at the picture, Annie could swear she saw the slight nod of her mother's head.

She reached and touched the empty space between their parents' photographs, where Abby . . .

After all, Nora won't be three forever, she told herself.

25

The moment ended.

Annie inhaled a gut-deep breath and stared at her own reflection in the glass covering the photograph of her parents. Her wide, unblinking eyes took in her taut expression and windblown hair.

Windblown? In the dining room?

Did I imagine this . . . or?

She edged away and tiptoed to the living room, stopping with one hand on the stair rail. Listening for a moment, she heard Nora crooning "Jesus Loves Me" in her childish lisp. When she sang *Bible,* it came out *Bi-bo.* She hadn't yet mastered *L* sounds.

Hearing her little daughter sing in her high, imperfect pitch, sounding so *ordinary,* Annie let her shoulders drop and loosened her grip on the railing, waiting until Nora finished the song.

Nora's voice wound down the stairs. "Okay, Mr. Bear, you s'posed to clap for me now. Here. I show you how."

Annie lingered a moment longer, not wanting to interrupt this tender moment.

"Thank you, Mr. Bear. Now—"

Annie looked at her watch. Noon o'clock, as Hank always said. "Nora, I've got the picnic ready. Please come down so we can go. And don't forget Mr. Bear. I know how much he wants to go with us."

"Okay, Mommy."

Waiting at the bottom of the stairs, Annie heard a drawer slam, then running footsteps.

But then it sounded like Nora stopped at Mayra's room. Annie heard another door close. *What was she doing?*

Nora appeared at the top of the stairs, clutching Mr. Bear and her favorite sneakers she'd worn earlier. She sat down, put the bear beside her, shoes on her lap, and scooted down on her seat. She held Mr. Bear by the collar, and he scooted right along with her.

Mayra had taught her to come down like that one day after Nora had fallen down four steps and almost hit her head. It'd been a good day for Mayra. As a reward for helping her baby sister, Annie had treated her to an impromptu shopping trip.

She watched Nora come down, a happy smile planted on her small face. "Good job, honey. You remembered what Sissie taught you. And I see you've taught Mr. Bear too."

"Yes, Mommy. I don't want him to fall like I did." She scrunched up her face in a frown. "It hurt."

"You're a good friend, sweetheart." She pointed at Nora's shoes. "But maybe you should put your old shoes on—those are your good ones. They might get dirty."

"Please, Mommy? I want to wear them. I promise I be careful."

Annie bent to tie the glittery laces for her—a birthday gift from Mayra. "Okay, if you promise. Honey, why did you go into Mayra's room?"

"I didn't. I just looked in."

"Why?"

"To see if she was there."

"She's at school, silly girl."

"I heard her talking, Mommy."

"But—" Annie stopped. "What did she say?"

"I don't know. I looked and she wasn't there." Nora jumped to her feet. "Are we going now?"

What in the world? Can this day get any weirder?

Annie thought the sooner she went outside into some fresh air and took a walk, the better. Maybe none of this would follow her, and maybe it wouldn't be waiting for her when they returned. "Yes, we're going now. How about we get your trike and you can ride it to the park while I walk?"

"Can Mr. Bear ride in my backpack?"

"Of course."

Annie reached for Nora's coat. "I'm not sure you'll need this, but we'll bring it just in case."

Nora rode ahead of Annie, Mr. Bear's furry brown head poking out of her backpack. The sun was bright overhead, playing hide-and-seek behind big fluffy clouds. A perfect park day, even in winter. Annie hoped the unseasonably mild weather would hold for a while.

As they passed Mr. Gruber's house, who lived next door, Annie saw him sitting on the porch as usual. She turned her head quickly, not wanting to make eye contact.

She heard a chest-rattling cough and turned to look at him again. Maybe he was sick.

Roger always called him Mr. Grubby. He'd always been the nosy kind of neighbor and continually harassed Roger about "keeping up the yard"—though why, Annie didn't know. Their yard was beautiful, but if the cranky old man saw even one dandelion, he'd holler at Roger if he was out in the yard and tell him to take care of his weedy grass. He didn't want any of those yellow buggers in *his* yard, by gum!

Roger usually grinned and waved at him. Annie wondered why he didn't tell the grumpy old man to mind his own business, but he always said life was too short to argue and Mr. Grubby was harmless anyway. And maybe annoying the neighbors was the only entertainment the old man had left.

Annie picked up the pace as they came abreast of Mr. Gruber's porch.

But Nora had other ideas. Straddling her tricycle, she planted her feet on the sidewalk and waved. "We're going to the park for a picnic. Wanna come with us?"

Oh no . . .

Annie was relieved when he peered over the top of his newspaper, shook it, then disappeared behind it without a word.

Nora's face scrunched up. "Mommy, he looks sad."

Annie didn't see anything different about his expression, but now she had to acknowledge to herself that he did look sad. Strange she'd never noticed it before. "Oh, honey, he looks the same as usual." Which was true. "Come on. Let's go."

Nora sat back down on her trike and pumped furiously.

"I bet you can't catch me, Mommy. I'm gonna beat you—"

Annie took off, jogging up behind her but letting her stay ahead. Nora's giggles wound their way into her soul and soothed the vague anxiety roosting there since yesterday.

Maybe today she could leave behind the fear that niggled around in her brain, the reason for her fences and schedules and love of *as usual.* Ellen would approve.

26

They turned into the park, using the same path she'd taken last night.

Annie saw they wouldn't be alone. Other parents who, like herself, had older children in school dotted the play area, sitting on benches and pushing their children on the swings. The climbing area buzzed with activity, tiny bodies moving in and out of the colorful castle, sliding at breakneck speed from the top, landing in heaps on the sand, and riding the merry-go-round.

"What do you want to do first, Nora? Eat or play?" Annie already knew what she'd say.

"Play!"

"I see your friend Olivia over there on the swings. Do you want to go over and say hi?"

Without answering, Nora sped away, her backpack thumping behind her, Mr. Bear's head bobbing up and down, and her bright-pink sneakers with the shiny laces making a splash on the brownish grass.

Annie followed, her own backpack straps tight across her arms, carrying the mini-cooler in one hand and towing the trike with her other.

Finding an unoccupied bench near the playground area, she parked the trike, set the cooler down next to her, and opened and guzzled a small bottle of water.

Settling on the bench, Annie took her phone out of her jacket pocket. As she did, she received a text from one of the moms in the group, asking if she'd heard about Ellen. It was a long text, saying how sad it was and what would her husband and kids do without her? On and on it went.

Annie skimmed it but decided not to answer right then. She thought it'd be a lengthy conversation and didn't want to get into it now.

She tried never to be distracted when she was in the park—or any other public place—particularly with Nora and Kimmie. She saw too many parents glued to their screens while their children played.

And there were always the horrific stories of snatched kids that started with the parent saying to the police officer, "But I just turned my back for a second!"

And then that one second became the rest of the parent's life.

Annie clicked her phone to Silent, made sure Roger's and the schools' numbers were on emergency bypass, then put it in its pocket in her backpack. She leaned back, turned her face to the sun filtering through the trees and stretched both arms along the back of the bench, listening to the gleeful shouting of children, parents talking, and dogs barking in the backyards that bordered the park.

She was glad she'd come. Not too cold, no wind, and for the first time since last night, she felt halfway normal, whatever that was these days.

She watched Nora and Olivia play, taking turns pushing each other on the swings, then sitting on the teeter-totter. Up and down, up and down. The predictable rhythm soothed her. She caught sight of Olivia's mother across the play area, sitting with another mom. She waved at Annie. Annie hoped she wouldn't come over—she didn't feel like small talk right now.

Apparently, however, Olivia's mother already had a captive audience. It looked like a serious conversation from Annie's viewpoint, both women gesticulating, faces intense, glued to the other. Annie briefly wondered what they were discussing, but she decided she didn't want to know. She'd had enough intensity the last eighteen hours. She leaned back again and looked up toward the tops of the massive trees ringing the park.

Maybe it was time to ask that question. The one Pastor Mike said she should ask. *Well, what about it, God? Are you trying to tell me something? About tomorrow?*

Annie heard a scream and jerked herself upright, her heart jumping painfully in her chest. But it was just the girls playing keep-away with Mr. Bear.

She turned her attention back to the question. She'd rather God would just come out and say it—she'd never liked riddles. *Are you trying to tell me I'm going to die tomorrow?*

There. She'd asked it in plain language. Hopefully, he'd answer the same way. She took a deep breath and took another swig of water. She wondered how long she'd have to wait.

She looked away, down the winding pathway that ended on the other side of the park where there were several covered picnic areas. An elderly man made his way toward her, his cane tap-tapping as he shuffled along. She watched as he came closer.

A dapper little man, no more than a shade over five feet tall, with thinning white hair—straggling under his narrow-brimmed hat—matched by a trim beard and mustache. He wore a black suit with a red bow tie. Very formal and correct for a walk in the park.

The tie reminded Annie of old black-and-white movies, ones

with Gene Kelly, Cyd Charisse, and Fred Astaire. Her mother had loved those old movies—filled with music from a bygone era.

One of Annie's fondest memories from her teen years was when she and her mother would drink tea and munch sugar cookies through their favorite musicals. Her mother's melodic voice—belting out "Singin' in the Rain"—now lifted on the breeze in the back of her mind, following the path through the park and floating away above the trees.

The little man was now just a few feet away.

The sidewalk curved away behind her bench, but instead of going on by her, he stopped and looked toward the play area, smiling in Nora's direction. One gold tooth glinted in the sunlight.

The flash of that gold tooth caused a buzz of alarm in Annie's brain.

27

The little man took a few more steps, reached her, and grasped the back of the bench on the other end from where Annie sat. "May I trouble you to sit on this end of the bench, miss? I'm quite winded." He punctuated his polite question with a charming little bow.

He had a faint accent Annie couldn't place. German or Austrian? It reminded her of the voices in another of her favorite movies—*The Sound of Music.* Now that he was closer, she decided he was harmless. "Of course, sir. There's plenty of room." She moved Nora's coat out of his way.

He settled himself and balanced his cane against the end of the bench. "Nice day for it, wouldn't you say, miss?"

"Yes, it is. And my name's Annie."

"All right, Annie. My name's . . . Well, today you can call me Achar. That's A-c-h-a-r."

"What a curious way to put it. Does that mean you might be someone else tomorrow?"

"Tomorrow?" He turned his face to hers. "After all, what is tomorrow? It doesn't yet exist. Who can say who we will be tomorrow if it doesn't yet exist?"

Annie turned away from him, looking for Nora. She sat in the sandbox with Olivia, her bear resting on a small hump of sand. Out of the corner of Annie's eye, she saw the man gaze in Nora's direction.

"Is there a child out there who calls you mommy?"

The buzz of alarm in Annie's brain now sounded like a thousand sirens coming her way. "Why do you ask?" she demanded.

He put up both palms in a sign of surrender, waving them in front of her. "I'm so sorry. I didn't mean to make you feel uncomfortable."

Annie unclenched her fists, knotted in her lap. "I'm sorry, but—"

"Please don't apologize. I see I'm right though, am I not? Else why would you react with such motherly vehemence?"

Annie adjusted herself on the bench to face him head on.

"You must realize that parents are always on heightened alert these days . . . Achar, did you say?"

"Yes, yes, I realize that. Again, I apologize. I can assure you that I quite understand. And yes, it's Achar."

After another sideways glance at Nora, she said, "If I may ask, what does your name mean? Is it a nickname?"

He chuckled, looking toward her but not quite meeting her eyes. He reached up and tugged on his bow tie, settling it again around his neck.

"It's not a nickname. It's my given name—I think my mother must've been able to see into the future to what kind of child I would be. It's Hebrew. It means 'to disturb' or 'to trouble.' And believe me, as a youngster I lived up to it."

"You're Jewish?"

"Yes. Russian Jew, but born in Israel and immigrated with my parents to America when I was just a *yeled*—a lad."

"Do you live around here? I've never seen you in our neighborhood."

"I actually live quite close to this park."

Annie's gaze roamed the nearby houses. "Oh? Where?"

He waved his fingers vaguely over his shoulder, as if Annie would know exactly where he lived by the gesture. "I come to the park often in fine weather, but usually earlier in the day. Perhaps that's why we've never met."

They sat in companionable silence for a few minutes, watching the children at play.

Achar cocked his ear toward the sounds of laughter. "Does it ever make you want to be so carefree again, Annie? Watching children, I mean. Look at them. Hovered over by attentive parents and nannies, safe in their world of make-believe, never wondering if tomorrow will come for them. Never worrying that it won't."

Annie slewed around to face him. "What did you say?"

"I'm glad you decided to come today—to bring Nora to play in the park."

"But . . . I never said . . . how did you know—"

Achar stood with difficulty, reaching back to pick up his cane, which he put in front of him.

It was only then that Annie noticed the cane was white.

"You're . . . you're—"

"Blind? Yes, I am, Annie. But today I can see quite clearly that you are on the right path. Not like the last time we met."

"But—"

He tipped his hat gallantly and walked away, humming a tune and tapping his cane to the beat.

It didn't help her nerves that the tune he hummed was "Jesus Loves Me."

As she watched him stroll away, Annie realized with a painful jolt why he seemed familiar. She was sure of it—it was the gold tooth that gave him away. And the accent.

But . . . it couldn't be. It just couldn't—

Achar, or whatever his name really was, had been a maintenance worker at the high school she'd attended.

It had to be him. But why had he appeared now? And how did he know Nora's name?

Annie clutched her stomach, eyes closed.

She remembered him now as he was then, a short, thin, quirky man in his mid-thirties.. Always sweeping, shuffling up and down the hallways, sometimes watching the students at their lockers but never talking to them. But back then his name wasn't Achar.

What was it? Annie clenched her teeth with the effort to remember. *Yes. We called him AJ.*

She'd never heard his last name. His first name might have been Achar, she thought now. Maybe he didn't tell them because he didn't want to explain what it meant, like he'd just done with her. He probably thought he'd be laughed at. After all, he was just a janitor.

Some of her girlfriends were scared of AJ, thinking it likely he was some kind of criminal, a drug dealer—or worse. Annie used to tell them to stop being so paranoid, that being a bit peculiar didn't automatically mean he was an axe murderer.

Another memory popped into her brain. He'd take smoke breaks behind the gym. If any of the kids caught him, he'd yank his cigarette out of his mouth and put a finger to his lips, then drop the butt on the ground, step on it, and saunter away.

Behind the gym.

One more memory slammed into her brain. The one that kept her up at night, the one that had effectively changed the trajectory of her life.

She tried to stop its arrival, but she might as well try to stop a speeding car with a wave of her hand. It catapulted front and center, obliterating everything else.

It was Achar who'd found her . . . that night when David . . . Annie couldn't finish the thought. She remembered lying on her back, David grinning at her like he'd just won the lottery. Then she'd blanked out. When she moved again and opened her eyes, it was AJ who stood over her.

He'd raised her up, helped her brush the grass off her ruined blue dress, and walked her out to the sidewalk. She remembered he was kind, asking her if he could help her get home.

She'd told him no, that she just lived three houses down.

He let her go, saying he'd watch her until she was inside her house.

As she'd reached her front door and fumbled for her key, she turned and glimpsed him still standing on the sidewalk outside the gym.

The wretched memory faded as soon as she turned the key in the door latch.

Annie rejoined the present and found she'd gripped the edge of the park bench so hard, her palm had slivers in it. She plucked them out as best she could, then hunched forward.

How can this be?

She'd asked God a simple, straightforward question, and Achar was his answer? Why was God so hard to figure out? Why were his answers so inexplicable? A person practically had to have a PhD in theology to figure God out. A God who promised to always be with you shouldn't be rocket science, for heaven's sake.

Annie jerked her gaze around to Achar's retreating back, her mind straining to come to grips with the last few moments.

Would this never stop?

28

Annie stayed motionless on the bench, watching Achar until he strolled around a bend in the path, out of sight. She half expected him to disappear in a puff of smoke.

Nora's piercing laugh jolted her, and Annie turned to see her swinging so high that her blond curls streamed straight up as she fell back to earth.

A sudden vision of floating through the picture frame earlier today smote her . . . and swinging in the park that day with Mommy and Daddy, both taking turns pushing her until she screamed in delight. Then her parents squeezing themselves into the swings on either side of her, pumping their legs, rocketing higher and higher, their squeals of laughter melting into hers.

Does it ever make you want to be so carefree again, Annie?

She heard Achar's question in her ear, almost audible.

Annie's throat tightened, tears burning her eyes. Did God walk around in community parks looking like dapper little men in red bow ties pretending to be blind? Or would he impersonate someone in a Seahawks sweatshirt and leather jacket . . . and call himself Joshua?

Absurd!

She focused her gaze on Nora again. Olivia had been summoned by her mother and sat next to her, munching from a bag of chips.

She watched Nora's short legs pump harder and harder, trying to push herself as high as possible. At the apex of each swing, she was almost parallel with the top cross bar. Annie smiled. Her youngest was fearless. Mayra and Kimmie had been so timid at this age. Even a younger Hank hadn't matched Nora's spirit of adventure.

And herself? Forget it. Roger came the closest to Nora's adventurous spirit.

Ellen was especially partial to Nora because of it—*had been*, Annie corrected herself. Would she ever adjust to thinking of Ellen in past tense? Maybe never.

She wondered what Ellen would've said to Achar and what Ellen would say to her right now. Annie had no idea, but a fierce longing to see her friend again, to sit at their favorite coffee shop and unburden herself, rose up without warning, threatened to undam those tears gathering behind her eyelids.

Annie blinked them back and watched Nora's back-and-forth motion on the swings, lulling her, mesmerizing her.

What should I do? Report the old man? For what? For being kind to me? For asking a question that made me think?

His question. She jerked herself up, palms grasping her thighs. *Does it ever make you want to be so carefree again, Annie?* And it struck Annie like a lightning bolt. She *didn't* want to sit on the bench while Nora played.

The old man was right—she longed to be in that make-believe world populated with other three-year-old Noras who didn't know the meaning of worry. Who lived to the full in each moment and didn't try to speculate about the next. To play without restraint, to love without angles, free to be their own little selves without having to adjust their masks when they slipped. To trust without

180

reservation that the people who cared for them would care forever. To not dread the unknowable or the unknown.

To be unafraid.

Annie felt her heart would burst from her chest with longing. She finally knew what she wanted, desperately wanted, and where to find it. It was here—it'd always been here.

She leaped off the bench, sprinted to the swings, and wedged herself into one next to Nora. She pumped her legs madly, going higher and higher until Nora screamed with delight.

"Mommy, you're going higher than me. I want to go that high. Will you push me that high?"

"Ahh—just let me swing a minute, honey, then I'll push you."

Nora held her furry friend over her head, his face pointed at the clouds.

"Mr. Bear, look at our Mommy. She's going up to the sky—"

Annie pumped her legs harder and harder as Nora's laughter filled her heart. Each time she reached the top of the arc and fell earthward again, she felt a small chunk of her adult being break off and drop. Her soul felt lighter with each downward drop as the burden of tomorrows, or no tomorrows, floated away on the wind.

Does it ever make me want to be a child again?

Yes, but the child in her lay buried under endless planning and schedules, stuck behind self-made fences with no gates. And fretting over a day that hadn't yet seen a sunrise. She used to know how to play with her children, with Roger. When had she forgotten?

Nora stopped swinging, her sneakers hanging limply, shoelaces twinkling in the bright sunlight. She sat with her hands gripping the chains, clearly entranced, watching her mommy become a child again. Her eyes widened as Annie's little-girl self, hidden deep inside her, giggled out loud. Nora giggled with her, and soon they were shrieking at the sky in gleeful abandon.

Oh the beauty of it—the wonder. Annie, for the first time

since last night, didn't care if tomorrow never came for her. This day, this hour, this moment was enough. She closed her eyes and saw the twinkle in the old man's eyes.

She slowed to a stop. Then she twisted the chains, letting them go, and shouted with laughter as she flew around in circles.

Annie saw the other parents staring at her like she'd lost her mind, but she didn't care.

"Mommy, Mommy, do it for me. Do it for me—"

And she did. Annie jumped down and pushed Nora until she could push her no higher, then set her swing to spinning until Nora begged her to stop.

And that was when Annie knew. Knew that heaven would be a playground just like this. Green grass, tall trees, playgrounds, and picnics.

We'll be children again, no cares, no worries, only everlasting love and laughter and play.

No need to grow up and lose ourselves in adulting.

No death. . . only life.

In that secret place in her mind—where fear slithered—she saw again the four shiny caskets, two flag draped, that had changed her and Roger's lives forever. And the vague outline of a tiny box she'd never seen—Abby's.

And yet another casket. The one that held her childhood, ripped from her one night under a star-studded sky. Prom night— the night that promised to be the magical fulfilment of all her girlish dreams, but instead buried those dreams in the muddy ground behind the school gym.

No, no more of that in this heaven in her mind. Only love and laughter, bright skies and unbroken dreams.

Maybe tomorrow . . .

But tomorrow didn't exist yet. Maybe never would. And for the first time, Annie didn't care.

In this moment, this magical moment, it didn't matter. Nothing mattered except right now, Nora, the bright sky overhead, and the sandy playground under her feet.

Annie gazed at the sky as her swing slowed to a gentle rocking, her toes scraping the ground.

Nora tried to match her movements, and soon they were keeping time with each other, side by side, with only the creak of the chains heard above them.

But no, Annie heard something else. She came to a stop and focused on the sound. It was Ellen's riotous laughter reminding her, as always, that tomorrow really was overrated.

29

When they tired of swinging, Annie and Nora rode the merry-go-round, the trees blurring as they flew around in dizzying circles. Then they sat opposite each other on the teeter-totter—up, down, up, down—laughing each time the other's hair lifted straight up. They played in the sandbox, Annie sitting right down in the warm, sunshiny sand with Nora. They built a city and decided Mr. Bear was the town boss. Nora renamed him Mr. Bossy Bear. He perched on a small plastic bucket placed upside down in the center of the city square.

Nora fussed over the sand that now covered his small vest and pants, brushing it off with her chubby hands.

"Never mind, sweetheart. He can take a bath when we get home."

"A bath for Mr. Bear? Mommy, you're silly—"

"Yes, aren't I? I forgot how fun it is to be silly, my silly little daughter! You're teaching me how fun it is."

Nora's giggles were a balm to Annie's heart. It'd been too long since she'd played with such reckless disregard for adult decorum. She remembered, as she patted the roof of Mr. Bear's city hall, how she and Roger, *BK*—before kids—had played tag, hide-and-seek, and kick the can. They'd often wondered what their parents were thinking, letting them marry so young. Neither she nor Roger could envision letting Mayra settle down at nineteen, four short years away.

But would they have listened to their parents if they'd objected? Probably not. And here they were, married twenty years with four children of their own, and so busy rearing them that they'd forgotten how to play with them.

Annie could cry for the pity of it.

They'd forgotten that children fly highest when they spread their wings and soar on the gusts of imagination.

Nora patted Annie's sand-covered leg. "Mommy, you have your sad face on again."

Annie scooted closer to her and grasped her soft face between her hands. "Not sad. Just remembering."

Nora squirmed away, rubbing her cheeks. "Mommy, you got sand all over my face!" With a pert grin, she stood and picked up a handful and threw it at Annie, hitting her square on top of her head.

The sand wars began. Nora shrieked when a blob hit her in the chest. Soon they were throwing handfuls two at a time, running around in circles in the sandbox, giggles accompanying each throw when they managed to find their marks.

Annie, turning suddenly to avoid Mr. Bear sitting on his bucket, tripped and fell, landing squarely on city hall. With a fiendish squeal, Nora jumped on top of her and they rolled over and over, completely flattening the sandy town they'd built so carefully.

Finally they lay quiet, Nora splayed out on Annie's belly. She felt Nora's soft breathing against her chest, where she'd spent hours as a baby, reminding her of where Nora had lived before birth—right under her heart.

Annie saw, out of the corner of her eye as she stroked Nora's sand-salted hair, several moms staring in their direction again. She ignored them. *Probably wondering if I'm unhinged, allowing my child to throw sand at the park. So what? We may never get to throw sand at each other again . . .*

She heard a gentle cough behind her. She twisted and saw the elderly gentleman—Achar—standing on the grass at the edge of the sandbox.

Sitting up, Nora nestled on her lap, she realized she must look a sight—sand and leaves covering her clothes, smudges on her face, one shoe off and resting in Mr. Bear's lap. She gazed sheepishly at Achar, reaching up and smoothing her hair self-consciously. Then she remembered he couldn't see her.

"No, my dear," he gently admonished, blind eyes twinkling. "You look quite delightful. I wouldn't change a thing."

He nodded once, winked, and stepped back onto the path and shuffled away, his cane tap-tapping in front of him.

Annie jumped up, spilling Nora out of her lap. She paced onto the grass, watching his slow progress. Was the old fool pretending to be blind? *Or did he see with other eyes?*

She watched until he was out of sight, heading down the side-walk that ringed the park. Her mind spun crazily, her thoughts landing on last night. It'd all started with Hank's question, Mayra's essay, and the dropped fork. Where would it end?

Was that only last night? It seemed like a lifetime ago.

The day was only half over, but Annie couldn't ever remember a roller-coaster ride like the one she was on.

She shook herself and shifted back into the present. Turning, she expected to see Nora right behind her, on the sand with Mr.

Bear. The impression of her body in the sand remained, right where she'd landed when Annie had leaped to her feet. Mr. Bear was there, an accusing look in his eye. She touched the small crater where Nora had sat. Cold. How long had it been? She could swear she'd turned her back just for a moment.

Annie's gaze surveyed the play area. "Nora! Nora!"

No answer. She must be hiding, the little scamp. . .

The park had almost emptied of moms and kids. She looked at her watch and was shocked to see it was almost one o'clock—nap time for most toddlers after a busy morning of play.

Where Nora should be headed right now. Except Nora wasn't here.

Annie felt the heat of the sun on her face and a cold trickle of sweat on her neck. She stood motionless, the park spinning around her. She closed her eyes, then opened them again. The spin slowed and stopped, but the light filtering through the trees was wrong, like the sun had moved from its place.

At the sound of a faint rustle, Annie looked down. Her eyes widened at the sheaf of documents clutched in her left hand. She looked closer at the dog-eared paper on top and gagged. A police report, dated almost four decades ago. Abigail Louise Walters, aged four.

How. . . what . . .

Annie's brain shut down. The park spun again, tree limbs bending, leaves blurring—like they had when she rode the merry-go-round with Nora barely half an hour ago.

She dropped the papers, watching them drift toward her feet . . . and evaporate before hitting the ground. Gone.

Clutching her stomach, Annie settled to the grass, her thoughts gliding and wheeling like a murder of crows through her mind. She opened her eyes. Once again the spinning stopped and the sun was back where it belonged.

What had just happened? She'd read that police report more than fifteen years ago. It'd sickened her then, as now, seeing her sister's name in block letters at the top.

The hideous words returned to her mind.

Abby had been taken from a park in a small town not far away from where she and Roger lived now. Mom had moved in with her parents while Daddy was stationed at the naval base in San Diego. She'd taken Abby to the park to play and stopped to buy her an ice cream cone from a truck.

She turned and looked down to where Abby had been playing not five feet away from her. She'd vanished.

Her body had been found three months later on a Thursday, in a ravine on I-82. Annie still remembered every word of the description of the body. She couldn't get the cruel words out of her head. They'd become part of her DNA.

She pressed her eyelids shut and then jerked them open. *This is not about Abby . . .*

Why was she just sitting here?

Jumping to her feet, Annie flung her gaze in all directions. She saw nothing. Heard nothing.

Managing to push her fear down somewhere within her, she walked carefully around the sandy play area looking for footprints. Aha. There were some pointing toward the castle.

She poked her head inside. It was dark and too small for her to crawl into. "Nora? Are you in here somewhere, sweetie?"

No answer. She stood still, listening for the tiniest noise, a breath, a whimper. She moved to the other side and repeated her actions. Still nothing. She straightened, feeling the slick fear glide up her pant leg, crawl inside her T-shirt, and wrap itself around her belly.

No! This will not happen. . .

30

Annie called to two women who occupied nearby benches. She hadn't noticed them before—they must've just arrived. "Have you seen my daughter? She was right here. Did you see where she went?"

"No," replied one mom. Her son sat next to her, munching potato chips. "What does she look like?"

The woman's bland, uninterested tone made Annie want to scream. "She . . . she has blond hair, she's about so high, and she's wearing a pink shirt and pink sneakers with butterflies on them. Are you sure you didn't see her? I've been playing with her for an hour—"

The woman shook her head. "Sorry. Didn't notice her. I've been reading."

Annie turned first one way then the other, wondering where to run first.

The other woman looked up. "My son and I just sat down while you were talking to that gentleman in the red bow tie. I'm sorry."

Achar! Was he involved somehow? Maybe her high school friends had been right and he was evil, a predator. Even though deep down she thought it was a stretch, she sprinted down the path to the sidewalk where the old man had disappeared. Looking both ways, she saw no one except a young man walking an absurdly big dog half a block away. Annie watched them disappear in the distance. The sidewalk was now empty in both directions.

She turned and walked back down the path, past the play area—both women who'd sat there were now gone.

Annie hurried to the other end of the park. This was an area she didn't frequent often, the largest play area being at the opposite end, where she'd come from. Stepping off the path frequently, she scanned behind bushes and trees, even looked up into the trees. Her heart lurched each time she heard a distant child's laughter, but she kept going.

She reached the end of the path, where it connected to a parking lot. Two cars sat in the lot, both unoccupied. Annie stepped out to the street bordering this side of the park, scrutinizing the sidewalk in both directions and staring at the front yards of the houses facing the park.

Nothing. It was like she was the only one in the world—and Nora wasn't in it.

Annie crumpled right there on the sidewalk and lowered her face into her hands. Her heart raced. Unable to breathe, she couldn't formulate a plan, couldn't take the next step.

A random thought thrust its ugly head into the forefront of her mind. *Had Nora ever existed?* Annie moaned and gagged into her hands.

Ridiculous! Of course she existed! Why am I even going there?

The old image crashed again through the barricade she'd erected in her mind, the barricade that kept out the unthinkable— the police report she'd held in her hand four years after she and

Roger had married. The same ghostly papers she'd watched just a few minutes ago as they'd drifted toward her feet and disappeared into thin air in this very park. It came into focus in her mind, like her iPhone camera sharpening an image before she snapped the picture.

The memory of the faded, old-fashioned typewritten print—computers were not yet common in police stations—complete with a dropped letter *e* throughout, captured her and pinned her to the sidewalk. No matter what Annie did, she knew she couldn't stop the images.

Phrases from the 1982 police report drifted through her mind again, unbidden, unwanted, like specters from the past—all the while her mind screaming Nora's name at her heart.

But these memories now held her hostage on the sidewalk.

Four-year-old female homicide victim. Body—frozen and partially wrapped in a bloody sheet—discovered in a ravine along I-82, near the Fred Redmon Bridge, which spans the Selah Creek at a height of 325 feet. Victim was found halfway down the eastern slope on the north side of the bridge.

ME estimates victim had been deceased between one and two months when she was found. Forensics at the scene indicate body was transported from another location and dumped.

Cause of death probably blunt-force trauma to the head and chest.

Extensive damage to genitals, tearing in the vagina, indicates forcible rape over a period of time.

Burn marks on back, thighs, and upper arms. Fingernails broken and split, both thumbnails completely missing. Condition of scalp indicates hair pulled out by the roots.

Evidence of animal scavenging, specifically superficial postmortem markings to the head and shoulders consistent with teeth marks, and disarticulation of the left foot at the ankle joint from apparent scavenger activity, possibly coyote, due to their large presence in the area.

This was not the image of her older sister she'd seen hanging on her parents' living room wall for years and which she'd inherited. Not the little girl, clad in a blue dress, who'd smiled out of the frame on her own wall. The only thing left of that photo now was a few marks on Annie's family room wall, because years ago, right after Hank was born, Annie found she couldn't look at Abby's face anymore. Because of the police report that tromped through her consciousness—and the fact that now she kept seeing Nora's face where Abby's was—she'd relegated the photograph to a box. She couldn't face explaining to her children who Abby was and what had happened to her. Just the idea of the retelling made her gag.

Annie bolted upright. The police report stomping through her brain, leaving its bloody footprints, blew away and was replaced by sudden realization. *This must be how it'd been for Mom. When Abby . . .*

This paralyzing inertia, sitting here in a puddle of cruel guilt, unable to make a decision, take action, or even think a coherent thought. Hideous images wearing Nora's face paraded through her mind. Her brain felt sluggish, like it was just waking up from a dream.

Annie looked up the street again. Far away down the block, she caught sight of a petite woman, belly swollen in pregnancy, running toward her. The woman's long chestnut hair escaped from an old-fashioned fringed black scarf tied over her head. Her arms waved, and her mouth opened in a scream. She ran closer, until Annie heard her frantic words.

"Abby! Abby! Honey, where are you?"

The woman dashed right up to Annie, leaned down into her face, grasping her shoulder in a vise grip. "Have you seen my little girl? Right over there. I was just buying her an ice cream cone . . ." The woman whipped around and pointed down the block at the old-fashioned ice cream truck that had somehow materialized.

As the woman faced her again, terror stretching her face to the breaking point, Annie knew the truth. It slammed into her without warning, causing her lungs to empty.

She knew that scarf, that voice, the wide, frantic gaze that pierced her own. It was her mother who stood before her, shaking, screaming in panic, demanding an answer.

Annie tried to answer. Opened her mouth, retching on the words stuck in her throat. She pinched her eyes closed, hoping that when she opened them again, she'd be magically transported back to the present. She didn't want to feel what her mother had felt.

She opened her eyes a millimeter at a time, and Annie knew she'd been wrong to wish to be out of the past and into the present.

The face on the woman had changed. It was her own face stamped there. She saw herself in her own eyes, blazing with panic. Annie yelled at Annie to find her little girl. To find Nora.

Annie grabbed her hair and yanked hard. The pain cleared her head. *This can't be happening . . . Please, God. This can't be happening. Make it stop.*

This other Annie crumpled to her knees, clawlike fingers grasping Annie's legs. Then she faded away inch by inch, once again her tortured eyes the last to go.

Annie hyperventilated, then snagged a breath. She rubbed her face, smoothed her hair, and sat up again. The frightening images had disappeared along with her mother who'd become herself.

Once again, she was alone, looking for Nora. Once again, her limbs and her brain were paralyzed, not knowing what to do.

The dead silence unnerved her. Neighborhood parks shouldn't be so quiet. Annie sat a moment longer, willing her heart to beat normally and her stomach to settle. She rose to her feet, locking her knees so she wouldn't collapse again. Fists balled at her sides, she made her way back to the play area.

Now her brain took her in another agonizing direction.

What would she tell Roger? That she lost his daughter, that she wasn't paying attention, that she took her focus off their youngest and allowed some deviant . . . She couldn't keep going there.

Should she call . . .

Annie jerked to a stop and slapped a palm to her forehead. Why hadn't she called 911? What was wrong with her?

She felt in her back pocket for her phone, then in the other one. Checked her front pockets, then the back ones again.

Her phone wasn't there. It was in her backpack, which she'd left . . .

Oh God, no . . .

She'd turned it off and put it in her backpack so she wouldn't be distracted by it. On the bench where they'd planned to eat lunch. She always put it away in public so she could concentrate on Nora. Always Nora.

That's right.

Annie breathed, hearing Nora's voice in her head saying she wanted to play first—*of course Nora existed.*

Of course she had tomorrows.

Sobbing, Annie charged back toward the play area, somehow finding the strength to run all the way back.

Please, God, make her be there. Give her back. You . . . you can't take her.

31

It was the longest run of her life.

The path wound around trees and frisbee golf areas, a fenced-off creek meandering through the middle, picnic spots, and a small dog park.

She rounded the last corner, sweat pouring down her face, dripping between her shoulder blades and wetting her underarms. What if someone had taken her stuff? *Why did I run off and leave everything? Stupid!*

Looking toward the bench, she saw that Nora's trike and their bags still sat right where she'd left them.

Another thought popped into her tired brain like a jack-in-the-box with a crudely painted face. She'd hated that toy when she was young, but here he was again. He sprang out of his box and jeered at her for not checking the bathrooms near the parking lot at the other end of the park when she'd been down there.

Of course . . . Nora must've needed to use the bathroom and had gone by herself, wanting to be a big girl. Always competing with her older sisters and brothers . . . that was her Nora. *That has to be it. Oh, God, please . . .*

Annie stopped dead, whipped around, left the play area again, and ran back toward those bathrooms. She was winded when she arrived, chest heaving. She wiped her nose with her sleeve and pushed hair out of her damp face. She heard traffic noise in the distance, a dog barking, and chattering crows and magpies in a nearby tree.

Nothing else, not a single human voice.

She headed toward the bathrooms, situated near the street, with bike racks lining the side of the building. She walked around the perimeter of the small structure first, looking for God knows what, then finally went inside, breathing as shallow as possible against the stale smell.

Looking around the filthy sink area, she saw nothing, not even a drop of water. Annie decided she must open the stalls. Hoping to see something, yearning to see nothing . . . because if she found Nora's shoe, or a hair ribbon, then that'd mean she'd been here without her mother, without her protection, fair game for the same kind of filth who'd stolen Abby and . . . done things to her.

Things no parent could see and then unsee.

The bathroom stalls were empty. Annie carefully checked all four men's and ladies', searching for any sign that Nora had been here. Not even a shoe scuff. In fact, it looked like no one had used this bathroom in a long while, nor had it been cleaned. February wasn't usually a busy month at the park, she guessed.

Annie realized now, wiping the sweat from her neck, it'd been ludicrous to chase all the way down here.

Nora would never have walked all this way to use the bathroom without telling her. She always needed help in the bathroom. She was only three, for God's sake! *What was I thinking?*

Annie knew the answer. She was beyond thought, acting and

reacting, bumping from life to death, from faith to fear and back again like a pinball. Like she'd done her entire life.

Annie darted out, letting the heavy metal door crash against the side of the building. She stopped, planting her feet so hard she almost stumbled. Surveying the same scenery again, frantically hoping against hope, she saw and heard nothing but empty grass, empty walkway, empty air—just like her empty heart. A world empty of Nora's sweet giggles and piercing three-year-old wisdom.

In the space of just a few wretched moments, Annie lived every moment of Nora's three years, from the first time she and Roger had seen her, until this very moment. Both parents had known, from the first moment they'd held her, that their family was now complete.

Then they'd taken their precious bundle home and let each of the three older children hold her briefly, even Kimmie, who had been four at the time. The same age as Abby when . . .

She raised her fists to heaven and screamed her frustration at the sky. "Why? Why are you doing this to me? Why does it have to be Nora? Make it me, God! Make it me! She needs her tomorrows—she's only three. Take mine. I've lived enough. Give her back, God! You can't have her yet. D'ya hear me? You can't have her yet!"

She clapped her hand over her mouth. Miserable with shame, her heart seized. What in the world was she doing, shrieking at God like a madwoman in a public park? How dare she scream at God like that? *Because I'd dare anything for Nora. If God were here in front of me, I'd say it to his face. Nora belongs to me, not you . . . not yet.*

She glanced around quickly. Across the street, she saw a curtain flick back into place.

911. What's your emergency?

There's a crazy lady yelling in the park. Please come quickly before she . . .

Before she what? What did parents do who lost their children? Annie could guess. They camped out at the local precinct making a nuisance of themselves.

Go home, folks. We'll call you if there's any news at all.

They went quietly crazy, yelled in public parks, suspected any man who looked remotely strange, even those who were blind and wearing a red bow tie.

They refused to answer questions asked by their younger daughter. Annie knew what those parents did—her own parents had done it.

They stopped eating, they argued and fought, blamed each other, then Daddy moved out. Then he came back. They couldn't move far enough past the first child to play with the second.

Those parents made flyers, the child's pleading eyes staring out of the picture at the world. They nailed them to every square inch of the city. Annie had found those flyers—Abby's—stacked in a box in the garage when she was fifteen.

Now she was one of those parents, stuck in a nightmare with no way out.

Annie knew what she must do. She must get back to the swings, back to Nora. *Back to before.*

She dashed off to the play area, away from the murderous thoughts that crowded her mind. Except they followed her like so many demons, their invisible bony fingers stretching out to pluck at her shirt, her hair, grab her shoulder, nip at her heels.

She ran faster, ponytail flying behind her, feet pumping like she was ten years old again, trying to outrun Ellen on the school playground.

As she ran, the park pathway stretched out in front of her— longer than it had ever been—just like when she ran cross country in high school and thought she'd never reach the finish line.

Her mantra now, as it had then, repeated itself over and over again in her head. *Finish, just finish.*

And today . . . *Nora will be there. Please make her be there.*

Chest heaving, spittle flying out of her mouth, Annie ran through the tomblike park.

She didn't think she could run all that way again, but she did. Her legs felt like hard, thick driftwood. Her heart pounded like it would burst, her shoulders aching as she rounded the last corner and the play area came into view.

Her eyes zeroed in on the bench where they'd sat. No Nora, but her bag still rested right where she'd left it. Her phone—she must get to it and call for help. Nothing else mattered now.

Annie ran to the bench and grabbed her backpack, fingers gripping the zipper. It stuck. She groaned and tugged at it, almost tearing it from its stitching.

She reached in. But her phone was not in the pocket where she always kept it.

The demons that had chased her all the way across the park now surrounded her, spinning in a mad dance, cackling their maniacal accusations. With each shriek, Annie felt the poke of a bony finger.

Bad, inattentive mother.

You deserve this. You should have been more careful.

You should've fixed your fence.

She's with us now. You can't have her back.

The voices went on and on until she spun around and yelled at them to stop. They clicked off so fast it startled Annie. But the silence was worse. And then became horrific . . . Nora's precious giggles turning into screams of frantic terror, calling her name over and over.

Mommy! Mommy . . .

32

Annie sat on the bench, trying to breathe, a fresh cascade of sweat rolling between her shoulder blades as Nora's frantic screams faded into the ether. Wiping her face, she upended her bag and shook it, begging God to produce her phone.

Her keys, a wallet, loose change. Nothing else.

Annie searched all the pockets, then opened the lunch bag, thinking she'd put it there by mistake. Not there. She searched her jeans pockets again and through the jacket she'd left draped over the bench. No phone. It'd disappeared into thin air, like Nora.

She stood and searched along the bench, finally kneeling in the grass and brushing her hand along the underside of the bench and down the legs, thinking it might have gotten stuck. Then she searched the other benches nearby. Could it have fallen out of her pocket during her mad dash through the park?

She stared down the path, the thought of walking all the way to the other end again jackhammering the top of her head. She knew she couldn't manage it. And anyway, she distinctly remembered turning it off and putting it in her backpack. She knew it hadn't been in her pocket.

Annie collapsed on the bench. She'd have to go all the way home and call 911. But how could she leave the park? Nora had to be here somewhere. She knew she couldn't leave the park—she just couldn't. It was the last place Nora had been, the last place Annie had heard her voice, the last place she'd had a tomorrow.

Gripped by indecision, Annie hunched forward, tears raining down her cheeks. The roller-coaster she'd ridden since last night had turned deadly. She felt herself free-falling into unimaginable grief.

The grief of a mother who was no longer a mother. The grief for which there was no answer, no medicine, no healing, and no escape. The thick, rusty bars of guilt would imprison her forever, and there existed no key to turn the lock.

She rocked back and forth, eyes pinched shut, arms wound tightly around her middle. She felt her muscles lock in place, her jaw clenched so tightly her teeth must surely break off in her mouth. Yet Annie couldn't stop her mind from going where it would go, to a well-worn path she'd trod before, but this time she had company.

The shrieking specters gripped her hands and dragged her down and down into a black tunnel. She felt another behind her, pushing a bony finger into her spine. Then once again, the images came.

Every news article about missing children, every movie she'd ever watched about kidnappings and evil predators—and what they did to their victims—now streamed through the Netflix of her brain, frame by sickening frame. *What was happening to Nora right now? Oh, I can't think this—I can't!*

She put her hands over her face, trying to block the gruesome images, but they only grew in intensity, there behind her eyelids. Naked children found in dumpsters, in alleys, in forested areas. Children chained to dingy mattresses in musty basements until the next customer arrived or a buyer could be found. Container ships filled with cages, their cargo disgorged on some foreign shore, never to be heard of again.

Innocent faces on milk cartons.

In her fear-racked brain, a picture fell into place out of nowhere—Nora's cherubic countenance on the side of one of those cartons, her frightened eyes seeking her own.

Have you seen this child? Missing since . . . today.

Another image took its place. Her beautiful, feisty Nora on tonight's evening news—sitting on her brand-new trike given to her on her third birthday, grinning ear to ear. Underneath the picture, *Child goes missing from local park.* An 800 number to report sightings of the child flashing red at the bottom of the screen. The news anchor's glum voice describing the park and the rabid mom racing from one end to the other, calling Nora's name. Witnesses talking about Annie's odd behavior.

Then at the end of the story, the local correspondent, posed in front of the castle in the play area, intoning in a funereal voice, "The authorities questioned the mother, particularly about why she didn't call 911 immediately. The distraught mother seemed to have no good answer. The investigation is ongoing. Tune in to the late news for updates."

Headline—with Nora's picture underneath—in the local paper, dated tomorrow: "Child Disappears from Neighborhood Park." The first line in the story: *Massive search mounted, but no results as yet. Distraught, unstable mother questioned. Investigation is ongoing.*

Her thoughts spun, making her dizzy. Round and round, always ending in the same place.

It should be me, God. Nora's only three. She hasn't had time to live, grow up, to fall in love. Please, God, give her back. Take me.

With the mention of God's name, the demons retreated, and

Annie stopped rocking and stood. She must leave the park and find a phone. This was insane, sitting here expecting a miracle.

Expecting to find Nora without doing something—*anything*.

She gathered up her backpack and the forgotten lunch. Nora's pink trike with the ribbons fluttering on the handlebars stood where it'd been parked, along with her backpack.

Mr. Bear still sat in the sand, his baleful eye turned on her, one short furry arm flung in her direction, like an accusing judge. She heard the gavel slam. *You—you didn't pay attention. You let her get lost. You are sentenced to die of guilt and grief for the rest of your natural life.*

Annie jerked Mr. Bear up and stuffed him in Nora's backpack. She put both backpacks on her back, then hooked the lunch bag over the handlebars of the trike and picked it up.

She managed three steps, then stopped.

She put the tricycle down and wiped her eyes, blocking all thoughts except this one. She must get home and call 911. And Roger. And what should she say to him? *Hey, honey, Nora disappeared today. What do you want for dinner?*

Stupid.

She looked at her watch, astounded to see it was only one forty—barely forty minutes had passed since Nora had gone. She hadn't known an entire lifetime could be lived in only forty minutes.

Annie gathered herself and took two more steps. She was now on the path out of the park and heading toward the sidewalk leading home, only five minutes from the house if she hurried and didn't have to stop and put everything down again.

She grunted and took another step. The load she carried, inside and out, threatened to put her on her knees again.

Another step. She stopped, pinched her eyelids shut, and saw them again.

The demons were back, wrapping her in chains, taunting her

with scenes of how the next few hours and days would likely play out.

Neighbors asking what happened. She caught their wary glances at herself and Roger. After all, parents were always the first suspects, right?

Yellow crime scene tape around the playground. And around their house.

Policemen in and out, looking at their computers for pornography, downloading their phone data, going through Nora's drawers, bagging her blue snowman pajamas and her tiny pastel-colored underwear. Turning their backs, whispering in corners, throwing narrow-eyed frowns at them.

Max's incessant barking at the strangers taking over their home.

Grim-faced, hardened detectives sitting in her dining room, putting a tap on their phones in case there was a ransom demand.

Ransom? We have no money. We have nothing anyone would want.

No overflowing bank account, no stock shares, no real estate.

Just Nora—an innocent three-year-old with blond hair and sparkling blue eyes. A fearless little girl who trusted everyone. The darling of the family—the light of their lives—would become a statistic. Ruined. Butchered.

She saw neighbors ten, twenty years from now, pointing at them from their yards, saying things like, "They've never been the same since . . ." Or telling a newcomer "the sad story of the little girl who went missing from the park just down the street . . . what was her name? Oh yeah, Nora. Sweet little thing. Her mother's always been a little off though."

Sickening, paralyzing dread squeezed her heart, sucked the breath out of her lungs.

She imagined telling Roger. The light in his eyes shrinking to pinpoints and becoming twin lasers aimed at her. His face cement-like, never to laugh or crinkle into a smile again. He would point at her, accuse her, like a wraith pointing a sharp-clawed finger and pronouncing judgment because Nora's mommy was the one who'd lost her in one instant of carelessness.

Just like Abby's mommy. Like mother, like daughter.

The love she and Roger had shared since they were eighteen would rot and die because Nora's face—her beautiful golden face— would always be between them. Her eyes always seeking them.

Where are you, Mommy? Help me, Daddy.

Oh, God . . . it'll kill Roger. I can't . . .

Annie couldn't force her feet to move. Her imagination was quicksand, pulling her under, burying her alive in memories of Abby's going and anguish for Nora. Always, when she closed her eyes, she'd see Abby's tortured body lying in that desert ravine, raped, beaten, and burned . . . but now wearing Nora's face.

A new demon, larger and more terrifying than the others, stealthily approached. His hot, acrid breath in her face blew another nightmare her way.

How would Mayra, Hank, and Kimmie be able to bear this? How could she ever explain what happened? How could they possibly understand why anyone would do this? Explain to seven-year-old Kimmie what anyone would want with her baby sister?

They'd be interrogated by the authorities. Would Mayra or Hank be suspected? Would they be encouraged to *just tell the truth about your parents? It's okay—you won't be in trouble.*

Her brain seized at the thought of her children pitted against her, suspicious, confused. She leaned over and gagged bile, letting it drip to the ground.

Her family would have a Nora-sized hole in it forever. Her children would become fearful, suspicious, distrustful adults, never wanting to try their wings . . . just like their mother.

As Mom and Dad must've been after Abby . . .

Annie watched her carefully constructed, fenced world—a world of faith, peace, and order—crumble into gray ruins, turn into dust, and blow away on the winds of mourning.

She brought the ring to her face and stared at the words. Is this what life had become for her?

She sobbed and stepped onto the sidewalk, turning left toward home. A home that was no longer a place she wanted to be. A pristine house, created just so, but now a hollowed-out space without Nora.

The fear that had slithered up her leg now had a chokehold on her. It'd done its work.

She took three shaky steps, stumbling over a tree root embedded in the sidewalk.

Annie looked back at the play area, then away again. The swings where she'd left her anxiety-filled adulthood behind while Nora watched, now mocked her. So much for becoming a child again. It was all a farce. She'd never sit on those swings, never be whole, nor believe in butterflies again.

Silly Annie, you can't go back to before, back to when things made sense, when Mommies and little girls were never parted and nothing bad ever happened to them. It's all a lie.

Dread clung to her, its odor like the pungent stink of the skunk Max had tangled with last fall. She'd never be rid of that enemy now.

She was sentenced to a life of guilt and unimaginable heartbreak. And as far as she was concerned, she deserved it. She was an unfit mother. She hung her head in disgrace.

She heard her mother's voice shaming her. "Didn't I tell you, Annie? Never turn your back, never . . . like I did. You just don't listen. Now look what's happened. You'll never see her again, never hold her, never give her butterfly kisses, never buy her a prom dress."

And the last damning statement . . . *She's with Abby now.*

Her mother's voice wound through her brain, down into her throat, and settled in her chest, fading and resolving into another boulder she'd carry there for the rest of her life. She'd never be rid of it, never escape . . .

Annie's head jerked up. Another voice had pricked her ears, eddied to her on the breeze.

Who was it? She scanned the sidewalk, looked toward the windows of the homes in the neighborhood. She didn't see anything, but now she heard the sound again. It sounded familiar. Someone crying?

"Mommy!"

She spun and looked toward the swings, dropping her bag in the process. Annie squinted. She saw pink spangly sneakers twinkling from across the park. Tiny hands fluttered.

No! It can't be. I'm losing it . . .

"Mommy! Where is you is?"

Annie heard the babyish words—words inimitably Nora's—and sobbed out loud.

She charged forward, stumbled, and face-planted in the damp grass. She sprang up, almost fell again, but managed to stay on her feet as she ran, keeping her eyes glued to Nora's small body, afraid to look away.

"I'm coming, baby. Don't move, honey," Annie called, arms and legs pumping madly.

Thank you, God!

33

nnie flew across the grass, half expecting Nora to disappear like a vapor. But she stood at the edge of the sandy play area, solid and warm, eyes drooping with sleep and clutching Annie's phone to her chest.

Annie scooped her up in her arms and dropped to the grass, both of them rolling over and over.

"Nora! Where were you, baby? I was so scared when I couldn't find you."

"Mommy—"

"I looked everywhere for you." Annie sat up and crushed Nora in her arms.

"Mommy, you're squeezing me too tight!"

"I'm sorry. I'm just glad you're here and not—" She clamped her lips shut.

Annie loosened her grip and turned Nora around on her lap to face her. She smoothed her hair back from her forehead and cupped the toddler's face in her hands. "You must tell me where you were, honey. I thought . . . I thought you were lost. I went everywhere in the park looking for you."

"I was playing hide-and-seek. I was in the castle."

"But—"

"And I stayed real still so you wouldn't find me. I hided good, like Mayra and Hank said. And I was quiet, even when you called me."

"But I looked there—"Annie's gaze jerked to the castle. Nora must've been hiding in a corner she couldn't see.

"And when you didn't see me, I came out. But"—she spread her small hands in a helpless gesture—"you weren't here. I looked everywhere for you, Mommy. So I got your phone and went back in the castle."

Annie grabbed her hands and kissed them. "But why did you take my phone?"

"I played *Peppa Pig* while I waited for you. You showed me how, 'member? Then I fell asleep. Then something walked on my ear and I woke up. It was a big buzzy—gross, Mommy!" She flapped her fingers at her ear to illustrate. "I came out fast, and I heard you make a funny noise. And here you are!" Nora threw her hands up over her head, like a miniature cheerleader.

Annie threw back her head and laughed at Nora's childish wonder. "Yes, here I am, my little love. And here you are. And I love you so much."

"I love you too, Mommy."

Annie lost control then and couldn't help her tears.

Nora reached up and touched her index finger to the puddle under Annie's right eye. "Why are you crying?"

Annie hugged her and murmured into her soft hair. "Because you have a tomorrow."

She drew back and rubbed her thumb over the wrinkle between Nora's eyes. "Never mind. We have to get back home. Come on—

our stuff's over there on the sidewalk, waiting for us."

Nora looked back to the sand box, anxiety clouding her eyes. "Where's my bear, Mommy? I forgot to take care of him, like you told me to. I left him in the sand all alone. You told me to take care of him like you take care of me."

Her frantic voice clawed at Annie's heart, reminding her of her own fear. Reminding her she didn't want the same monsters who'd hounded her all her life to chase away Nora's innate courage and daring. *Please, God . . .*

Annie stood and took Nora's hand. "Yes, honey, I remember. But Mr. Bear is safe in your backpack, just like you were safe in the castle."

She let go of Nora's hand and struck a pose, like a runner at the starting block.

"Come on. I'll race you!"

Nora giggled, matched Annie's stance, and took off.

Annie watched her chubby legs churn up the path. She let Nora get several yards ahead of her, then sprinted after her. This time there were no demons chasing her, no ghostlike fingers grasping for her. She felt the wind flow through her hair and delicious, childlike joy propel her from behind. Fear was left in the dust again.

Nora crowed her victory. "Mommy, I beat you!"

"You sure did, you little speedster. How did you get so fast?"

"Hank taught me how to run faster—like this." She pumped her arms. "Wait till I tell him I beat you!"

Nora plopped herself onto her tricycle, breathing hard as she leaned on the handlebars.

Annie leaned over and hugged her curly head, then picked up the bags. With Nora pedaling next to her, they headed for home, the sun warm on their backs.

The familiar peace surged up through her toes to her heart when her feet touched their lawn. Home. Safety. With Nora by her side. The terrors of the last hour fled like leaves before a gust of wind, taking the wraiths with it.

She would get inside, lock the door against the demons, put Nora down for a nap, and have a cup of tea. Like every other day before this one.

And like tomorrow would be.

34

nnie awoke with a start. She looked at her watch, astonished to see she'd only been asleep for thirty minutes—it was only 2:15 p.m.—but it felt later. She hurried into the kitchen to make sure her watch hadn't stopped. No, the clock on the stove and the grandfather clock read the same—now 2:16 p.m. She still had almost forty-five minutes before she'd wake Nora and go pick up the kids at school.

She wandered back into the living room and looked out the window. A car and a flatbed truck had pulled up to the Baxters' house across the street. Several people exited the vehicles and walked up the path to the porch—the porch where she'd seen John and Eleanor holding hands last night. What was going on?

Annie rubbed the back of her neck, trying to remember what had awakened her. A dream—she'd had a dream. How odd. She hardly ever dreamed, and now she'd had two within twenty-four hours.

And one in the middle of the day? It must have been a powerful one—she hadn't been asleep that long. She sat in her chair and willed herself to recall the dream.

Something about feet? Try as she might, she couldn't force any details to her mind.

But now she remembered what had awakened her—a sound, a jarring sound in the quiet nap routine of her home between one and three on weekday afternoons.

A giggle, strange and out of place, long and high pitched, coming from somewhere behind Annie's chair. But there was nothing but the large paned window giving a view of her pink hydrangeas planted along the picket fence in the front yard. Her mother had helped her plant them when she and Roger had first moved in. It was almost the last thing they'd enjoyed doing together before . . .

She stood and scanned the landscape, trying to see the source of the giggle. Nothing but grass, two trees, the hydrangeas, and the unusual activity at the Baxters' beyond her fence.

Annie shook her head, mystified, and sat again. She closed her eyes and concentrated on recalling the dream. A kaleidoscope of colors floated in front of her vision, finally resolving itself into her neighbor's front yard. She'd dreamed of Mr. Gruber? *How odd!*

Behind her eyelids, she focused on Mr. Gruber's porch. He wasn't there. Like one of those wide-angle pictures on your camera you can pan all the way around, she rotated slowly around his yard. His rose bushes came into view. He was proud of those roses. He called them Jean's roses. Then the brass yard lamp he'd installed a few years back at the corner of his yard by the sidewalk.

The camera lens in her mind panned left. His mailbox, out by the street, rotated into view. She stopped. Moved right again. A pile of old clothes lay by the sidewalk.

She squinted and zoomed in. Mr. Gruber was in those clothes! His head lay on the sidewalk, his feet dangled over the curb. He was barefoot. Annie's vision zeroed in on his bare feet—it disturbed her to see the old man shoeless and sockless, like he was a homeless person. Except he wasn't homeless. He lived in the house next to them—had for twenty years.

Annie's eyes popped open.

Something had happened to the old man. What was she doing just sitting here? He lay on the sidewalk—dead or alive, she didn't know, but she must go out there. *And what about that insane giggle that woke me up?*

She jumped out of her chair, rushed to the front door, jerked it open, then stopped. She must make sure Nora was still asleep.

Leaving the front door standing open, she ran back to the stairs and took them two at a time. She tiptoed to her own bedroom door—she'd let Nora sleep on Mommy and Daddy's bed as a treat—and pushed the door open wider.

The child's pink-and-blue blanket lay rumpled on the bed. Nora and Mr. Bear were nowhere to be seen.

Annie's heart thumped, sending pain through her chest and sweat to her brow. She rushed into her bathroom, then ran to the kids' bathroom, then into the bedroom Nora shared with Kimmie. Not there.

A groan escaped. She lurched through the doorway, banging her shoulder on the frame.

Annie ran downstairs and searched the house, then raced out the back door to the garage and backyard. She zoomed back into the house and out the front door, gazing wide eyed around the yard and neighborhood. She went to the edge of their property and looked both ways up and down the street.

No Nora. But no Mr. Gruber lying next to his mailbox either.

The shiver started in her fingers and traveled up her arms to her shoulders, then down to her thighs.

Clenching her fists, she heard the unnerving sound of a hiss behind her, and paralyzing fear took her. Just as her knees buckled and threatened to drop her where she was, she heard the giggle.

But this time she recognized it. She whipped around and froze, uncomprehending.

35

Nora sat on Mr. Gruber's front-porch steps.

The old man perched beside her, wearing the overalls and long-sleeved shirt he wore every day. He held Mr. Bear, moving him up, down, and sideways, talking to Nora in a growly bear voice.

"Miss Nora, you must always mind your mommy and daddy—" He broke off, noticing Annie.

Nora looked her way and waved. "Hi, Mommy! I woke up—"

Annie spread her arms with a jerk. "Nora! What are you doing over there? Get over here this instant!"

"But, Mommy—"

"No buts, missy."

Nora froze at Annie's tone and scooched closer to the old man.

Annie stalked over to Mr. Gruber's porch and yanked Nora to her feet. "You scared me to death, honey! Why did you come outside without telling me?"

"But, Mommy, you were sleeping so good. I went by you on

my tippy-toes because I didn't want to wake you up."

"That doesn't matter. You should have told me where you were going. I've told you and Kimmie a thousand times—don't go anywhere without telling me."

Nora looked down at her feet. "I'm sorry, Mommy. I promise I won't—" She burst into tears and grabbed Annie's legs, squeezing them and wetting her knees.

Annie's heart broke. "Nora, Nora, don't cry so. I'm sorry I got mad, but I was scared."

Annie lifted her gaze to Mr. Gruber's distraught face, his white hair lying in wisps on his forehead. "This will not happen again."

Mr. Gruber reached and patted Nora's back, smoothing her hair. He handed Mr. Bear back to her and stood, heaving himself up with difficulty, turning to go up the steps to his wicker chair.

Then he slewed back around, clutching the railing to keep from falling. "This is probably all my fault, Mrs. Lee. She heard me on my porch and came out to see, well, to see if something was wrong." He looked down at Nora. "You have a kind little girl. You should be proud of her."

Annie gazed down at Nora's tear-streaked face, one fist rubbing her eye.

He turned again to retreat up to his porch. "Sorry if I'm speaking out of turn," he mumbled.

Annie's curiosity took center stage. "What do you mean, 'to see if something was wrong'?"

Mr. Gruber faced her, focusing behind Annie and over her head. His face reddened. "I . . . well, I was—" He stumbled over his words and fell silent, wiping his dripping nose with the back of his hand.

"He was crying, Mommy. I heard him through the window when I was on your bed."

Annie looked up at her bedroom window—it was open an inch

to let fresh air in. Then she looked at the old man, now seeing faint tear streaks on his cheeks. In her desperate panic over Nora, she hadn't noticed.

Her anger melted. "Is there anything I can do for you, Mr. Gruber?"

"No, my dear. Or, wait—"

"Yes?"

"You can call me Jake. That's my name."

"Yes, it's on your mailbox."

"Well, I think after twenty years, you could call me by my given name, Mrs. Lee."

Annie smiled and stuck out her hand. He took it and patted it.

"Annie. You can call me Annie, Mr.—I mean Jake."

Jake laughed and leaned down and patted Nora's head. "And perhaps, with your permission of course, you would allow this little one to sit with me on my porch once in a while?" His eyes clouded. "I had a little daughter like her once."

Annie gazed into the old man's sad eyes and knew why he'd been crying. She picked Nora up and hugged her tightly.

"Please, Mommy? I like him. And he makes Mr. Bear talk to me in a funny bear voice."

"Of course you can, honey. But you must always ask me, remember?"

"Okay, Mommy. I 'member."

Annie leaned into Nora's face and gave her a butterfly kiss on the cheek.

Jake winked at Nora. "When she comes over, I'll be sure to let you know. I promise. And of course, you are always invited to come with her. A visit now and again would be delightful."

"Thank you, Jake." She put Nora down and took her hand. "And now we must go."

"Goodbye. Say hello to that strapping husband of yours."

"Yes, I will."

She stepped down to the yard.

"And, Annie."

She turned around again, impatient now to be on her way. "Yes?"

"Please stop by anytime. I'm always here." His voice thickened. "And always alone. I really don't have anyone except your family."

Annie gulped. The poor man.

"Of course, Jake. I might have time to sit and talk tomorrow."

"Tomorrow. Yes, tomorrow would be lovely." He nodded and turned away, hand on the screen door.

Annie looked at her watch. "Wait." She stepped back to the porch. "We have time. I don't have to leave for another thirty minutes or so. Could we stay and visit now? Why wait for tomorrow when today's right here in front of us?"

His poor old eyes lit up like the morning sun. "Yes, we should seize the day, as Jean always used to say. And you're right—tomorrow's not here yet, is it? Come on up. I'll get us some coffee."

He disappeared inside. When he reappeared, he balanced a coffeepot and two white cups in his hands. He set them on a small table, then gestured to the two chairs on the other side of the table from his.

Annie lifted Nora into the white wicker rocker, set Mr. Bear on her lap, and took the other rocker next to her.

Jake poured the coffee and handed a cup to Annie, then smiled at Nora. "And I just happen to have a little something for you." He took a wrapped cookie out of his shirt pocket and glanced sidelong at Annie. "With your mother's permission, of course."

"Of course. Nora, say thank you to Jake."

"Thank you, Jake . . . I mean Mr. Goober."

"Oh, I'm sorry, Jake. She has a little trouble with your name."

The old man slapped his knee and laughed. "No, my dear, don't apologize. I've been called worse. Mr. Goober will do just fine."

Annie sipped her coffee, admiring Jean's pink roses. She was glad she'd stayed.

Leaning forward, she tapped Jake on the knee. "I'd love to hear your story, Jake. You must've lived an interesting life. Would you mind?"

Jake's eyes met hers. It was as if he looked through her to memories scattered like leaves in the yard. His eyes darted here and there, as if picking and choosing which ones to share.

Annie backpedaled. "You don't have to. I certainly don't mean to pry."

He waved her words away. "No, I think I'd like to. I'm not sure how interesting it is, but I'll give it a go." He grinned. "You must reciprocate someday, my dear."

"Deal."

Jake rose and paced from one end of the porch to the other, his chin cupped in his hand. "The thing is, where to start."

"You could start at the beginning."

"Can't start at the beginning—I'm too old. We'd be here until a month from next Tuesday."

Annie giggled, warming to this neighbor she'd barely taken the time to know.

He returned to his seat. "How 'bout I just tell it like I'm giving a speech or something. Just the parts that paint me as I am."

"Works for me."

He closed his eyes for a moment, then opened them and squinted at Annie, a smile lighting his face. "I'll start with Jean, the best part of my life. But first I have to go back a bit."

"However you want, Jake. I'm all ears."

"Thank you, my dear." He sat back and took a deep breath.

The look on the old man's face made Annie wonder what she'd gotten herself into.

36

"Here's the thing. Nobody really likes me—I know that, and most of the time it doesn't bother me. The neighbors avoid me, except for Roger. He's a decent-enough guy, but he really should take care of his dandelions. He lets just one get established, then my yard is filled with the little yellow devils." He darted a glance at Nora. "Excuse my language."

Annie shook her head. "Just talk the way you talk, Jake. We're not offended. And by the way, *we* like you, me and Nora. And so does Roger—he says so all the time."

Jake's mouth lifted at the corners. "Well, I've never cared much that no one likes me. I'd just as soon not have to talk to anyone. My wife, Jean, used to give me heck for that." His face stilled. "She was different from me though. People always liked her. Jean's the only reason we had any friends at all. She had a way about her. She could cozy up to someone and warm them from top to bottom without even takin' the time to blink. People just knew she cared. Me? People always knew I didn't care."

"Sorry—don't believe that."

"Believe it. My dad didn't care about people, and neither did my mom. He drank and she knitted. That's all. I'm seventy-four now, and the only memory I have of my dad is the back side of his hand comin' at me. I got pretty good at duckin'. I remember my mother's tears though, and I despised them. Weak."

He was silent, clearly sifting through hard images of the past. "I always wondered why she didn't do him in with one of her knitting needles. I know I thought about it plenty of times."

Annie raised a finger, and Jake paused. For the first time, she worried about Nora hearing this, but glancing at her, she saw she was playing with Mr. Bear and not paying attention.

She signed to Jake to continue.

"You sure?"

"Yes, it's okay. Right, Nora?"

Nora didn't even look up. "Huh?"

"Nothing, honey." Annie turned to Jake and grinned. "You see? Go ahead."

"I'll try to be more careful. Now, let's see—where was I? Oh yes . . . Dad died of drink—liver failure—and Mom died of a broken heart. My brother died in a car chase. He and his buddies robbed a convenience store and wrapped their car around a tree just outside of town. Don't know if Mom's broken heart was over that or the way Dad abused her and caroused with other women."

"Oh, Jake, I'm so sorry. That must've been hard."

He shrugged. "I left as soon as I could. Enlisted and headed for the sunny shores of Vietnam at the ripe ol' age of eighteen. Just squeaked by and graduated, then dressed up in my shiny new uniform and boots and hit the beaches after boot camp. We landed in a hail of gunfire, and I figgered my life would end quickly."

"Our dads were deployed to Southeast Asia toward the end of the war, before we were born. They were in the navy, so their tours didn't last long. I think they mostly served in some kind of advisory capacity."

"Navy, huh? I knew there was something off about you two." His voice was gruff, but by now Annie wasn't fooled.

He patted his chest. "Marines. The best of the best."

Annie dipped her head. "Thank you for your service, Jake."

"The ones who deserve your thanks are the ones you can't thank, the ones who gave it all. Somehow, though, I made it back home in one piece—well, almost one piece."

"You were wounded?"

"In the worst way. I left my mind back there—you know, the part that thinks you're invincible, that the world is an okay place. The part that says you can make something of yourself. I struggled with PTSD for five long years after coming home. Maybe struggled is too strong a word—I didn't really fight all that hard against it. Mostly numbed it with the bottle and with pills."

"That must've been so hard for you."

"Wives had it the worst, as I recall, even though I didn't have one yet. I had my bottle and my pills—that is, until a sweet young nurse tripped over her own feet and landed at mine in the hall of the VA hospital one day. Dark-brown hair tucked under her surgical cap, trim little frame that would just about start the fireworks all by itself, and green eyes wide and deep enough for a soldier to get lost in. I helped her up and asked her out all in a blink. And the wonder of it was, she said yes!

"We were inseparable after that. Six months later we got hitched and settled down in an apartment on the other side of town from the hospital. We waited to have kids—mostly because I didn't really like the little demons. It's a wonder we ever did. Jean said she refused to get pregnant until I told her I *wanted* to be a dad. Seeing as how the only role model I'd ever had was Dad's abuse and a mother who couldn't do anything but cry over it, there didn't seem much chance of it. There had to be something better to do in life than to bring another generation into this sorry world, then send them off to some godforsaken place to fight in another war."

Jake paused in his story, his hands tight in his lap, a faraway look in his wrinkled old eyes.

Annie leaned in. "I like Jean already. She sounds like my grandmother—now there was a scrapper. I used to spend summers with her, and she could whip out a willow switch ten feet long and flick me with it on my bare leg so fast, I never had a chance to get away."

Jake sipped his coffee as she spoke, then laughed and sprayed it all over his shirtfront. He set the cup down and grabbed for a napkin. "I think Jean could've given your grandma a run for her money." He wiped the napkin on his shirt. "And she never, ever gave up once she'd made her mind up."

"Grandma too."

"Over the next year, I watched Jean. With friends, with people she worked with, the neighborhood kids. Especially after we moved to this house. She loved kids. And they loved her."

"This must've been long before we moved in, right?"

Jake grinned. "You were still just a twinkle in God's eye, I'm sure."

"Now, Jake, I'm older than I look. I've got four kids, remember?"

"Anyway, Jean started letting some of the neighbor kids come to our house and play games on the porch and in the yard when she wasn't working. And she'd bake cookies for them. She'd sit and talk to some of the older girls about dating and boys and hair and whatever else girls chatter about. They liked her. She let them call her by her first name, and she remembered all of theirs. She was invited to birthday parties. Sometimes I'd tag along just to watch her. She was amazing, a beautiful sight to behold."

"She sounds wonderful. I bet Mayra would've liked her."

Jake smiled. "That Mayra's a real go-getter, and she looks a lot like you, Annie. You must be very proud of her, and the rest of your little brood."

"We are. But they are a handful. Sometimes it's all we can do to make sure everyone is where they should be when they should be."

"Noticed. Especially you. You don't seem to take things in stride the way Roger does."

Annie looked down at her hands.

"Oh, there I go, speaking out of turn again."

"You're very perceptive. It's something about myself I'm trying to change."

"Before life passes you by?"

Annie swallowed hard. "Something like that." She raised her head and winked at him. "Jake, please continue your story. You have to wait for mine, remember?"

He nodded and sipped his coffee. "After a while, I started getting brave. I started thinking maybe being parents wasn't such a bad idea after all. Jean seemed to have a handle on it. With her next to me, I just might turn out to be a decent father. After all, she'd taught me a thing or two about how to be a husband."

Jake turned his gaze to Nora, feeding Mr. Bear a bite of cookie. A tear slipped out. "So I told her one day that I was ready. Six weeks later, I found a pacifier by my breakfast plate. Eight months after that, Rosie Grace was born. The most perfect baby girl ever. Spittin' image of Jean, right down to her dark hair and tiny hands and feet. And she was a little scrapper too, just like her mama."

"Oh, Jake, she sounds beautiful."

"The first time she looked at me, I lost my heart and never found it again. I could barely stand to leave her to go to work. I hurried home every night and took over with her while Jean cooked dinner and cleaned up. After work was Rosie Grace and

229

Daddy time. I couldn't get enough of her—"

He stopped, put his head back against the chair cushion, and closed his eyes.

He was quiet so long, Annie thought he'd dozed off. "Jake?"

He sat up and pointed his index finger at the porch ceiling. "You know, I never was much a one for bothering God about the hard stuff, but after that day in 1979, he and I had a few tough conversations, let me tell you. I gave it to him with both barrels and never let up. But it didn't do no good. What happened still happened and there wasn't nothin' to be done about it."

Annie tensed and threw a quick glance at Nora, dreading where his story was going.

"After what day, Jake? What happened?"

37

"She lived for five years. Born in 1974 and died in 1979. I gave God a piece of my mind that day—never spoke to him again."

Annie gasped and clutched her collar. "Oh, Jake—"

"Jean's eyes were never the same after the doctor came to the waiting room shaking his head. The life in 'em just drained away. 'There was just too much damage,' the doc said. 'She never had a chance.'"

He leaned forward, his face in his hands. "A little girl on a tricycle is no match for a full-size truck."

Annie blanched at the harsh image, words trapped in her throat.

Jake sat up and eyed her, clearly wondering if he should go on.

"I don't know what to say—"

"I was right there, fussin' around with Jean's roses. Saw the whole thing. Rosie Grace sailed down the slope of the driveway to the street. I threw my shovel down and ran like the devil to try to catch her, but I was too late—couldn't reach her in time. She got to the bottom of the driveway and rolled into the street between two parked cars. Don't think the truck driver even got a good look at her."

"I threw her mangled tricycle in the dumpster at work the next day. Didn't take any time off. Why should I? There was nothing here anyway—Jean never did come home from that hospital. Oh, she was here, her body drifting around the house, dusting, straightening, cooking. Even washing Rosie's clothes. I ask you, what for? But Jean was somewhere else—in the grave with Rosie Grace, I suspect."

Jake bowed his head and swiped at his eyes. "If I'd only known, I'd never have—"

Annie reached for him and patted his hand. "Never have had her?"

His head jerked up, staring at her with eyes like glittering stones.

Annie withdrew her hand. "I'm sorry. Maybe I shouldn't have said that."

"A year we went on like that. But then Jean died in her sleep. Heard her cough once in the middle of the night, and she was gone for good the next morning."

Annie bowed her head, trying to hold back her tears.

Nora got up and climbed into her mother's lap. Annie hugged her close.

"I sit on my porch now and watch the world go by. I have no interest in it. They can fight their wars, take their drugs, build their empires. It has nothing to do with me. I'm waiting to see Jean and Rosie Grace again. Then maybe . . . maybe something will matter again."

He fell silent, staring vacantly across the street, ignoring Annie and Nora as if they weren't there.

Annie wondered if he would speak again, say something encouraging. That he'd found peace again somehow, that he was glad he'd had them for a while. All those soft words people say when harshness took over their lives.

But Jake was clearly spent with the telling, and it was time for her and Nora to go.

Annie stood, then knelt by Jake's wicker chair. Taking his gnarled hands in hers, she said, "Jake, I am so sorry. And I'm sorry never to have gotten to know you before this. Neighbors should know each other, watch out for each other. I haven't done either."

Nora stood on the other side of his chair and patted his knee. "Don't cry, Mr. Goober."

Jake withdrew his hands and patted Annie's arm. "Now, my dear, it ain't your fault. It's mine. I'm not easy-like with people." He turned and took Nora's hand. "But this little one—Jean would've loved her in an instant."

"Well, whoever's fault it is, let's stop being so foolish, okay? You can visit with Nora whenever you want. And Roger and I, we'll have you over for dinner sometime soon. Would you like that?"

His leathery cheeks crinkled in a smile. "Yes, I believe I would. Maybe I can give him some advice on dandelions."

"He'd like that." She glanced at her watch. "Okay, then. Now we'd better scoot to pick up the rest of the tribe from school. Come on, Nora. Say goodbye."

"Bye, Mr. Goober! Thank you for the cookie."

He patted her head. "See ya later, sweetheart." He stood and laid his hand on Annie's shoulder. "Remember something for me, my dear."

"What?"

"You never know when you're having the last conversation with someone you love."

He dropped his hand and turned away, leaving her weak-kneed and breathless.

Annie and Nora walked back through the hedge dividing their properties and up to their porch. Nora ran into the house ahead of her. Annie heard her tromp up the stairs, telling Mr. Bear how good he'd been while Mommy talked to Mr. Goober.

Dear little scamp . . .

Annie hesitated at the open screen door, then rotated and looked over at the old man, now ensconced in his chair with his newspaper in front of his face. Twenty years they'd been neighbors and that was the longest conversation she'd ever had with him. She'd always thought of him as a mean, miserly old grump and had never wanted to speak to him. His jabs at Roger about their yard always annoyed her, even though Roger never seemed bothered by it.

She turned and followed Nora in, letting the screen door close on its creaky hinges. She must remember to ask Roger to fix that.

Annie turned to make sure the door had latched and caught sight of Jake's mailbox over the tops of the shrubs. A chill crept over the back of her neck as she recalled her dream. Mr. Gruber— Jake—lying on the sidewalk at the curb, bare feet hanging in the street.

"You never know when you're having the last conversation with someone you love."

Annie shook her head and went in.

38

Annie shut and locked the front door, then leaned against it, relaxing the tension in her neck and shoulders. She felt the fear slide back down her pant leg.

She must get going. She couldn't stand here in the doorway a minute longer. She was already behind schedule.

Nora bumped back down the stairs on her seat and ran over to her. "Are we going yet?"

Annie nodded and grabbed her purse and Nora's hand. They'd have to make tracks—dangerous these days to keep children waiting around at their schools.

She pulled out of the driveway thirty seconds later and noticed a knot of people standing in the Baxters' yard across the street, the flatbed truck now backed up to the porch. She wondered again and glanced at her watch.

She decided to take the time and find out what was up with her neighbors.

She pulled into the curb, intending to walk across the street and ask. Then she saw Jake at his mailbox and lowered the front passenger window.

He turned, empty handed, and shrugged. "No mail. Guess I'm too early. I'll have to check later—"

"Jake, do you know what's going on at the Baxters'?"

His mouth tightened in a straight line. "Oh. I guess I thought you knew. That's why I didn't mention it before. John collapsed last night with a heart attack."

"Oh no—Roger said he heard sirens late last night. But we had no idea—"

Jake leaned into the open window, pointing with his chin. "Their children and grandchildren are moving her in with one of them."

He looked at Eleanor being helped down the front steps by one of her children. "They don't expect him to make it, I heard from their son."

"Poor Eleanor. I'll have to see if I can send her a card or something."

Jake nodded. "He was ready, I expect."

A tremble started in Annie's hand. "What do you mean?"

"He told me just yesterday he'd done everything he needed to do."

"But . . . you mean, somehow he knew?"

Jake shrugged. "How should I know? But he told me about this quote from old Ben Franklin. 'One today is worth two tomorrows'." His gaze pierced Annie's. "Smart guy, huh? I believe old Ben knew what he was talking about."

He winked and shuffled away, making his way back up his walk and into his house.

Annie gripped the steering wheel. The ring's stone winked in the sunlight, casting a reflection on the headliner of the vehicle.

She inched away from the curb, looking back at the Baxters' front yard.

"Mommy, where are Mr. Goober's shoes?"

"What?"

"Mr. Goober's shoes are gone."

Annie twisted in her seat and looked toward Jake's front porch, but he'd already disappeared inside.

"Are you sure? Why would he be barefoot outside in February?"

"He was, Mommy. I saw his toes."

Should she check on him? *No . . . I'm not going in there. This is utter nonsense!*

She gunned the engine and peeled out, leaving the demons behind on the asphalt.

39

ank's and Kimmie's schools were adjacent to each other, sharing a soccer field. Hank's day ended half an hour before Kimmie's, so his job was to wait outside the grade school for his sister, then both were to meet Annie in front of the fountain, located by the front doors.

Many other parents picked their children up in the same spot, and there was always an assigned teacher and an aide outside with them.

Each day it was the same—Annie didn't relax until she turned the last corner and saw the two of them right where they were supposed to be. Today was different.

"There they are, Mommy. I see Kimmie."

But Hank wasn't with her. Kimmie sat on the fountain, one of the teachers sitting near her.

Annie craned her neck, trying to find Hank. She reminded herself that sometimes he was held up by PE, his last class of the day.

She tried not to worry. "Yes, I see, Nora. We just have to wait in line with the other parents until we're close enough."

Usually, Ellen's son Shane waited with Hank. But of course, not today, which turned Annie's thoughts back to Ellen. The tide of emotion rose to the surface again—she'd managed not to think about it the last few hours—bringing with it worry about where Hank was.

The teacher's aide, Sophie, waved Annie through, and she inched the car forward, setting aside her sorrow once again. She knew she needed to grieve, but this wasn't the time.

Sophie, who also attended their church, looked through the window. Annie could tell she was in for a round of "I'm so sorry for your loss" statements about Ellen. She steeled herself as she rolled the window down and forced a cheerful smile. "Hi, Soph. What's up with you? Did your husband get that job?"

"We're still waiting to hear if he gets called back for a second interview. He's so excited—like a kid getting his first job. It's really his dream job, what he's been working for ever since we started dating in college. And there's so much room for advancement. If he gets it, he's promised I can go back to school and finish my degree." Pause. "Annie—"

"Well, I'm sure he'll get it. From what I know of him, he's perfect for it. The help he gave Roger rewiring when we did that kitchen remodel last year was super. Roger was impressed with his knowledge."

"Annie, I—"

Annie cut her off. "Have you seen Hank's class come out?"

"Not yet. Annie, I heard about—"

"Oh, there he is now. Gotta go." She put the window back up as the kids raced each other to the van.

Hank threw his backpack in the backseat, slammed it shut after Kimmie, and opened the front passenger door.

"Uh-uh, Hank. You know better. Get in the back."

"Mom—"

"Now, Hank."

Annie waited for him to get out and switch to the back. She saw Sophie out of her side vision, still standing next to her window, staring at her. She waved at her and pulled away.

She supposed she'd have to apologize to Sophie on Sunday, but she just didn't feel like dealing with her excessive chatter today, or her sympathy.

"Mom, can we have KFC tonight? We haven't had it for a long time." Hank loved KFC to the point he'd eat it for breakfast, lunch, and dinner if given the chance.

"Maybe this weekend, son. I've got something else planned for dinner tonight."

"Yeah, what?"

The truth was, she'd hadn't even thought about dinner yet. She white-knuckled the steering wheel again. Her usual orderliness, which included planning ahead for dinner, had been sucked into a black hole in her mind.

"Well, what are we having?" Hank insisted.

"It's a surprise. Now drop it."

"Ow, Hank! You hit me—"

"Hank, knock it off. Kimmie, are you all right?"

"It was an accident, Mom. I didn't mean to hit her. I needed my backpack, and her face got in the way."

Annie heard the smirk in his voice and sighed. *Maybe my—what— insanity? Maybe it's affecting them.* She looked at him in the mirror. "Hank, just be more careful. Kimmie, answer me. Are you okay?"

"Yes, Mommy. It didn't hurt that much."

"See, told ya so—"

"Hank, give it a rest. I'll think about KFC for tonight, but no promises. If I decide to, we can pick some up on our way home."

"Yay."

"But no soda pop. You'll drink milk with it. Or water. Got it? Don't even ask for soda."

"Yeah, got it," Hank grumbled. Then he blurted out, his voice tinged with anxiety, "Mom, did you hear about Shane?"

"Yes. Drop it." Shoulders tense, she jerked the wheel. She wasn't ready for this.

"Drop it? His mom died. Last night. You heard?"

"Yes, I heard. Let's talk about it later."

"But it's Ellen. She was your best——"

"Hank! Stop!" She glanced at Nora in the rearview mirror. She couldn't bear it if Nora asked again what *die* meant.

Hank evidently didn't get it. "It's all over school that Shane wasn't there today because he's the one who found her. And——"

"I'm not going to say it again, Hank—stop talking about it. Now."

That seemed to get through to him. His glare lit up the mirror.

Annie didn't care if he was mad. He'd get over it. She wasn't so sure about Nora.

Five minutes later, she pulled into the high school lot, searching for Mayra as she slid into a parking space. She wasn't waiting in her usual spot by the big stone planters near the main doors. Annie spied a resource officer on duty nearby, talking with Eric, one of Mayra's friends. It looked like a serious conversation, the husky officer standing close to Eric. The boy stared at the ground with his hands in his pockets.

"Wait here, kids. I'm going over to talk to Eric. See . . . right over there. Maybe he knows where Mayra is."

"She's probably with Cassie, and I bet Eric knows where Cassie is——"

Annie turned around. "What's that supposed to mean?"

Hank's dark eyes danced with mischief. "Oh, nothing."

"Something!"

Hank drummed his fingers, exactly like Roger did when he felt nervous or uncomfortable. "Never mind, Mom. Just a smart remark. Sorry."

Annie stared, recalling Cassie jumping nervously earlier this morning at the church. And Hank hardly ever apologized. Annie wasn't convinced. But she didn't have time right now.

She opened her door and grabbed her purse, then stuck her head back in.

"I'll just be a minute. Behave yourselves. Hank, watch your sisters."

Annie walked quickly to the resource officer—Danny, according to his ID badge.

"May I help you, ma'am?"

"I just have a quick question for Eric."

"And you are?"

"I'm Mayra Lee's mom. She's usually waiting for me right here."

"Okay. Go ahead and ask."

She looked up at the muscular young man—a star tackle on the football team. "Did you see Mayra after school?"

"Umm—yeah. She was by her locker just a minute ago. She was talking to . . . to . . . one of her friends."

"Cassie?"

"Yeah."

"What's Cassie doing here? Isn't she homeschooled?"

"Yeah, but she takes one class here on Fridays. Music."

She noted the moisture on his upper lip. "Is there something wrong?"

"Nothing's wrong, Mrs. Lee. I just need to get going."

Annie pinned him with a stare and thrust her finger in his face. "You don't fool me. Now what's going on?"

Danny stepped closer to her. "Mrs. Lee, maybe you should calm down a bit."

"I am calm. Eric, are you sure you don't know where Mayra is right now?"

"I'm sure."

"Okay, but if I find out . . ."

Annie adjusted her bag, then faced Danny. "Sir," she said in a calmer voice, "I need to go in and look for her."

"I'll come with you. Do you know where her locker is?"

"Yes. She's a sophomore this year, so it's near the science wing."

"Okay, let's go." The officer looked at Eric. "Eric, you coming? We can talk on the way."

"No . . . no, that's all right, Danny. Maybe some other time. I really gotta go."

Danny put his hand on Eric's shoulder and gave him a gentle shake.

"Anytime you need to talk, I'm here, okay? Just come and find me."

Eric nodded. He turned and looked at Annie—or in her general direction. He seemed to have difficulty making eye contact.

"'Bye, Mrs. Lee. I'll see you around."

"Maybe at church? Haven't seen you there for a long time, it seems."

"Yeah—maybe," he said, face flaming. He turned and strode toward the parking lot.

They watched him reach the lot and turn toward the street in the distance.

"Kids," Danny said, running his hand through his hair. "Glad I don't have any yet."

"They can be a handful. Better wait until you're ready. Can we go in now?"

"Sure."

Annie glanced back at her minivan. She saw the vehicle bounce a couple of times, like a small earthquake had taken place inside, then heard a squeal from one of the girls through the open window.

She threw up her hands in frustration. "Danny, I'll be right back." Running to the van, she stuck her head in the open window.

"You guys settle down and stop horsing around. I have to go inside and get Mayra. Will you be all right for a few minutes?" She addressed the question to Hank, who drew himself up straight, squaring his shoulders.

"We'll be fine, Mom. I'll take care of the girls," he said in his Roger voice, laced with self-important swagger.

She smiled. "Okay. Thank you, Hank. I know I can count on you. Girls, mind your brother. Hank, make sure the doors are locked. And put this window up, okay?"

Hank nodded.

Annie ran back to where Danny was waiting, and he led her inside.

A few moments later they stood by Mayra's deserted locker. The hallway was empty and too quiet, like the park earlier today.

Not again . . .

Annie's brain shut down, wall posters and lockers slow-spinning around her. She closed her eyes. Danny's voice, asking her if Mayra had a phone, faded away. When she opened her eyes, nothing was familiar to her.

The paint on the walls had changed color, the locker numbers were different. *But . . .*

Wait, *not* unfamiliar.

This wasn't Mayra's school. And this wasn't Mayra's locker. Not even Mayra's world.

Annie stood in shock in front of her own high school locker. She looked right and saw Ellen's locker, identifiable by the black-and-green sticker on the front—with the words *Break All the Rules* emblazoned on it.

Looking down, Annie saw her own overstuffed book bag at her feet and a locker key clutched in her fingers.

Danny had disappeared. Kids wearing thirty-year-old fashions streamed around her, laughing and shoving each other. The music blaring from overhead speakers contained lyrics Mayra and her friends had probably never heard.

She gazed down the hall, reaching into her mind to get her bearings. She caught sight of Ellen hurrying down the hall toward her, red hair blazing like a beacon.

Ellen? She waved a high five as she threaded her way toward Annie through the sea of students.

The breath whooshed from her lungs, leaving Annie in a puddle of weakness. She took a backward step, stumbled over her bag, and sagged against the bank of lockers.

Ellen reached her and grabbed her elbow, giving it a shake. "Hey, Annie. What's up? You look like you've seen a ghost."

She turned away from Annie, stuck her key in her locker, and opened the door.

"Ellen, what's happening. Why are you . . . why are we here?"

Ellen faced Annie with her characteristic impish grin, flyaway red hair sticking up in all the wrong places as usual. "Don't be afraid, Annie. You'll see."

"See what? Ellen—" Annie's grab at the back of Ellen's fringed jacket was too late.

Ellen had already flipped back around, stepped inside her locker, and pulled the door shut behind her with a loud clang.

Annie froze in place. Her face felt stretched to the breaking point. Grabbing the handle of Ellen's locker, she tried to yank it open. Locked.

She lowered her forehead to the locker door and breathed in Ellen's favorite citrussy scent.

Annie groaned and squeezed her eyes shut again, reaching for anything to steady herself before she collapsed completely.

Oh, God, what's happening to me? I can't take any more.

40

"Hey, Mrs. Lee. Are you all right? Do you need to sit down?" The concern in Danny's voice forced her eyes open and slowed the whirl of the hallway to a stop. She found she was clutching his arm. Heat washed over her face as she let go of him and rubbed her thumb nervously over the ring.

"Yes . . . yes, I'm fine."

"You don't look fine. You're as white as a sheet, like you've seen a ghost. Can I get you some water or something?"

"No, please. Just let me get my bearings for a minute, okay? I . . . haven't been feeling well." Annie didn't like to lie—but still, it was partially true, she told herself.

"Okay, take your time."

Annie looked up and down the empty hall, heard no voices, saw no kids scrambling to leave the school to get home or to athletic practices.

"Danny," she stammered, trying to block the last few minutes out of her mind. "Where could she be? Eric said she was right here."

He patted her shoulder. "You know girls, right?"

She shrugged him off—she didn't need to be comforted. She needed to find Mayra.

He folded his arms across his chest. His dark eyes locked to hers, and he attempted a weak smile. "Now, Mrs. Lee, she's here somewhere. Even though I don't have kids of my own, I know how girls are. And I have three sisters. Mayra and Cassie are probably just hunkered down somewhere gossiping about boys and clothes. Why don't you go back out to your car and wait?"

Back to my car? Mayra's not out there. She's not anywhere . . . get ahold of yourself . . .

Annie gripped her purse and planted her feet. She tried to stare Danny down. "No, I'm not going anywhere until I find my daughter. Now, where else can we look? The cafeteria? Another building?"

"Listen to me for a second. You shouldn't leave your other children too long. I'll take a quick look around in the usual places, find her, and bring her out. How's that sound?"

His expression contrived to be reassuring, but Annie saw a glint of worry in his narrowed eyes.

"Mrs. Lee, I'm going to have to insist. This is the best plan."

Annie gave up. "Okay, I guess. But if you don't find her right off, you must come out and tell me."

"I'll do that. And don't worry. You have no idea how often this happens. I can guarantee you they're just being irresponsible. Now, off you go." He flicked his fingers toward the parking lot, then headed to a side door in the opposite direction. He turned at the last moment, grinned, and gave her a cheerful thumbs-up.

Annie ran down the hall and out the front door, willing her eyes to see Mayra waiting for her at the van. She wasn't there. Annie's heart lurched.

Why, of all days, did she have to be late picking her up?

She slowed her pace, eyes scanning the parking lot. Maybe Mayra was sitting *inside* a car now, talking to her friend. She stopped and squinted against the bright sun, peering inside the cars nearby. She saw no one. She walked down the sidewalk to the end of the row, then back the other way to the other end of the parking lot, keeping a wary eye on her own parking space.

All Annie saw were rows of cars with empty seats.

She looked across the street at the Taco Bell—a favorite after-school hangout. Should she go over there? No, she couldn't leave the other three kids alone in the parking lot. And she refused to run from one end to the other, like she had in the park.

Annie wanted to scream with fear and frustration. The parking lot shrank in her vision to just her vehicle in its slot and Mayra's empty seat. The familiar crushing sensation swept through her chest. Fists knotted at her sides, sweat trickling between her shoulder blades, she slogged back across the lot to her vehicle.

As she approached, she heard Nora's high giggle through the glass. Her chubby legs kicked straight out as Hank tickled her. Kimmie snuck a hand under Hank's arm and tickled him at the same time. Then Hank had both sisters shrieking uncontrollably, tickling them with a hand apiece.

How can they laugh when Mayra's gone?

Nora's question whispered on the breeze and slithered into Annie's head.

What's die, Mommy?

Annie slapped both hands hard on the front of the van. Instantly, the laughter inside switched off as the children stared at her through the windshield.

Hank opened the sliding door and climbed out. "What's wrong, Mom? Where's Mayra?"

Annie trudged around the front of the van and stood in front of Hank. "I don't know—"

His voice turned shrill. "What do you mean, you don't know?"

"She's got to be here somewhere, Hank. Calm down."

"But—"

"Danny, the resource officer, went to look for her. He knows the school layout better than I do, and he can look for her faster. We just need to wait here."

Hank clearly wasn't fooled by her false confidence.

"Get back in the van, Hank. Keep Nora and Kimmie occupied. Can you do that for me?"

"Are you gonna call Dad?"

Annie hesitated, then shook her head. "No—"

"But, Mom—"

Annie shoved her desperation down where Hank wouldn't hear it. "She's here somewhere. I don't need to call Dad—yet." She shook Hank by the shoulder. "Get back in, Hank. Help me with your sisters."

Hank pulled away from her and jerked the car door open.

Annie recoiled at the glare of hostility he threw over his shoulder. *Never mind,* she told herself sternly. *I'll deal with it later. Right now I just have to find Mayra.*

She took her phone out of her pocket and stared at it. *Should* she call Roger? Her finger hesitated over his name. She bowed her head and closed her eyes. *Please, God, let her be here somewhere. She's only fifteen. Please let her be here.*

Annie slid her phone back into her pocket and slumped against the driver's door. Checking her watch, she was surprised to see that only twenty minutes had passed since she'd parked. Another lifetime had passed in her heart as she'd envisioned new, horrendous scenarios. She was getting good at this.

"Mom!" Hank's voice yanked her mind out of the hell it had spiraled into.

41

He pointed toward the athletic field to the left of the building. Annie jerked her glance in that direction and shaded her eyes. Mayra walked toward her, flanked by Danny and Cassie.

Tears of gratitude washed down her cheeks, splashing onto her jacket. Then anger surged like a tsunami. Annie tried to keep herself together as the three approached.

A moment later they stood in front of her. Both girls stared at their feet.

"Mayra?" Danny laid an index finger on Mayra's shoulder.

"Sorry I worried you, Mom," she mumbled. She raised her eyes to Annie's face. "Mom, were you crying? It's not that big a thing. We were just talking. We went over to the bleachers for some privacy."

Annie couldn't control the harshness in her voice. "Your privacy is not the issue here. *You* might think it's not a big deal, young lady, but it is. Why couldn't you have waited in your usual spot? You could've done your gossiping later."

Cassie's head flew up, and she backed up a step.

Mayra threw a glance at Cassie, then draped an arm around her. "Mom, you don't have to be mean. You don't even know what we—"

"Mean? You haven't seen mean yet." She turned her frustration on Cassie.

"And what about your mom? D'ya think she might be worried? Is she here looking for you?"

"No, Mrs. Lee. I called her and told her I'd be a little late. I'm within walking distance."

"Oh, so you called *your* Mom."

Mayra huffed. "Mom—"

"Umm, yeah, Mrs. Lee. This is really all my fault. I needed to talk, and Mayra was just trying to help . . ."

"So you think it's your fault that she didn't call me, text me . . . *something* to keep me from worrying? I don't think so—that's on her."

Cassie shrugged. "Maybe I'd better start walking." She looked at Mayra. "I'll see you tomorrow. Thanks for . . . for . . . listening. You're a good friend. I'll figure this out. I promise."

For the first time, Annie heard the despair in Cassie's voice and wondered if she'd been too tough on her.

The girls hugged each other.

With supreme effort, Annie forced her anger into retreat. "Cassie, do you want a lift home?"

"No, I'd rather walk. I need to think . . . and it's only a couple of blocks. Thanks anyway."

She turned away and soon stood at the walk light on the street.

Mayra stared in her direction. Cassie lifted a hand and waved, then strode across the intersection.

Annie nudged Mayra's arm. "Please get in the van. We need to go."

Clearly angry, Mayra stepped away from her, jerked the front passenger door open, and slid in. She slammed the door so hard, the van shook.

Annie rubbed her temples. *Another evening of crises . . .*

As she started around to the driver's side, she saw Danny still watching her. She'd forgotten he was there. "Thank you, Danny, for helping me find the girls. I'd better get them all home."

"You're welcome, Mrs. Lee."

He glanced at Mayra through the window. She sat with arms crossed, staring straight ahead, obviously sulking.

"If I might just say—"

"What? You think I was too hard on them?"

"No, no. I wouldn't presume to say that, Mrs. Lee. It's just that . . . well . . . maybe you could ask her what they were talking about? You might be surprised at how smart your daughter is. Even though she definitely should have called you—" he finished, red-faced.

"Okay. I'll ask her *after* I read her the riot act. Thanks again, Danny."

He stepped back, waved at Mayra, and disappeared inside the school.

Annie stood rooted to her spot, watching him. She glanced down at the ring, the words on the stone glinting at her. Nausea lay just below the surface, threatening to wash up on shore.

What had those girls gotten themselves into?

She recalled several situations from her own teenage years— herself and Ellen closeted together, conspiring how they could pull one over on their parents—and imagined Mayra and Cassie in a far worse scrape. After all, the internet made vulnerable girls far easier prey in this day and age.

Her imagination was in overdrive again. She needed to nip this in the bud—now.

Mayra and Cassie will find out just how hard it is to fool me. After all, I'm not stupid. They would not succeed in getting away with whatever they were up to. She remembered a few tricks her own father had employed to keep herself and Ellen in line.

And whatever it was they were into, Annie determined to ferret it out . . . tonight.

It was time to circle the wagons and close the breach in her fence.

42

Hank won the argument over dinner options. By the time Annie had stopped for gas and headed for home, the thought of coming up with something to eat was the last heavy straw. She couldn't do it.

She pulled into the drive-up at the local KFC and was immediately ambushed by all four children yelling their preferences.

"Stop it. Just stop it!"

Their voices switched off.

"Geez, Mom, get a grip," Hank complained. "You've been a grouch all day. What's up?"

"Hank—"

"Mommy, are you mad?" Nora's question ended on a tearful whimper.

Before Annie could respond, Mayra laid a hand on her arm. "Mom, you're sweating. Are you sick or something?"

"No, I'm not sick. Just tired. I'm sorry if I sounded mad. Now if you all don't mind, I'll choose the dinner items. This may come as a shock to you, but I've been your mom for fifteen years now, and I happen to know what you all like. I'd appreciate complete silence while I look at the menu—"

"Can I help you? Are you going to order?" The disembodied voice startled her.

She answered with more irritation than she'd intended. "Can you just give me a minute, please?"

Mayra gave her a pained look. "She's asked twice now. Didn't you hear—"

"Mayra, please. Be quiet while I think."

"Fine. Think. I didn't know ordering dinner was nuclear science."

Annie pushed her frustration down to share a bench with her anxiety as she looked over the menu board. She ordered a bucket of half regular and half extra crispy, along with several different sides.

Hank complained when she ordered coleslaw, but she reached backward and thrust a palm at him. He buttoned up.

Kimmie, who'd been the quietest of the bunch—as usual—spoke up. "Soda? Please, Mom?"

"Don't even."

After paying and waiting longer than usual, they were on their way again. Annie just wanted to get home and settle Hank and Mayra at their homework and Kimmie and Nora up in the play-room for an hour or so before Roger arrived home from work and the nightly dinner circus started. She desperately needed some downtime after this roller-coaster day.

Part of Annie's daily routine was to have that downtime so she wasn't a frazzled mess when Roger walked through the door. He spent his day in an orderly world managing other people's finances, meeting new people—some of them rich women with nothing to do all day except spend their money—and she didn't want him comparing her with them. She knew her friends thought it was an archaic notion, but she didn't care. She wasn't about to take chances with her marriage.

Keeping good habits were important. Routine. As usual. She clung to her mantra now, hoping to dispel the ghosts roosting in her chest since last night.

Tonight's dinner would be back to normal. No surprises. No tension. Friday night—good family time. And no nightmares for Nora, please God.

Annie felt her spirits rising. Tonight would be a good end to the week.

Two minutes later, she knew she was wrong.

Nearing their neighborhood, the ghosts snatched her coveted mantra with knobby claws and streaked away, screeching like maniacs—leaving Annie sweating and clutching her steering wheel again.

43

She turned the corner to their street and was stopped by a police officer straddling a motorcycle, palm out. Beyond him, two yellow barricades blocked her way.

Annie looked past him at the police cars and emergency vehicles spread out across the end of the cul-de-sac.

She glanced at the Baxters' house, now deserted. What could have happened?

Annie's brain spun in circles again as she searched the street and the yards. Eyes wide, leaning over the steering wheel, she brushed dust off the windshield. Leaning back against the seat, she pinched her eyes shut, then opened them again.

Her heart lurched and stopped, then slammed against her breastbone.

It was true . . . She saw a pile of clothes ending in bare feet next to Mr. Gruber's mailbox.

"Mom? What's going on?" Hank leaned forward from the back seat.

"I . . . I think it's Jake—Mr. Gruber. Something's wrong with him."

The police officer dismounted his motorcycle and approached. She lowered the window. "What happened here?"

"Ma'am, you can't go any further unless you live here. I'm sorry."

"But we do live here."

He took a small notebook out of his pocket. "Name and address, please? And are these your children—all four of them?"

"Yes, they're mine. My name is Annie Lee." She gave him the address.

She heard a whimper from the backseat and looked in the mirror. Nora had a fist in her eye, rubbing tears away.

Kimmie patted her shoulder, then leaned over and whispered in her ear.

Annie glanced at Mayra, wide eyed and stoic, but the tremble in her bottom lip gave her away.

"Mayra, I'm sure—"

"Sure of what? That he's dead?"

"Mayra, please. Watch what you say."

Mayra turned her face away and pressed her forehead to the passenger-side window.

"Way to go, sis. Make everything worse like you always—"

"That's enough, Hank." Annie leaned out the window. "Officer, I really need to get them home."

He looked up from his notes. "Okay, ma'am, your name's here. You can proceed to your home. Please take your children inside immediately and stay there. It's likely we'll be here for a little while longer."

"Can't you tell me what happened to Mr. Gruber? He's our next-door neighbor . . . our friend—"

"Ma'am, I'm sorry, but I can't give you details. But I can say that, unfortunately, he expired this afternoon. We'll be notifying his next of kin. Do you happen to know any of his family?"

Annie's eyes filled with tears. *Expired? Police-speak, I guess.* "I don't think he has any living family. He told me just today that we're his family."

"Then, again, I *am* sorry for your loss, Mrs. Lee. You can go on through now. And remember"—he glanced into the back-seats—"all of you, stay inside. It'll be safer."

The officer stepped aside, moved one of the barricades, and waved her through.

She drove past him, nosing slowly through the tangle of vehicles ranged across the cul-de-sac.

The emergency team had already laid Jake on a gurney and rolled him to the back of the ambulance.

Nora's shrill voice jarred her. "Mommy? Where are they taking Mr. Goober?"

Hank corrected her with a big brother sneer. "Gruber—it's Mr. Gruber. Why can't you say it right?"

Mayra looked back at him. "Knock it off, Hank. Don't be so mean—"

"All of you—just be quiet." Annie thought her head would explode. She wondered if the kids could hear the pounding. Waiting until the ambulance drove away, she pulled slowly into their driveway.

Mayra clicked the garage door remote. They watched in silence as the door climbed at glacial speed.

Annie parked and the kids piled out of the car, Mayra helping Nora out of her car seat. They hurried into the house, no doubt raiding the refrigerator within moments.

Annie sat, staring at Roger's tools again. It didn't work this time. His orderly arrangement mocked her day . . . filled with chaos and disorder . . . and fright.

Her mind reeled as she thought back over each incident, beginning with dinner last night.

What would I do today if I knew I'd die tomorrow?

The rings.

The strange conversation with Ellen last night.

The man in the park.

The newscaster this morning.

Ellen . . . dead.

Abby. *Abby? How could she be part of this?*

The meeting with Pastor Mike.

Nora gone from the park.

The dream. Dreams.

Finding Nora at Jake's—and his tragic story. Rosie Grace.

Watching Ellen disappear into her locker—for some reason, that was the most disturbing of all.

Mayra—missing for what? Ten minutes?

And now Jake, dead, like in her dream. She'd just had her first long conversation with him, gotten to know him a little, to like him, even care about him. And now . . .

The last thing Jake had said to her sprang unbidden to her mind. *You never know when you're having the last conversation with someone you love.*

"Mom, are you coming in or what?"

Annie jerked her head to the slit of light showing at the door from the garage into the house—Hank's head silhouetted there.

I guess I can't stay out here all night.

She dragged herself out of the van, carrying dinner in one hand and her bag in the other, and shuffled to the door leading from the garage into the laundry room.

Roger's tools—hanging neatly and in order, like so many trolls frozen in different positions—winked at her in the slit of sunlight showing through the garage windows.

Annie stopped and glared at them. She itched to sweep them all off their hangers and throw them in the dumpster.

They mocked her yearning for order and sameness, for *as usual*, uneventful days and peaceful nights. Rules followed, fences built, and mantras repeated had no power to keep the dread away. It wouldn't matter how high she could swing, how many silly games she played with Nora and Mr. Bear as she tried to leave her grown-up self behind and become a child again, the trolls would always find a way in. Today's joy in the park had become yesterday's misery and sorrow, fueled by fear and anxiety.

The little devils were right—life wasn't like Roger's tools. It should be, but it wasn't.

And if it wasn't, she didn't know how she'd survive. She might as well *not* have a tomorrow.

Fine. Bring it on.

She jerked the door open and went in, locking it behind her.

44

Annie cleaned up the kitchen after the kids blew it up with four different snacks, then herded them upstairs to their assigned tasks—Mayra and Hank at their homework, and Kimmie and Nora occupied quietly in the play room.

She glanced at the clock. Exactly seventy-one minutes until Roger would be home.

She was glad she'd given in to Hank and bought the chicken for dinner. For once, she didn't care and she didn't feel guilty. Ellen would be proud of her.

A stab of sorrow pierced her chest. She'd barely had time to mourn today. Another piece of baggage to unpack. Maybe she should call Mark and see how he and the boys were doing.

Annie retrieved her phone from her bag and punched his number in. Voicemail. She didn't leave a message—didn't know what on earth to say.

Probably just as well. Too soon.

Wandering over to the window in the living room, she peered out at the street. Someone stood on the sidewalk across the street, staring at Jake's house. Annie didn't recognize the man. He turned and walked away after a minute. Maybe someone from the next street over who'd heard the sirens. No doubt news of his death had already made it around their cozy neighborhood grapevine.

She breathed a sigh of relief as she sank onto her chair in the living room. The police and ambulance were gone, and the street was quiet once again.

Annie determined she *would* think through this strange day and make sense of it. She would find some kind of order—she had to. She'd go crazy without order and routine. And once she made sense of it, she could tell Roger.

Not until, though. Annie was afraid he'd think she was losing her marbles if she just blurted it all out to him without a plan. She suspected that was the real reason she hadn't called him yet today. Even the telling of her bizarre, *un*usual day needed to be done from a prepared outline.

Especially the part about Jake. Maybe she wouldn't tell Roger the dream she'd had about their neighbor. It was the craziest part of this crazy day.

But that didn't sit too well with Annie. She always told Roger everything.

Annie reached for her Bible on the small table next to her chair and opened it at the bookmark. She tried her best to read a little each day, but she'd fallen behind. She found the place where she'd stopped four days ago. Ecclesiastes 3:1. "For everything there is a season, a time for every activity under heaven."

She stopped with her finger on the page. She'd always liked that verse. To Annie's mind, it was a balm of orderliness, a regimented concept rooted in sameness. She felt settled as she read it.

She thought about the seasons of the year, how they always returned at their appointed times.

And clocks. Annie liked clocks—no surprises there—no deviation. Nine o'clock followed eight o'clock every day of every month of every year. Sunrise in the east, sunset in the west—every day, every time.

Unless the earth stopped spinning. Thanks, Hank. She thrust that thought away.

And calendars—July *never* came before June.

She looked around her orderly living room—every chair, sofa, and table placed just so for maximum efficiency with just a touch of elegance. Not a speck of dust, nothing out of place.

Like Roger's tools. Like this Bible verse. Even the children's voices drifting down the stairs soothed her, because they were *where* they were supposed to be *when* they were supposed to be.

Every day after school—snack time, then homework time, then playtime. Then Roger arrived home and a different season began. The dinner hour—family talk time. And after dinner, sometimes a walk together down the street to the park or a nature program on TV. And at bedtime, no roughhousing, no scary stories—just calm play, one parent supervising while the other cleaned up after dinner.

Every day the same routine.

For everything there is a season, a time for every activity under heaven.

Her life formula, practiced from the time Annie was a teenager—from the very day after that wretched scene behind the gym on prom night. And she'd redoubled her efforts after the discovery of what had happened to Abby, and after the births of each of her children.

Her eyes and finger moved down the page. *A time to be born and a time to die.*

She looked at the clock again. Sixty-one minutes until Roger arrived home.

Since I will die tomorrow, what haven't I done today that still needs doing?

Annie frowned. The question had changed. It was no longer a question of *if* she'd die tomorrow. That was a given now.

Hope fluttered into her mind like one of her bright-orange butterflies. Strange. What'd happened today to drive away her fear?

. . . a time to die.

Annie zeroed in on the word *die*, but now it didn't mean much to her. She could think of it without the fear that had glided through the door, snakelike, last night. Less than twenty-four hours ago it'd put a tremble in her hands and sweat on her brow. But now, considering it here in the safety of her home, it was no longer a concept to dread but to embrace.

Achar had said it. *After all, what is tomorrow? It doesn't yet exist.*

How could she be afraid of what didn't yet exist? *But still, something's changed.*

She thought back over the events of the day. Remembering . . . picking up one scene, discarding it, picking up another. At last her thoughts drove her like a cattle prod to the swings in the park. Not the scene from last night, but from today, when she'd played with Nora.

But what did that have to do with it? She'd thought the trolls in the garage had destroyed whatever joy there'd been on those swings.

Annie leaned her head back on the chair and closed her eyes, her finger still resting on the Ecclesiastes passage. It was as if the words on the page traveled through her finger, up her arm, and through her forehead into that cavern of fear in her mind. She hesitated at the entrance, then stepped in. But instead of the darkness she'd come to know, blinding light shone around her.

In a moment of lightning clarity, she knew. She opened her eyes and willed her brain to capture the one moment in this day when she'd understood, that had meant something. The one moment that had changed everything.

It wasn't the ring she twisted on her finger, nor the man in the park, nor her fear for her children. Annie groaned as she thought of Jake Gruber, his bare feet hanging over the curb, his soul winging its flight to Jean. But it wasn't that either.

She knew now.

It *was* the moment she'd flown high in the sky, hair streaming out behind her. It *was* Nora sitting on the swings, watching in awe as her mommy swung higher and higher and became a child again. No worries, no tension, just today. Not tomorrow.

She sprang out of her chair and rushed to the laundry room door leading out to the garage. Opening it, Annie looked left, where Roger's workbench was. She pinched her eyes shut, then opened them again. Tools, just tools hung there. Not the mocking trolls her mind had conjured.

She locked the door again and retreated back to the living room.

A new thought pressed in. Tomorrow only existed in the mind, in her severely regimented mind as she planned her days, as she scurried around—cleaning, cooking, corralling children—sticking to her inviolable routine, staying behind the white picket fences surrounding her heart.

No time for play, for giggles, for butterflies, for castle building, or for long conversations with a stuffed bear.

God, what had she missed? What joy could have been hers while, instead, she'd spent her whole adult life waiting in fearful expectation of *tomorrow*, the next tragedy, the next heartbreak, the next betrayal . . . or, as Roger teased her . . . for the other shoe to drop?

What had her fear done to her children? Stripped from them the spirit of adventure, the can-do mindset that marked successful people? Had she doomed her children to a life of mediocrity because *she* feared to venture into the unknown and to live her life governed only by the limits of her own imagination?

Ellen had said as much to her once. She recalled her harsh sentence like it was yesterday, but it'd been spoken ten years ago, when Mayra was but five years old. Annie now cringed, remembering what they'd said to each other, especially herself.

Mayra insisted she was old enough to ride the bike Roger had bought for her at a yard sale. Roger wanted to let her try, but Annie steadfastly refused, saying Mayra had to wait another year.

She told Ellen about it the next day, whining that Roger had disagreed with her, that he didn't seem to care about keeping Mayra safe. She still remembered the look of disbelief on Ellen's face, shadowed by disappointment.

She should've known Ellen would take Roger's part. And Ellen never minced words, didn't care about trying to be nice or delivering the truth couched in gentleness. It wasn't that she didn't care about people's feelings. She did, but she'd often said that pandering to feelings distorts the truth.

"Annie," Ellen had said, "let her try. Don't turn her into you—you'll ruin her. What's the worst that could happen? You'll be right with her, won't you? If you don't let her try, you're going to make her in your own image, too afraid to try something new, a little scary, a little dangerous. Just like you've been all these years, after that night—"

Annie had cut her off and told her to mind her own business, to take care of her own kids and let Annie take care of hers.

Now, Annie wished she could retrieve those words. Ellen had been right, so right.

She looked at the clock again. Now fifty-one minutes until Roger would be home. She grabbed her phone to call him, to tell him. Voicemail again.

Annie leaped from her chair, pushing her damp hair off her forehead. She surveyed the living room. Pristine as usual. One wild thought—what her mother would've called a hairbrained idea—thrust itself into the forefront of her mind and wouldn't let go.

Maybe she was delusional, maybe her family would consider commitment to an institution . . . or maybe, just maybe it would mean the final eviction of those bony-fingered demons of fear taking up residence in her soul like a bunch of squatters.

Squatters who'd been calling the shots for her since Abby. Since prom night. Since Mom and Dad . . .

Annie had to try.

Tomorrow will be no match for me, she screamed at herself.

45

She strode to the bottom of the stairs. "Kids! Come down here."

"Why?" Mayra's voice surged through the floorboards over Annie's head.

"Now—and bring your quilts and blankets and pillows."

"But my homework's not done."

"That's okay."

Hank appeared at the top of the stairs. "Our blankets?"

"Yes. Please do as I say. Drag them off your beds and bring them down."

Hank stared with slit eyes. "Mom, what—"

"Please, Hank, just do as I say. You'll understand."

He threw up his hands and backed away, retreating down the hall.

Annie heard a whispered conversation with Mayra—her room was closest to the top of the stairs.

"It's 'okay' that my homework's not done? What's up with that?"

"I don't know, Mayra. She's actin' weird. She's been weird since last night, and it's just getting worse. We should tell Dad."

"You first, bro."

They moved off, voices fading, and Annie got to work.

She moved her chair closer to the sofa and tugged the coffee table to the other side, to form an open square. Then she ran to the dining room and brought the chairs into the living room one by one. She lined them up opposite the sofa.

Giggles and indistinct questions wound their way down to the living room. As she grabbed the sofa cushions and arranged them on the floor inside the square, she heard four pairs of feet tromping overhead.

Annie stood back and turned a critical eye on her handiwork. *Still not right.*

She stepped to her chair, which she'd lined up at a perfect ninety-degree angle at the corner of the couch. Shoving the leg of the chair with her foot, Annie knocked it out of alignment from the couch.

She'd never thought crooked could be so satisfying.

Then she tossed a blanket into the middle of the pillows she'd carefully arranged. With a final stroke of genius, she unarranged the pillows on the floor into a colorful jumbled pile. She stood back again and took note.

Complete, beautiful disarray. Perfect.

Annie tipped her face to the ceiling, hands cupped around her mouth, and bellowed, "Hey, what's taking you guys so long?" She smirked, imagining the shocked looks on the kids' faces. Her children knew she never *bellowed*—that would be rude and unladylike. *There's a first time for everything*, she thought, standing inside the crude, lopsided square formed by the living and dining room furniture. All it needed was the kids' blankets and pillows—and the kids themselves—to complete it.

Annie rubbed her hands together in anticipation of what came next. It'd been so, so long.

A wad of bedding landed at the foot of the stairs. Hank heaved another load, then Mayra another. Soon all four came down, Nora and Kimmie dragging their blankets behind them.

The children stared at Annie—her hair no doubt sticking up in unusual places, mimicking the jumble of rearranged furniture.

"Mom?" Mayra's eyes widened in confusion.

Annie squatted and stacked a red pillow on top of a blue one, then straightened and faced them. "It's okay. I just had this idea."

Mayra's too-grown-up voice sounded indignant. "What, to trash the living room?"

Hank surveyed the room, a scowl darkening his face. "Yeah, Mom. What happened to 'there's a place for everything and everything needs to be in its place'?"

Nora put her thumb in her mouth and sat on the bottom step, clutching her blanket.

Kimmie saw, leaned toward her, and wrapped her arms around her baby sister.

Annie rubbed her forehead. "Don't worry, you guys. I know it looks weird, but it's gonna be fun. You'll see."

"The question is, *what's* gonna be fun—" Hank's gaze jerked to the window. "Dad's home. Why's he so early?" He locked eyes with Annie again. "Mom, what's going on? This—all of this—it's not normal. Do you have a fever or something?"

She stepped to Hank and cupped his face in her hands. "No, I don't. You can feel my forehead if you want. And no, it's not usual—and isn't that great?"

"Yeah, right . . ." Hank shook his head and backed away from her, his expression changing from clear concern for her physical health to definite unease over her mental health.

"I'm telling Dad. Maybe he can talk some sense into you."

"Hello? Tell Dad what? And where is everyone?" Roger's firm step sounded in the kitchen. "I took off early today—" He appeared in the archway and stopped abruptly, staring. "Who in tarnation did this?"

Mayra plopped onto the sofa with a scowl. "Don't look at us."

Hank's gesture encompassed the entire room. "Dad—Mom's off her nut—*she's* the one who made this mess in here."

Roger looked at her across the room, forehead wrinkled. "Annie? What's going on?"

Annie flew into his arms, almost knocking him over. "I'm so glad you're home early—"

"Why? To help you straighten up the house?" He grinned as he picked up a pillow.

"No . . . and put that pillow back. But . . . I do need your help. Would you please bring Grandpa's bench in from the dining room? It's too heavy for me to carry."

Roger didn't move. "Grandpa's bench?"

"Please? I'll explain, I promise. Just put it right over there in front of the bookcase."

Roger stared at her for a moment, then beckoned Hank. "Come on. You can help me."

"What? Dad, are you gonna just—"

"*We're* gonna just."

Hank followed his father to the dining room, muttering under his breath. "Where's Mom? I want the real mom back—"

Annie heard a whispered conversation, Hank's voice strained and anxious, Roger clearly trying to calm him. She waited, then relaxed as she heard sounds of the bench being lifted.

They carried the heavy one hundred-year-old bench in and placed it where Annie directed. Then they turned as one and looked at her—both standing with their hands on their hips, like two peas in a pod—Hank's head just reaching his father's shoulder.

He was growing up so fast. They all were. Annie's throat tightened. She loved them so, so much.

Roger spoke first. "Well? It's your turn. Explain what's happening here."

Annie started to explain, really wanted to explain. But she realized she needed something from upstairs. Something that would help them understand.

Instead of answering, Annie backed toward the stairs. "I'll be right back."

She ran lightly up the stairs, her stockinged feet making no noise.

Mayra's voice followed her like angry hornets. "Great! What's she doing, Dad?"

As she turned the corner at the top of the stairs, Hank added his frustration. "Dad, are you gonna just stand there? Aren't you going to do something? There's obviously something wrong with her."

Annie was too far away to hear Roger's answer, but she could imagine it.

He'd calm them with some made-up explanation, then later he'd take her to task. He was so good with the kids. She should tell him more often how much she appreciated his balance. And optimism. Something she'd never had in abundance. He'd always made up for what she lacked.

Annie entered Mayra's room, looked first one way then the other, not seeing what she'd come after. She edged to the desk where Mayra's backpack sat, and unzipped it. There it was, the red notebook that had been under Mayra's pillow last night.

Annie opened it to the first page to make sure, then headed back downstairs.

Oh, I hope this works . . .

She hated to imagine what'd happen if it didn't.

46

Mayra recognized it immediately. "Mom, what are you doing? That's my essay—and it's private."

"Yes, sweetie, I know. I . . . I'd like to read it. Please? It'll help explain so much."

Mayra's lips pressed together in a straight line, her arms crossed in front of her. "I don't see how. What's my essay got to do with . . . this?" She punctuated her question with a wide sweep of her hand. "And anyway, you probably shouldn't, Mom. It's gonna upset you."

Annie thought for sure Mayra would veto her request, and if so, she'd have to abide by her wishes. She held her breath and prayed silently for a yes.

"But I guess so, if it's so all-fired important to you."

Mayra threw a fierce look around the room, jabbing a finger at each of them in turn. "But it's nobody else's business, you guys. You will not mention it outside this room, hear? If you do . . ."

Annie breathed again. "Yes, Mayra, we won't say a word. Now, will you—all of you—please sit down? I have a story to tell you."

Hank threw up his hands, pointing at the small clock over the bookcase. "What about dinner? It's past dinner time. And we still have homework. And—"

Mayra frowned at her brother. "Yeah, since when are you so worried about homework on a Friday night . . . or any night, for that matter?"

Hank threw her a glare. "You either, know-it-all."

Annie intervened. "Dinner can wait. KFC, remember? It'll be quick. And tomorrow's Saturday. You can do your homework then."

If a boulder crashed through the front window, it would have had less shock value than her words. Annie knew her family had never, ever heard her say such reckless words before, that a standing rule—like the correct time to eat dinner or do homework—could be broken.

Roger and the kids froze in various stages of finding places to sit in the living room jumble she'd created. Except Nora, who hadn't moved from where she sat on the bottom stair, thumb still in her mouth and Mr. Bear clutched to her chest.

Every eye, owl-like and uncomprehending, focused on her.

Annie's tongue stuck to the roof of her mouth. How could she make them understand?

Roger shifted his stance, holding out an invisible microphone in front of her. "I just have one question, ma'am. Who are you and what have you done with my wife?" He spread his arms wide. "You know, the wife who would've had a stroke walking into *this*—"

Annie blew out a breath and giggled. "I'm still me. Just not the same me who kissed you goodbye this morning." She frowned. "A better me, I think." She motioned for him to sit.

Roger sat, then gestured to Nora, who ran to him and snuggled down in his lap.

"Come on, kids. I think we should give your mother the floor."

Hank clearly couldn't resist a grumble. "Yeah, she can have the floor as long as she's the one who has to clean it up." He plopped onto a pillow.

When her family had settled themselves, Annie paced in front of them, head down.

Where to start. The rings? The essay question? No . . . none of those. Something closer to home.

Ellen? No.

She stopped pacing. Her eyes gravitated to a grouping of pictures on the wall by the stairs.

Her family, all six of them, smiles plastered under professionally coiffed hair, stared out of heavy silver frames edged with delicate filigree in each corner.

They'd paid a photographer to take the pictures last year, in the park where she and Roger had spent so much time before and after kids—and where she and Nora had played today. The weather had cooperated, and the children, for once, had been on their best behavior. After the photo shoot, Roger had treated them to cones at a nearby ice cream parlor that had graced the town for more than half a century.

She had scoured nearby antique stores for a week, until she'd found the perfect frames. Then she'd dickered with the owner for a discounted price for all seven. It'd taken Annie another week to hang them. She'd first drawn a diagram. A large group picture in the center, with the smaller single pictures surrounding.

Each picture just so, perfectly spaced, perfectly matched. Like Annie wanted life to be.

A beautiful day. It stood out in Annie's memory as a day crafted by herself, a day that would bar its door to any hint of unpleasantness or sadness. No evil had been allowed to rear its ugly head *that* day—or it would have to deal with her. The pictures told the story of the Lee family, on a special day, in their best clothes, wearing their best smiles.

Annie's critical eye now zeroed in on Hank's picture hanging slightly crooked. A tiny urge licked at her heels. She recognized it. It followed her everywhere—must right the wrong, straighten the twisted, and never, ever deviate from the *as usual* path.

She stepped to the wall and reached.

Before her fingertips brushed the frame, she heard Ellen's voice in her head—from a conversation they'd had decades ago—urging her not to do it.

It was the day they'd almost missed their senior-picture appointments. They'd planned to go together to the studio—located in Seattle—with their moms, then out to lunch at a swanky place on Puget Sound.

Annie had been unable to decide what to wear. Three different outfits mocked her from her bedspread. Then, after she finally decided, she couldn't get her hair to behave.

Ellen was beside herself, their mothers were frantic to get going on the two-hour drive over the mountains, and Annie was having a meltdown. All because *perfect* wasn't happening for her.

Ellen took her by the shoulders and gave her a shake. "Annie, you can't have perfect. It doesn't exist. Just close your eyes, point to an outfit, and stick with it. And don't worry about your hair. That won't be perfect either, but who cares? Anyways, perfect's overrated—"

"'Anyways' isn't a word."

Ellen had groaned. "As usual, you completely miss the point."

Now, as Annie's fingertips brushed Hank's frame, Ellen's voice screaming in her head to *just let it go*, she dropped her hand to her side. Ellen's voice clicked off—in the middle of her rant—like Annie had pulled a switch.

Tilting her head sideways, Annie saw Roger and the kids watching her, clearly knowing what she was about to do. What she *would've* done . . . yesterday.

She smiled to herself and swung back to the wall. Her hand flew from her side. She knocked another frame slightly askew, then faced her family, beaming her smile all around the room.

Roger's eyebrows were perched at his hairline.

Mayra and Hank stared at her, then at each other.

Kimmie leaned into Mayra, who took her hand in hers.

Annie caught sight of herself in the mirror across the room. A stranger looked back.

Her face stretched with dread, but not for the usual reason. She was afraid, but not afraid the way she'd always been. She was afraid they wouldn't understand, wouldn't believe her, would think she'd gone crazy. Her face was ugly with fear. Was this how they always saw her? No wonder her children's faces were drenched in anxiety.

She relaxed and smiled wide. Better.

Nora sank back into Roger's chest and tugged her blanket up to her chin. She pulled hard on her thumb, the sound of it noisy in the silence.

Annie backed up and sat on Grandpa's bench, her family spread out at her feet.

"I had a strange day. Let me tell you about it."

She started with last night—Hank's thousand-mile-an-hour winds, Mayra's essay, and the dropped fork—and kept going.

Ellen's call, the walk to the park, Joshua, the ring box.

Roger gasped when she held up her right hand. "Annie, where—you mean that man gave it to you? How did he get your mother's ring?"

"I don't know . . . I just don't know. And—I don't think I care. Let me finish."

Roger settled back against the couch and snuggled Nora closer. "Okay."

The TV news anchor, the broken butter dish.

Ellen, the visit with Pastor Mike, the trip back in time through the picture frame.

The park with Nora, Achar.

All of it.

Then the hardest part of all. Annie reached deep into her fear and hauled it up.

The shame of losing Nora, running frantically through the park, acting like a crazy woman without a plan.

Nora pulled her thumb out of her mouth and hid her face in Roger's lap. Roger stroked her head, his eyes never leaving Annie's.

The telling reached the end of her day, up until this very moment. She left nothing out. When she stopped, her lips clamped shut and a tear slipped down her cheek.

Annie dropped her gaze, unable to hold her head up, afraid of what they thought of her. Afraid she'd killed any trust her family had in her, that they'd never see *as usual* again.

Silence descended like a thick blanket and muted even the whoosh of their shallow breaths.

Annie knew her ship had sailed far away from normal and now chopped through rough, unknown waters. She took with her the man she had loved fiercely and forever since she was eighteen, and the children for whom she'd gladly give the last breath out of her lungs.

No turning back now. Would they come with her?

They'll either get it or have me committed.

47

"I don't—" Annie's words sounded garbled to her ears, like she spoke through a mouthful of cotton.

The crushing silence was breached with those two words, though, and released a tidal wave of emotion and questions.

Roger stood, spilling Nora out of his lap. "Ellen—" Roger's voice was like molasses, heavy and dark. "Honey—" He leaned down and bear-hugged her. "I don't know what to say. Why didn't you call me?"

"I don't know. I started to several times, but so much was happening—it was like I was caught in this giant grinder and couldn't get out."

"And Mr. Gruber? What happened to—"

"Jake. Today, he asked me to call him Jake." The old man's name caught in her throat. "And yes, they both—Ellen and Jake—passed away today. And did you hear about John Baxter—"

"Yeah, heard it from Eleanor's niece—Marie—you know she works in the office right down the hall from me. That's why I came home early today—to see if Eleanor needs anything." He shook his head and tugged on his ear lobe. "So much death—"

Nora burst into tears. "Mr. Goober's squished?"

Kimmie enclosed her in her arms again. "It's okay, Nora Bora." Kimmie had called her that from the moment of Nora's birth—when Kimmie was three.

Watching her two youngest girls, grief washed over Annie—grief that she'd never known Abby, nor felt her big-sister arms around her.

Nora shook her head. "No . . . no." She wriggled out of Kimmie's arms. "Not okay—"

"He was old, Nora Bora. It was his time. Right, Mommy?" Kimmie said.

Old words from such young lips. *For everything there is a season . . .*

Annie picked her way between the pillows on the floor and raised Nora up to snuggle her, glancing at Kimmie. "Yes, it was his time, Kimmie."

She drew back and looked into Nora's unblinking eyes. "He wasn't squished, honey. God took Mr. Gruber home to live with him. In the house where God lives with his angels."

Nora laid her head on Annie's shoulder. "Where his baby is? And his baby's mommy?"

Annie's heart seized. She didn't know Nora had understood that part of Jake's story. She locked eyes with Nora. "Yes, they're all together now, Nora Bora." She looked at Roger. "And . . ." She choked on the words. "Ellen's there too."

Roger stepped closer to her, tenderly brushed Nora's hair away from her face, then frowned. "Jake and Jean had a baby? I knew he'd been married, but he never said anything to me about a baby." He shook his head. "Twenty years, and I guess we didn't know him at all. What a shame, huh?"

Hank groaned and covered his face.

Mayra laid a hand on his shoulder. "Are you okay, brother?"

He turned stark eyes on her. "No. I'm not okay." He shifted to Annie. "That's what I was trying to tell you in the car, Mom. What's Shane gonna do without his mom?"

Hank's face shone white against the blackness of his hair, sweat clinging to the corners of his mouth, his unspoken question filling Annie's heart and stretching it to the breaking point.

What could she say? If she tried to answer, she'd have to confront Hank's real fear—facing life without his own mom. She could barely handle her own fears.

Keeping herself together for her children's sake, as she'd always done, now seemed impossible in the face of their confusion and heartbreak. Her white picket fences lay mangled around her, and she was helpless to stop the bad from busting in.

Roger leaned over and grasped Hank's knee. "He's gonna need you, son."

The clock in the dining room chimed six thirty, but no one mentioned dinner again. By this time, they should be eating, comparing notes, encouraging each other. It was what they'd done every weeknight since forever.

But Roger had said—just yesterday—*forever's not as long as it used to be.*

Annie put Nora back into Roger's arms and sat down in front of her family, Mayra's notebook in her hand.

"I want to read this to you. Mayra, thank you for letting me." Annie opened the notebook. "But first I have a question. When did you talk to Ellen? It couldn't have been today—"

"It was last week."

"But I thought you just got this assignment yesterday."

Mayra shook her head. "No, I never said that. We got it a couple of weeks ago. I just didn't tell you about it until last night.

I wanted to think about it." She twisted to look sideways at her father. "See, I did think about the question. And I wrote it last night during homework time. It's weird. Like Ellen knew—"

Annie touched her arm. "So you talked to Ellen before you talked to me?"

Mayra averted her eyes, looking at her hands.

"It's okay that you did. I just wondered why."

"Because . . . okay . . . Don't take this wrong, Mom. Ellen's cool, less . . . rigid about things. I wanted an honest answer, not a canned *Christianese* one. That's her word, not mine."

"I see. And you thought I'd give you—as you say—a 'canned' one?"

"Yeah. Sorry, Mom."

Annie looked down for a moment, the heartburn of regret seeping into her chest. "You're probably right." Her voice was soft. "I don't like to face the stuff that doesn't fit into my . . . my template for doing life. I learned that today. Probably not a hundred percent, but maybe—" She stopped.

If she died tomorrow . . . No, this was not the time.

"—but maybe I'm starting to grasp that there is no template for life. There's just life."

Roger cleared his throat. "Okay, Annie. So I'm getting that this strange day has made you think. The people you ran into today, the craziness about the rings, the man in the park last night. Jake and Ellen and John Baxter. And thinking you'd lost Nora . . . and Mayra. Frightening." He spread his hands. "And it's made you think about your own mortality? About the . . . the fragility of life? I'm guessing so. But . . . there's more, isn't there?"

Annie wrenched her gaze away from his intense brown eyes. "Yes. I hate to admit it, but I've built barriers . . . around all of us— or tried to. But it wasn't just to keep my family in and bad stuff out. It was to protect myself." She glanced at Mayra. "I thought if

I found this *Christianese* formula and stuck to it, never deviating from it, I'd be—we'd be—safe. Do you get it?"

She looked from one face to the next, hoping for understanding. She settled on Roger's familiar expression—the one she'd slept with and awakened to for two decades.

"I get it, Annie. From what you've told me about it, you started pounding the first fence post right after what happened on junior prom night. Am I right?"

Cool relief blew across her face. Of course Roger got it. He'd always understood her, from the first moment they'd met, although it'd taken Ellen to convince her of it.

"Yes, I think so." Annie looked down at Mayra's notebook, running her finger over the cover. "I guess I have always lived life waiting for the other shoe to drop."

Roger reached over and squeezed Annie's knee.

She covered his hand with her own. His tender expression and intense gaze reflected the many years he'd spent loving and protecting her. Annie knew that sometimes he'd even needed to protect her from herself.

He leaned closer to her. "I know it. I've tried to take that shoe away from you. When something bad happens, you run for cover and don't want to come out. Maybe now you're learning that life on earth is never completely safe. And that death doesn't end life."

Annie's grip on his hand tightened. "That's exactly what Pastor Mike said."

Mayra looked from one parent to the other. "Wait, what? Prom night? Was that what Ellen—"

"Mayra—" Annie bit off what she was about to say.

Roger waded in calmly and threw Annie a life preserver. "We can talk about that later."

Mayra frowned but didn't push it.

Annie opened the notebook to the first page and let her gaze rest gently on Mayra's middle name. She and Roger had deliberately chosen it to keep Abby's memory alive. But they'd never told Mayra why she was given that name. Perhaps it was time.

"Mom, are you sure?" Mayra's expression wore concern, not challenge. "There's stuff in there you might not want to read."

"You mean about Ellen?"

"How'd you know?"

"I hate to admit it, but I've skimmed the first two pages already. Last night while you were asleep. I'm sorry."

Mayra shrugged. "Guess it's okay then."

A fresh cascade of memories assaulted Annie as she looked down at the notebook again.

Finding out about Abby, a beautiful blue prom dress, graduation, marriage, their parents' deaths.

The births of each of her children—with each birth, Annie had to convince herself that nothing bad would happen to them. Spending her days so wrapped up in keeping them safe, she hadn't taught them how to live. Regret burned her chest again.

"I'd like to read this now, if no one minds."

Roger nodded. "Go for it."

Swallowing the lump in her throat, Annie knew this moment had the power to put her on her knees—or spread her wings. She didn't know which it would be.

48

NO TOMORROWS
by Mayra Abigail Lee

When I told my parents last night about this essay and the question I chose—*What would I do today if I knew I'd die tomorrow?*—they acted like it was too hard of a question for a fifteen-year-old. Like it was too deep . . . what's the word they used? *Grim*—too depressing for me to think about. But then Dad said it was an important question and I shouldn't be flippant in my answer. I wanted to say to them what was in my mind, but I was afraid to say it.

Fifteen-year-olds die every day. Why not me?

Anyway, I decided to do some research—I asked some of my friends. Yeah, I can hear my parents now. *You call asking your friends research?* But that's what I did.

Most were idiots about it. Figures—they wouldn't know a deep question if they fell into it and drowned.

Live it up for a day and get away with it. At fifteen, what could I possibly get away with?

Say goodbye to people. Exactly how do you do that, anyway?

Go see a dirty movie, 'cause you weren't allowed to before you were gonna die tomorrow. Really, Jason? You're so dumb.

Make sure the people you love know you love them.

That one came closest, I thought. But even that answer doesn't explain *how* to make sure they know you love them. What do I do? Kiss them, hug them, buy them something? The longer I thought about it, the more difficult the question became. I guess because most people either don't know they're going to die tomorrow, or they have some disease and can prepare. And I don't know which would be worse—just to drop dead or prepare to fade away by inches.

Then I decided to talk to my mom's best friend, Ellen.

You might be wondering why I didn't ask my mom. It's because I already knew what she'd say. She's been my mom for fifteen years now, so I've kind of got a handle on how she thinks. Her answer would be right out of the Bible or some Christian self-help book. I wanted a real answer—a scared-human one, not a parent lecture or one with fancy words. No thees or thous, thank you very much. Just the plain, unvarnished truth. Ellen would tell me the truth, what she really thinks, without the fluff. And she doesn't worry about rules like Mom does.

I wanted an answer I could hang my hat on.

So I called Ellen and asked her. There was this weird silence, like she wasn't surprised by the question, but still, she didn't answer right away. Here's how the conversation went, after she had a chance to think:

"Mayra, the only way I can answer that question is to pretend it's real."

"Okay, pretend it's real. You have twenty-four hours to live. So tell me."

"It's okay with you if I pretend? If I just make it all up, like some twisted novel?"

"Whatever works for you."

"When's it due? Can I give you my answer next week? I'll write it out for you. Can I do it any way I want?"

"Okay, sure, it's all good. I just need some ideas to run with. And thanks, Ellen."

That conversation was a week ago.

Ellen met me at my school yesterday and gave me an envelope. I didn't open it until I got home. I read through her answer three times.

It's the best ever. Here it is:

Mayra, God told me I'd die tomorrow. So the first person besides my own family I want to talk to is your mom. But I didn't get the chance.

Annie slammed the notebook closed, bent forward, and pushed a breath out.

Roger leaned over and grasped her shoulder. "Annie—"

"I'm okay. Just give me a minute."

Her chest hurt all the way through to her shoulder blades. The leftover remnants of their picnic lunch rose from the depths and threatened to erupt. She hadn't thought it'd be this hard.

She squeezed her arms around her belly and willed the sensation away. Moisture dripped from the tip of her nose to the notebook paper in her lap. She ran a finger over it and looked up.

"I'm fine. When I skimmed it before, I'd stopped reading where you said 'that conversation was a week ago,' so I didn't see that last line." She looked at Mayra. "You warned me, I guess. It . . . it . . . kind of hit me, here." She pointed at her chest, then smiled weakly. "Sorry I dripped sweat on your notebook."

"It's okay, Mom. I have to put it in a Word doc anyway before I turn it in." Mayra's eyes softened, something that didn't happen often. "You don't have to do this, you know."

"Yes . . . I do."

Annie clenched her lips together and opened the notebook, finding her place again.

Yes, I'm dead. I died early this morning around three o'clock.

Annie stopped again, staring at the time, working it out in her head. Three in the morning, last night. The same time that . . . in her dream . . . Ellen was in her dream?

She shook her head in wonder, then continued reading.

My name is Ellen Jarvis, and I didn't know I was going to die until about an hour before it happened. I wish I'd had more notice, but at least I got an hour.

Annie's my best friend—we've been friends since middle school. I remember the first time I saw her. We were lined up in the hall on the first day of fifth grade. The teacher walked down the line, assigning us "partners" to sit by when we got into the room. I prayed I wouldn't have to sit by a boy. I knew I'd be mortified, but as I watched, she was pairing girls with girls. Whew!

I looked to the right and saw her stop in front of someone I hadn't met yet. The school was small, but we'd just moved into town the day before, actually across the street from the Lees'.

So, anyways—yes, Annie, it's really a word—I heard the teacher call her Annie. She stuck out like a sore thumb, because she was wearing my clothes, the same ones I wore that day. Same jeans with the pink fringe on the bottom, same pink blouse, even the same color of socks and sneakers.

I didn't know if I should be mad or amused, but then the teacher saw us staring at each other, and boy, did she laugh. She said, "You two have just got to be partners, right?" So we ended up laughing over it, too, and sharing a double desk and our hearts for the whole year. And so much more—a friendship like no other, inseparable for the next three decades.

We could look across a room at each other and know. Our husbands say we don't email each other, we "fe-mail" each other.

Soul sisters. We always knew what the other was thinking—about everything from homework assignments to boys to the latest stupid fashion trends. We finished each other's sentences. Sometimes we didn't have to speak, just said what was needed with eyebrows and hand gestures. Yeah, some of those hand gestures, too. I see your smile, Annie. Don't try to hide it. I know what our parents would've done if we'd been caught flashing those gestures . . . The only thing as alike as us was our parents, right? Straight-arrow military all the way.

People sometimes called us names, like the "Bobbsey twins." We didn't know what that was about until we looked it up. But we were always together, always loyal to each other, and we always stood up for each other. That's a friend in my book, and we didn't care if they tacked a "Bobbsey" on it or not. We were closer than the closest of twins.

And the scrapes we got into, and out of . . . our parents never knew the half of it.

It lasted from the first day of fifth grade until three this morning. Or I should say two fifty-nine, since I died at three.

I woke up about two and knew right away something was way wrong. I'd had a nagging headache for a couple of days but didn't think much about it. I've got three boys—headaches are a dime a dozen around here. It came and went, but then it came and stayed. I felt a little sick to my stomach a couple of times, but I ignored it. I'm too busy to give in to a headache.

I'm the leader of the moms' group at church. We're meeting today—well, I guess they canceled the meeting because I died. I was supposed to give the devotional today. I'd picked the topic of how to help your little ones memorize the Scriptures in creative ways. Like, have your child draw a picture of the verse as she memorizes it. Talk about it. Make word pictures. Set the verse to a simple tune. Make snacks that remind you of the verse. I didn't come up with all that. I got it out of a book called Toddling with Parents—*great title, right?*

Anyway, I died, so the moms won't get to hear that. Or wait—maybe you could do it next week, Annie. Yeah, don't give me that. You're saying, "Oh, I couldn't possibly . . ." You can—you'll be great. Get Nora to help you with it . . . what an imagination she has. Don't know who she got it from—I'm pretty sure it wasn't you. Ha!

So at about two this morning, I woke up and couldn't move. I tried to roll over and get up and go to the bathroom, but I couldn't.

My body wouldn't behave itself. "Stuck like Chuck," as Shane would say. Oh, I can't think of him right now . . . good thing he has Mark, and Hank.

I just laid there, my eyes following the ceiling fan around and around as I listened to Mark snore. I couldn't even turn my head to look at him. I couldn't open my mouth to call to him. I wanted in the worst way to say goodbye to him, to hold him and have him hold me, to tell him to take good care of the boys or I'd haunt him the rest of his life.

Then I felt an odd tingle in my forehead, just above my right eye, and it gradually moved to my cheeks, then to my chin. That's when my brain kicked into gear, and I started praying. By the time my fingers were tingling, I'd covered my whole family—I asked God to please take care of them. I knew I would see Jesus in just a few moments. I don't know how I knew. I just did.

I saved Annie for last. Not because she isn't important, but because she is, and I wanted time to figure out what to ask. I'd ended with my three nieces, then I thought about Annie. I could see the clock glowing across the room. It said two thirty-five. I knew I didn't have much time.

Annie won't know what to do without me—I know that as sure as I know anything. She's a strong woman, but she doesn't know it yet. She always did say I was the brains of the outfit. That always made me laugh.

Like the time in seventh grade I talked her into skipping our last class—one of only two times I know of that Annie skipped a class. History, what a bore. We went to the arcade. I was the one who made up the cool story about the little old lady who was lost and Annie and I helped her get home. She would've never come up with that story—just me, the brains of the outfit.

I wish we'd had more time. I wanted to tell her how much I'd always admired her. I don't think she'd ever thought of herself as someone to be admired.

But I did admire her for a lot of things, things that now I'll never get to say to her.

She never got a chance to say goodbye to her mom and dad, to tell them it wasn't their fault about Abby. That she finally understood why they never told her. She was glad about one thing though—that they never found out what'd happened to her when she was sixteen. That was our secret, and I'm glad now it's going to my grave with me.

I was so proud of Annie and Roger when Mayra was born. And so heartsick that Mayra's grandparents would never hold her. It was hard, but Annie and I stuck together like we'd always done.

(PS to Mayra—you need to stick by Cassie right now—free advice. Make me proud, girlfriend.)

If Annie had been sitting on the side of the bed this morning when I was getting ready to die, what would I have told her? Could I make her understand that it's okay, that I'm ready for the exit music, the next act, that everything I needed to do was done?

That's the rub. If you're not dying, you're not ready to die. If it's *not your day, then you still have stuff to do.*

I'd tell her, Annie, be sure you finish everything you have to do today—only today.

Kiss your husband, hug your kids, and eat some of that fancy dark chocolate you love.

Leave the dust on the furniture and the cobwebs on the blinds, and go out into the sunshine and take a walk.

Take Nora with you and watch her admire a nasty slug, or pretend to be a butterfly, or blow you kisses. Swing with her at the park.

Take a picnic lunch with you and watch Nora feed Mr. Bear part of her PB&J sandwich.

Stop at your neighbor's house—you know, that cranky old man who always tells Roger to mow his lawn and kill the dandelions. Stop at his house, wave at him, call good morning.

Leave a message on Roger's cell phone—tell him you love him and to hurry home.

When the kids get home from school, do something silly with them, like build a massive fort out of blankets in the living room. Remember that? How long has it been since you built a fort with your kids?

Live, Annie, live.

Unpack all those boxes where you've hidden yourself from the bad stuff. Without the bad stuff, we'd never recognize the good stuff. Break the rules once in a while, take a risk. And for goodness' sake, hack up all those fences you've built—you won't need them anymore. God never promised to keep us safe from this bad old world, just that he'd be there with us, and that he'll take us away from it when it's our time.

My time is now, Annie.

Death doesn't end life—I heard that somewhere, and it's true. My paraphrase? Life starts when it ends.

Live for me. You'll have to be the brains of the outfit now, but I promise, I'll always be there for you to talk to. Just look up. You'll see me looking down.

That's what I'd say. Live today, because today is always worth two tomorrows.

So long. My tomorrow belongs to you now, Annie. I'm tellin' ya, don't squander it or mess it up, because I will *come back and haunt you.*

(PSS—Mayra, I can't wait until I see your mom and ask her how she liked my answer. She'll probably laugh and tell me I'm crazy. I don't care. We're that kinda friends.)

It's me again—Mayra.

That's my essay. I hope it's okay that Ellen wrote most of it. She wrote it last week and gave it to me yesterday. I added my part and put it all together last night. Then when I got home today, I had to add this next part. Because . . .

You might not believe it, but I swear it's true. I heard in school today that Ellen really *did* die—at three this morning, exactly the way she described in this essay. Strange, huh? Can't explain it, so don't even ask.

And here's something else. If I don't get a good grade on this essay because I didn't write the whole thing, I don't care. Sue me.

They're good words, words that I, Mayra Abigail Lee, intend to live by.

49

Annie closed the notebook and handed it to Mayra, touching her fingers as she did.

It felt like slow motion. Not a sound in the room. Not a sound outside. Time stopped while Annie stared at Roger and he stared back. And the kids—sitting on the floor on sofa cushions in their trashed living room—stared wide eyed at both of them.

Annie shifted on the bench and lifted her gaze over their heads, looking out the window. Twilight, that in-between time of the day, with streetlights and yard lights beginning to glow, neighbors coming home from work, vehicle headlights turning into driveways.

Just another evening in their quiet corner of the world.

But Annie's universe had shifted, and she felt the air surge with a strange electricity. *Same* was over—the sameness that'd been the center of her existence for as long as she could remember.

She slid her gaze around to the back of Roger's head as he stared at the skewed pictures on the wall. What was he thinking?

He looked back at her, the corner of his mouth lifting in a crooked smile.

"So you still want to know what I'd do if I knew I'd die tomorrow?"

Annie put a hand out. "I do, but let's start with the kids. I think we should talk about this."

"Really?"

"Yes, really. I know I was afraid before, but a lot's changed since last night."

Roger dipped his head. "Evidently." He looked at Hank, who sat on a giant green pillow, his back against the sofa. "What would you do, son?"

Annie hoped he wouldn't try to be funny. Such a comedian. But his wacky humor would ruin the *un-sameness* of this night. He didn't disappoint her.

Hank looked at the floor, then up at his dad, white circles around his tear-filled eyes. "I think I'd go see Shane. He needs me."

Roger gave him a thumbs-up. "Perfect, son. That'd be tough for sure, but I believe you're up for it."

He looked sideways at Kimmie. "Do you understand the question?"

"Yes, Daddy." She leaned over and squeezed Nora. "I'd play with Nora Bora. I think she needs her big sissie."

Annie couldn't see through the mist in her eyes. "Ah, honey, that's so sweet."

"Nora, if you knew you'd move to God's house tomorrow, what would you do right now?" Annie waited, hoping for no outbursts about squished people.

Nora put her thumb in her mouth, sucking noisily and staring at Annie. Then she pulled it out with a *pop!* "I'm playing with Kimmie—right, Kimmie? You promised—"

"Good one, Nora." Hank clapped her on the back.

Nora's face glowed.

Roger winked at Annie. "Can't get much better than this, right?"

He turned to Mayra. "You're up, sweetie—"

"Yeah, I know. Besides . . . you know . . . saying goodbye to you guys—"

Hank snorted.

"—yeah, you too, li'l bro." She continued with a stammer. "I'd talk to Cassie—again. I tried today, but . . . she wasn't having it."

Roger frowned. "What's up with Cassie?"

Mayra's face burned red. She looked out the window, clearly reluctant to answer. "She's pregnant. And hasn't told her parents. She's thinking about an abortion."

She turned and faced Annie. "Did you know? Cassie told me you saw her today looking at some crisis pregnancy brochures at the church."

"No, I didn't *know*—but I wondered." Annie dropped her voice to a tense whisper, hoping against hope. "What did you tell her?" Waiting for Mayra to answer was the longest few seconds ever. Most kids Mayra's age thought nothing of abortion, that it was the only viable solution.

Mayra thrust her chin up. "That she should tell her parents. Let them help her."

Roger beamed at her. "Well done, honey."

"And I told her she should definitely *not* have an abortion. What you said that one time when we talked about it—that there are always other options. And I told her I'd stand by her. She's my friend, and as long as she needs me, I won't let anyone hurt her. And I'll try to help her make the best decision."

Annie let out a breath. "I'm so proud of you, Mayra. Your answer was exactly right. And I think she'll come around—after all, she has you for a friend." She stroked Mayra's blushing cheek. "D'ya think she'll tell her folks?"

"I think so. I told her I'd help her if she wanted me to." She hesitated. "And by the way, I'm not putting that bit about Cassie—

the part that Ellen wrote about to me—in the finished essay for class. I don't think Ellen wanted me to . . . I'm sure that was just an aside for me."

Roger nodded. "I always said you're a smart cookie . . . just like your mom." He shifted his gaze back to Annie. "What were you doing at the church today, honey?"

"I went to talk to Pastor Mike about all this. I hadn't been to the park yet or talked to Jake. I have to say, his answers weren't—"

"Conventional? Are you surprised? His answers never are." He frowned at her. "What *did* he say?"

The clock ticked loudly while Annie decided if she should say what was in her heart. She didn't want to scare them the way she'd been scared today.

"After we talked about Ellen, I asked him if he thought God was trying to tell me I'd . . ." She stopped and watched Nora's face. ". . . go live with him tomorrow."

"And what did Pastor Mike say?"

"He told me he didn't know, that I should ask God."

"Have you? Asked God, I mean."

She looked at her family and decided to give them an un-canned answer. They deserved to hear her heart. "Yes, I did. He hasn't answered yet, except to tell me that this day, this time—right here, right now—is all that counts. I don't need to know ahead of time. Like Ellen said, just get done what I need to get done today. And it's not about doing tasks, fixing what's wrong, straightening the crooked parts of my life." She spread her arms wide. "It's about relationships, about all of you. Nothing else. I knew that when I was on the swings today with Nora."

Roger frowned. "What happened on the swings?"

Before Annie could answer, Nora piped up. "Mommy swang so high, Daddy . . . she almost swang up to the clouds—"

"Swung—"

"No, Hank," Annie cut in. "Swang is perfect . . . because it's a Nora word, and sounds just like her."

She looked around the room, then studied the family pictures again.

"Nora's right. I *swang* up to the clouds. And every time I went up there and looked down, I realized that it doesn't matter if tomorrow never comes for me. Tomorrow's an unwritten story. What I do—who I love on today—is what counts."

With her words, the mounting tension in the room whooshed out like wind rushing through a canyon. Annie saw in each face, even Nora's, understanding.

Roger's soft voice floated to her from across the room. "You kicked your fears to the curb, didn't you? I'm proud of you, honey."

Mayra raised her hand, like she was in class. "I have a question."

Roger waved a hand at her. "Okay. Go ahead."

"Why do people who say they're Christians get afraid when they know they're gonna die? I mean, what about that verse where God tells us that he's building houses for us in heaven and he'll take us there when we die? You'd think we'd jump for joy if we knew we'd die tomorrow, right? Instead, we waste our time trying like crazy to make it not happen."

Annie pushed an answer out past the lump in her throat. "Mayra, that's a great question. What do you think the answer is?"

"We talked about it at youth group one night. I think it's because we don't really believe what God says. We say we do, but when our time comes, we find out we don't." She looked up at Annie. "And I think Ellen said the same thing in my essay."

Roger leaned over and patted her knee. "I think you might be right. It's definitely something to think about and discuss, isn't it?"

In the silence that followed his comment, Annie heard the tick of the clock in the dining room, reminding her of a line in a movie she and Ellen had once watched together.

Time waits for no one.

After the movie, they'd had a snack at a local café and a discussion about that line. Actually, it'd been more of an argument, because as usual Annie was afraid and Ellen told her to stop being a wimp.

"Annie," she'd said, *"why are you always afraid of the truth?"*

Thinking about that line now brought Annie an odd sense of peace, and she swore she heard Ellen's giggle.

Annie jumped when Hank broke the silence. "Hey, Dad! What about you? What would you do today if you knew you'd—"

He paused and looked sideways at Nora.

"—go live with . . . you know . . . God tomorrow?"

Roger didn't hesitate. "That's easy. I'd mow the lawn."

His answer was met with a chorus of giggles and eye rolling.

Hank wagged his head back and forth. "Come on, Dad. Be serious. Mow the lawn? On your last day above ground?" He grinned. "Get it? 'Above ground'?"

More eye rolling from Mayra. "Uh, yeah, Hank, we get it—"

Roger waved her to silence. "No, really. I'd mow the lawn"—his soft brown eyes sought Annie's—"so your mother wouldn't have to worry about it for at least a week or two."

God, how I love this man . . .

Hank and Mayra chorused, "Sheesh, not the mush again—"

Roger held up a hand. "Okay, okay, mushy stuff is over. Now what? Annie, what would you do—"

"Not yet."

"But—"

Annie held up her index finger. "Wait. I'm thinking."

She gripped the bench with both hands, staring at the floor. Then got up and disappeared into the dining room.

The empty space on the wall—Abby's space—drew her. She knew exactly which picture belonged in that space.

She took a deep breath and returned to the living room. All eyes were on her.

"There's something else I have to do before I tell you what I'd do tomorrow if . . . It's been buzzing in my brain all evening, and I know I have to do this."

She backed to the stairs. "Wait. Just wait right here."

"And just where else would we be?" Hank quipped, always the funny guy.

She raced up the stairs and came back with the cardboard box.

Annie carried the box to her seat, the now-unsealed envelope riding on top of it. She sat, settling the box at her feet, and picked up the envelope with shaky hands.

Roger shifted in his seat. "Honey, what—"

He stared, clearly driven to silence.

"Now what's going on?" Mayra's shrill voice broke in.

50

"I'd like to introduce you kids to someone. Someone I should've told you about long ago." She took three sheets of lined paper out, covered front and back with graceful longhand. "First, I'm going to read part of this letter. It's from my mother to me."

Mayra's gaze was glued to the envelope. "From Grandma? She wrote you a letter? When?"

"Before you were born, according to the date. I found it just last night, when I was looking through this box. I couldn't read it right then, because . . . well, just because."

Roger's frown told her he was unsure. "Do you really want to read it here? What if—"

"I did go back and read it later—this afternoon, I mean. Yes, I want to. It's important. But there are some parts, kids, that are too personal. Understand?"

Receiving nods from all four of them, Annie looked at Roger. "Honey?"

"Go for it."

Annie looked down at the pages, looking for where to start. *At the beginning, of course.*

"'Dearest Anna Banana—'"

The kids howled.

"Mom always called me Anna Banana. I grew up with it. Corny, I know—"

Mayra grinned. "Like Nora Bora. Do all families do that?"

"Probably. All the best families, I think."

"Sorry, Mom. I interrupted you. Proceed."

Annie clutched the paper between both hands and looked down at the words swimming through the moisture leaking from her eyes. Her mother's voice, velvety smooth as it'd never been in real life, spoke to her heart as the words on the page circled through her tears. They finally settled into logical sequence.

"'Dearest Anna Banana,

"'As I write this, you have just graduated from high school. How proud we are of you—both of us. Dad has bragged about you to everyone he sees, even Mr. Hastings at the corner store.

"'I know we haven't always been as demonstrative as we should have been, but love and pride have always been in our hearts for you.

"'This might be hard for you to read, and for that, I'm sorry. Here goes.

"'One thing I've always regretted was not telling you about your sister, Abby. You shouldn't have grown up without at least knowing something about her, and that's my fault. I'm so sorry.'"

Annie felt, rather than heard, the breathing in the room stop as she read those words. She looked up.

"Bear with me, kids. I know this must be strange for you to hear."

Mayra huffed. "Strange isn't the word for it, Mom. Grandma's not the only one who should've—"

"I know, honey. But just let me keep reading, okay? I'll explain, I promise." She picked the letter up, feeling the tremble in her fingers again. This was harder than she thought it'd be.

"'You had so many questions, more and more the older you got. Your Dad and I just couldn't deal with them. We should have been able to, but we just weren't. We were broken for so long. That's why we finally took all the pictures of Abby off the walls—except for the one in our bedroom—and put them in this box. I'm sure you'll find it sooner or later, after we're gone, and then you can do what you want with them.

"'I'm going to tell you about her now—and why she left us. But first, I want you to understand something. I used to be like you, living life in fear of what would happen tomorrow. Especially after Abby, but even before that. When your father deployed to Vietnam, even though I knew he'd probably not see combat, every day was a struggle. Roger's mother went through the same thing.

"'A struggle to go to sleep, a struggle to wake up, to do the things I needed to do. I guess I thought if I took my mind off him for even one moment to think about something else, that'd be the moment he'd be gone. Even something as simple as a grocery list or an appointment—one moment of inattention—and he'd come home in a box.

"'It seems silly now. As if I had the power to so hold him in my thoughts, that somehow my thoughts would be a shield to keep him safe.

"'I lived like that until he came home to me. Such wasted time. I don't remember smiling from the time he slipped the ring on my finger when he left, until I saw him walk down the steps of the transport helicopter in one piece.

"'Annie, I didn't get the message of the ring then, the day he put it on my finger. I didn't get it until just a few days ago. Even after Abby left, I didn't get it. Her leaving made everything worse.

"'Now you'll be leaving soon, but not like Abby, thank God—

and I want you to get it. I don't want you to live your life waiting for the other shoe to drop. Waiting for the next bad thing to happen, as if you had any control at all.

"'Bad things will always happen. But, Annie, honey—don't live in fear of tomorrow. There is no tomorrow—only today. Live today. Let tomorrow take care of itself.

"'That's what the ring means. That's why your father put it on my finger. He didn't want me to miss my life while I waited for him to come home.

"'I'm so glad you and Roger finally met. I'm so glad you fell in love. And I'm happy that he's the son of your father's best friend. Somehow it seems the circle will close with your marriage in a few months. I'm so looking forward to that, and your dad and I wish you every blessing as you graduate and blend your lives together.

"'And now . . . Abby. The sweetest thing ever to happen to me. To us.

"'You look so like her. Her disposition, right up until the day she left, was like the brightest of suns and moons combined. I hope you have a little girl just like her someday.'"

Annie's gaze drifted to Nora. *I did, Mom. I did.*

"'When Abby left, God died inside my soul. It was the same for your dad. It wasn't God's choice to die—I killed him. The thought of him, the presence of him just . . . wasn't there. Abby's leaving was his fault—he let it happen the way it happened. So between the two of us, God and me—me for my carelessness, and him for I don't know what—we're responsible for it.

"'But God was reborn in my soul the day I first saw you lying there in my arms, looking so like her, but distinct in your own way. Sisters to the bone. Same eyes, different hands and feet. Same hair, but different nose and cheekbones. I loved you the moment I saw you.

"'Annie, honey, I know what you came to believe after you found out you'd had a sister that day when you were seven. Your anger gave you away at first, then your sadness. You thought the reason you existed was to replace her.

"'No, sweetie. A thousand times, no.

"'Here's the truth. No one could ever replace your sister in our hearts. Not even you.

"'But, Anna Banana, no one could ever replace you in our hearts either. We had you for you. I regret that somehow your dad and I could never make you believe that. I think you always thought of yourself as second string or something. Nothing could be further from the truth.

"'I hope you don't think that anymore. You were always you, and no one else.'"

Annie stopped reading and glanced at Roger.

His face softened. "She knew, honey. She knew. You were always, as long as I've known you, competing with a ghost. I tried to tell you, but—"

"I know." Annie looked down at the letter. "I lived my whole childhood and beyond thinking they had me because they wanted Abby back. But I did too . . . want her back, I mean." She smiled at Nora. "I would've done anything to have a big sister."

Nora laughed. "I have two big sissies, Mommy."

Roger hugged her tight. "Yes, you do. Aren't you the lucky one?"

Annie locked eyes with each of her children in turn. "I want all of you to know, right now, that your dad and I had each one of you because we wanted *you*. Never, ever forget that. Treasure each other. Don't waste a moment of today worrying about tomorrow. And," she added with a grin, "if we forget to tell you enough, you have our permission to remind us."

She looked down at the letter. She decided in that instant how she was going to handle the next bit.

There's no other way, her heart whispered.

51

She read the next three sentences out loud, then stopped.

"'Annie, this next bit is hard to write, but you deserve to know what happened to Abby. By telling you, I hope to lessen the guilt I've carried for so long, the guilt that perhaps I unwittingly transmitted to you and helped put the blinders on your eyes. Time to take 'em off and live without boundaries, honey.'"

Annie glanced at Kimmie and Nora. They'd become distracted by trying to straighten Mr. Bear's hat. She was glad. They were so young.

"The rest of the letter tells the story of my sister's disappearance when she was four years old, before I was born. I never met her."

Mayra made a sound, and Annie looked at her, surprised. Mayra hardly ever cried anymore, but here she was, mopping her eyes with her sleeve.

"Oh, honey. Please don't cry. I didn't mean to make you sad."

Mayra sniffed. "I'm so sorry, Mom. What happened to her?"

Annie threw a look at Roger, then cocked her head toward Kimmie and Nora. He clearly took the hint.

"Hey, Kimmie and Nora." He looked at his watch. "Geez, it's seven thirty. I hear we have KFC. How about you girls help me in the kitchen? We'll get the food on plates, and we can eat in here. It'll be a picnic."

The girls jumped up and ran into the kitchen ahead of Roger.

He turned at the archway and glanced back at Annie, lingering there until she blew him a kiss, then he headed into the kitchen.

Annie sat on the floor among the pillows, knee to knee with Hank and Mayra.

In a low voice, she explained what she'd learned when she'd done her own sleuthing before Mayra was born. Then she summarized what her mother had said in the letter.

Hank and Mayra were clearly shocked and angry.

"Did they ever catch the scumbag?" Hank's eyes leaked tears in the corners.

"No, not as far as I've ever heard."

Mayra leaned back on a pillow, forehead scrunched up. "Mom, how could you have kept this to yourself all these years?"

"I guess the same way that my parents did. When I got old enough, I pestered them unmercifully for answers. Got punished for it too."

"They should've told you. It's not fair," Mayra declared in her fifteen-going-on-thirty voice.

As if you know everything there is to know about life.

Annie kept her tone even. "*Life's* not fair, Mayra. Mom and Dad—well, they went through something no parent should have to. The death of a child changes a mom and dad in ways they have no control over—it's the way we're wired. They couldn't bear for me to know details. I was just too young. And by the time I was old enough, they'd died. I used to be mad at them over it, but not anymore. I understand, because . . . because I'm a mom now."

Mayra's glare said it all. Annie guessed she was angry because she'd been left out of the loop. She'd just have to get over it.

"Honey, you'll have to take my word for it."

Annie waited, knowing she had to give Mayra time to process these gruesome details.

Her face looked chiseled in stone. "Okay, Mom. Guess I'll just have to take your word for it."

"Thank you. Now, both of you. The manner of Aunt Abby's death is not for little ears, d'ya hear me? You are *not* to tell Kimmie and Nora."

Hank frowned. "So you're going to do the same—"

"—I want your solemn promise that you won't. You two are barely old enough to handle the information."

"But, Mom—"

"No buts, Mayra. Their innocent minds shouldn't be burdened with this kind of stuff. Your dad and I will tell them when they're old enough. And—hear me—this is for our family only. This information goes *nowhere* outside these walls. Do I have your word?"

She knew her voice was pleading too much. She should just lay down the law and be done with it. But she wanted them to understand the *why*, not just the *what*. She wanted them to protect their baby sisters.

"Yes, Mom." Hank's response was immediate.

"Mayra? This is important to me, honey."

Mayra crawled over to Annie and put her head in her lap. "Yes, Mom. I promise. I won't say a word to Kimmie and Nora, and I won't talk about it to anyone except you and Dad." For once, her voice didn't sound edgy and sarcastic.

Annie let out a breath and relaxed her hands.

"Hey, what about me. You can talk to me—" Hank sounded indignant.

"Oh yeah, and the *little* bro too." Smirking at him, she sat up and punched him on the arm.

"Thank you, both of you. It means a lot to me."

"Mom?" Hank stared out the window, his hands knotted in his lap. The yard lamp just outside the front door lit his face, showing the strain around his eyes.

Annie wished she could smooth away her son's obvious anxiety. "Yes?"

"All that weird stuff that happened today—the stuff you told us about. Do you think God was telling you that you're going to die tomorrow?"

Annie's throat tightened. *God, how should I answer him?* "No, I don't think so. But I have to be honest, son. I don't really know when I will die. Nobody does. But what I do know is that God wanted me to think about it. About what's really important. Does that make sense?"

Hank's anxious frown relaxed. "Yeah, it does."

"I don't want to live my life anymore by a schedule, always afraid that if I deviate from it something bad will happen. And I don't want you to live that way either. Like Ellen always said, rules were made to break, and life is about taking a chance on a dream."

Hank turned his gaze to meet Annie's eyes. "Do you think Aunt Abby's in . . . heaven? And Shane's mom?"

Her heart melted as her arms reached for him and he leaned into her. "Yes, son. I have no doubt at all. In that really big house we talked about earlier." She took Hank's and Mayra's hands in her own. "And something else."

"What?" Hank and Mayra leaned forward.

"I will see Ellen again, and we will all meet Abby someday."

Hank high-fived Annie. "Awesome!"

Mayra's glance strayed to the box. "Are we going to look at the pictures?"

"Yes, we are—"

Just then, Roger, followed by Kimmie and Nora, came in laden with plates, food, and drinks on a cart.

"—after we eat."

52

Roger and Nora passed out the plates of food while Mayra poured ice-cold glasses of milk. Kimmie and Nora sat on the floor, using the bench Annie had vacated as a table. The rest sat on the floor, balancing their plates on their laps.

Nora wiped her chin. "Mommy, this *is* like a picnic—"

Hank wiped greasy fingers on his shirt front. "Yeah, a carpet picnic. Hey, ya wanna hear my latest joke?"

Mayra groaned. "Dad, don't let him—they're always so cheesy."

Roger laughed but gave Hank a quick nod. "Sure, son, go ahead. We promise to laugh whether it's funny or not."

"Gee, thanks, Dad. Okay here goes. Support bacteria. It's the only culture some people have."

Even Mayra snickered.

Hank stood and took a bow. "Okay, what's the speed of dark?"

Roger chuckled. "Okay, okay. Enough for now. I think we're going to—"

"But wait. How fast *does* dark go?" Kimmie frowned at Hank.

Hank cracked up, collapsing to the floor. "Kimmie, that's—"

Roger put his hand over Hank's mouth. "Look at pictures now, right, Annie?"

"Yes. We are. Kimmie and Mayra, please take the dishes and leftovers to the kitchen. And how about if we move to the dining room table to open the box? Hank, will you help your dad take the chairs back?"

"I'll clean the kitchen if you want, honey."

"No, it can wait."

He bent and kissed her on the cheek. "I think I like my new wife."

"I was going to say, *you* can do it in the morning." She grinned at his stiff salute.

"Yes, ma'am, Sarge, sir, or whatever it is they say."

"Well, let's get to it. Everyone sit in your usual places—no wait. Sit in your usual places, then move one chair to the left. Then I'll start the pictures around."

Annie and Roger watched while the kids pushed each other into place, the two younger ones not sure which way was left. Finally, they were settled.

Mayra glanced around the table. "Wow, this looks weird. Everybody's out of place."

"I like it." Hank leaned over to Nora. "I never get to sit next to you, Nora Bora."

Nora rewarded him with a wet thumb in his ear.

"Yuck, Nora—" He wiped his ear with a napkin.

"Okay, kids, that's enough." Annie opened the box and sent the first group around the table. "Most of these little albums are organized by Abby's age—"

"Wow, Mom. This one looks like that picture of you in the family room. Look, I think you're wearing the same blue dress—"

see, it has the white collar." Mayra jumped up and came back with the picture. She held them up side by side. "What were you, about three?"

Annie leaned in close. "Yes, I'd say about three. Nora's age."

Tears sprang to her eyes when she realized the short-sleeved navy-blue dress with the crisp white collar was indeed the same as in the picture of Abby. She'd never noticed it before. A warm peace flooded her heart. She'd probably worn lots of Abby's hand-me-down clothes—she'd somehow never considered it before. That must've been hard for her mother, but living the military life, probably a necessity.

It's a connection. Thank you, Mom.

They continued digging through the pictures, warming Annie's heart with their oohs and ahhs, exclaiming *look at this one*, and the general hilarity over old-fashioned cars and clothes, even a shot of her parents' old tube TV, which sent Hank into fits of giggles.

"How'd you guys survive, anyway?"

Roger reached and thumped him on the head. "Oh, it was so difficult having to get up off the couch to turn the TV off, let me tell ya—"

Hank looked at Kimmie and Nora, who frowned in confusion. "They didn't have remotes back then," he said.

Kimmie giggled. "Really? No remotes. Wow—"

Hank jumped to his feet and put his fist up near his mouth, posing like he held a microphone. "Nope, and phones hooked with cords to the wall. You couldn't carry them around in your pocket. How 'bout that for weird?" He took a bow and plopped down in his chair again.

"Okay, Hankster. Enough with all the useless trivia." Annie grinned. "Leave them *something* to discover for themselves, okay?"

Roger looked at his watch. "It's almost nine. Hey, Annie, you haven't told us what you'd do tomorrow, if . . . you know—"

Hank broke in. "That's right, Mom. You never said."

She looked around the table, thinking she didn't want *this* story to end, that there was still another scene, another chapter.

Say it now. It's time . . .

53

Annie stood, pushed aside the box of pictures, and struck a theatrical pose. "I'd build a city, complete with castle and moat. Who wants to help?"

She backed into the living room and picked up a blanket rumpled at her feet, then shook it out and draped it over her shoulders like a cape. "I get to be the queen—who's gonna be king?"

"Yeah—King and Queen of the Castle—we haven't played this in forever," Hank shouted.

Even Max barked his enthusiasm and chased his tail, until Hank captured him by his bright-red collar.

Roger bent and scratched Max's ears, then glanced up at Annie. "He wants to play. Squire Bulger—what do you think?"

"Perfect! Let's find a cape for him."

"What is it, Mommy?" Nora had leaped to her feet, clearly not knowing why she was excited.

"Mom—Nora's never played before." Mayra counted on her fingers. "Has it really been that long?"

Annie nodded. It'd been at least three years since they'd played the game, begun when Mayra was Nora's age. It was riotous fun—the good queen kidnapped by the evil Squire Bulger, then rescued by the gallant king, aided by his trusty servants.

Somehow, in the busyness of rearing the kids, they'd let go of the joy of play.

Annie remembered her trip through the picture frame earlier—*was it real?*—and the simple pleasure of playing with Mom and Dad. It was time to build some memories of their own.

Annie stooped and gave Max a pat on the head. "Come on, everyone—you have to build the city for the queen."

Roger picked up a pillow. "Yeah, she can't just stand here in the middle of the wilderness—she needs a decent castle and a throne."

The free-for-all started, Roger and the children draping blankets over the furniture to make castle rooms, Nora squealing, "Why can't I be queen?" and a tug-of-war between Mayra and Hank.

Annie stood still, watching them scurry around the messy room. *Perfect.*

"Mom, how about this for a cape for Squire Bulger?" Mayra held up a multicolored fringed scarf given to Annie by a woman at their church. Annie had never liked the untidy, wild colors, but had accepted it just to be nice. She'd worn it a couple of times but then had relegated it to the bottom of a chest of drawers where other similar items resided.

"Mayra, that's brilliant. See if you can put it on Max."

Max, the soul of patience, sat still while she tied it around his neck.

"Honey, it sure looks better on Max than it ever did on you," Roger said, eyes twinkling with mischief.

"I agree. But no one is to tell Mrs. Henderson that, or that Max wore the scarf. Agreed?"

Hank ran his index finger over his mouth. "Our lips are sealed,

Your Majesty."

Roger swirled a blanket around his shoulders and placed a baseball cap on his head.

"Okay, I'm ready and crowned. Queen Anna Banana, let's get this show on the road."

Nora hopped up, eyes burning with excitement. "Who am I going to be, Mommy?"

"Why, you're going to be my princess! Here's your crown, sweetheart—"

Annie took her silver necklace from around her neck and draped it on Nora's head, the small silver cross resting on her forehead.

And then the real fun began.

Her family's shrieks of laughter and joy, accompanied by Squire Bulger's barking, filled Annie's heart to the brim, like crystal-clear water running into the dried-up crevices of her soul and washing away the dirt and grime of fear.

She wondered briefly if the neighbors could hear them or were standing on their porches, wondering what in the world was going on at the Lees'.

Annie decided she didn't care.

Let 'em wonder.

54

Hours later Annie drifted to the kitchen, leaving the blankets and quilts draped over the furniture in the living and dining rooms. The dark hidden spaces in the tents, once peopled by squealing child-sized knights and princesses, now lay empty and quiet. All knights and princesses, and King Roger, lay sleeping upstairs—where they should be, since it was after midnight.

She'd carried Nora upstairs behind the three older children, and they'd fallen into their beds, exhausted by their own imaginations. She'd looked in on Roger, recently the overlord of the dining room castle. He was turned away from her, snoring at the open window.

She stood in the middle of her once orderly kitchen, now a glorious mess. Pots and pans piled high, crumbs scattered over every inch of the counters, dribbles of chocolate frosting trailing in random spots on the floor and splattered on the cabinet opposite the stand mixer—still resting on the butcher block island.

How had chocolate splattered way over there?

They'd decided, at the ungodly hour of 9:45 p.m., to bake a cake together to celebrate the queen's rescue. She flinched at the mess, felt that niggle to put on her apron and get busy, but instead she resisted, standing still and sniffing. The sweet odor of dark chocolate swept over her senses.

She stepped to the mixer and drew her finger through the sticky darkness of frosting on the beaters and put it to her lips. It tasted thick and velvety sweet, like Nora had chortled hours ago. "Yum, Mommy! I made it myself!"

Another memory to tuck away before this night was spent.

She'd had to stop Mayra from wiping frosting from Nora's forehead. "Leave it be," she'd said. "She looks beautiful." Then she'd grabbed her phone and taken a picture.

Annie looked at the clock on the stove—12:37 a.m. It wasn't today anymore—it was tomorrow. Dawn in just four and a half hours.

She looked at the cake, inexpertly cut by Hank. Instead of neat squares like she would have sliced, Hank had cut geometric shapes, a different one for each of them. A triangle for Mayra, a circle for Nora, an oblong for Roger, a star for Kimmie. Annie had declined, saying she'd snacked enough on the frosting.

Hank had made each of them use their shape in a sentence.

Nora's sentence was the sweetest. "My piece looks just like us—a round line with no breaks."

Roger had leaned in close. "What do you mean?"

"A *sookle* of fun, and we're all inside it."

"A *circle of fun.*" *Dear Nora . . . God, please don't let her grow up too fast. I want more time to play with her, to learn from her.*

Before serving them, Hank had taken a picture of each piece of cake with Annie's phone, saying he'd turn it in for extra credit in his geometry class. What a clown he was.

There were two pieces left in the pan. She looked at the clock again—12:40 a.m.

Never eat sweets after six, said her exercise coach.

Really? Two pieces? This from her mother.

Chocolate isn't bound by a clock. Enjoy, Annie. Ellen.

Ellen won, like she always did.

Her heart hurt, thinking of her friend, wishing she could share this moment with her.

Annie picked up a fork and dug in, wolfing down both pieces, savoring each bite. As she licked the last bit of frosting off the fork, she waited for the guilt to pop up and jeer at her. It never did show its face.

Ellen had said once after a failed exam, "Guilt is overrated. When it comes, unless you're an axe murderer or something, knock its block off and tell it to scram."

At the time, Annie had been shocked at her unruliness. Now, she smiled at the memory and looked up at the kitchen ceiling, giving her friend a high five. *You were always right, weren't you? I should have listened more.*

After finishing her cake, Annie did decide to put on her apron. She put the cake pan next to the sink—she needed to at least organize this mess. How could Saturday morning activities happen with Friday night still in pieces all over the kitchen? She'd organize now, and Roger could clean it in the morning.

Annie gathered the pots and pans out of the sink, along with the chocolate-covered plates, and set them on the counter, trying not to make too much noise. Then turning on the faucet, she squirted some blue dish soap into the sink, watching fragile bubbles form and float upward. She popped one with her finger and giggled.

How long had it been since she'd played with bubbles? She faced her destroyed kitchen and thought, *Why not? It'll still be here tomorrow . . . if tomorrow comes, that is. And if it doesn't, double why not?*

Annie turned off the water and hurried into the living room.

Spying a bottle of bubbles—most lately Princess Nora's only defensive weapon against evil spells—where it had been left earlier, she grabbed it and went back to the kitchen, perching on a stool with her bare feet dangling.

Soon dozens of bubbles floated lazily around her, settling on the counters, the floor, the chocolate-covered mixer. She felt one land on her hair, and she reached up and felt the moisture.

Bubbles aren't like us, Annie thought. *They're there and then they're not, and they don't care about tomorrows. Like butterflies.*

She blew a few more glistening orbs, then replaced the cap tightly and left it on the table.

Magic.

She tiptoed to the photographs on the wall, staring at the light in her mother's eyes. No more sadness there. She reached and lightly stroked her right ring finger.

Annie looked at her mother's face and smiled.

She understood now. Maybe she'd visit Pastor Mike tomorrow and tell him what she'd learned. Maybe. Or perhaps she'd cherish the lesson all to herself.

The box of Abby pictures was her next stop. Sitting down, she wiped her bubble-sticky fingers on her apron, then pawed through the pile of small albums and loose pictures, looking for one in particular.

Four years of pictures, taken by first-time parents, added up to a sizeable number. Annie peered at them one by one, starting with Abby's baby pictures.

Birthdays, Christmases, Easters, jumbled together with family barbecues and hikes.

She tried to keep them in some semblance of order, but that was too time consuming. When she finished with one album, she tossed it in the box, not caring if it was in order or not.

She finally reached Abby's fourth birthday album—they hadn't gotten this far earlier tonight when they'd looked at them with the kids. She set the album in front of her and opened it with shaky hands. She knew what she'd find. She didn't know if she wanted to again.

But tomorrow is here, and I must get on with it before . . .

The first picture she saw, on the first page of the album, was Abby sitting amid a pile of gaily wrapped presents. Her mother sat on the floor with her, Abby's apple-cheeked face cupped in her hands, their foreheads touching. Abby held a stuffed bear in the crook of one elbow. Annie set that picture aside, thinking Nora would like to see her aunt Abby holding an older version of Mr. Bear.

She smiled. If she knew her daughter, it'd promptly be named Grandpa Bear.

She couldn't ever tell Nora that Abby's bear had been found shredded into pieces near her body. Annie wiped her eyes, thinking of her sister clutching that one comfort at the end.

Turning the pages of the album, hoping to see that one, she stopped on one she'd never noticed before.

Her mother and father standing in front of their home, Abby playing at their feet. Her mother looked down at Abby, but her father's gaze pointed over the head of whoever took the picture. It was almost as if he was somewhere else, his mind drawn outward, away from his family.

She rubbed her thumb over her father's face, wondering what might've been in his mind. On the heels of her wonder followed another thought. She didn't have to speculate. No, she knew what it was. Ever the soldier, always the protector. Scanning the edges of their world to make sure no evil could get through the walls he'd built. Just like her own fences.

That was why he'd stopped smiling, after Abby . . . in his mind, he'd failed.

A tear slipped down her face as she laid that picture aside. It wasn't the one, but Annie was glad she'd found it.

I love you, Dad.

She turned the page.

There it was, the picture she'd wanted to find. Back at Abby's fourth birthday party. Mom and Dad, posed in front of the fireplace, Abby standing in front of them, one hand on their mother's rounded belly.

The look of pride on her four-year-old sister's face took Annie's breath away.

She'd seen the same look on Mayra's and Kimmie's faces the first time they'd seen Nora and held her. They'd touched her face, her hands, her feet, exclaiming over how much Nora looked like her big sisters. From that day on, Nora was as much their baby as hers and Roger's.

Annie pried the picture out of the album and turned it over. On the back, in her mother's hand, was written, *We told Abby today that she's a big sister now. She said that was the bestest birthday present of all.*

She brushed her finger over the words. She turned it over again and stared at Abby's small hand caressing her baby sister not yet born. Annie sat as still as possible, trying to capture the touch of Abby's plump fingers.

She could swear she felt Abby's hand on her head, then sliding down over her hair to rub her back. Then a light touch on the back of her hand holding the photo.

She took the picture to the wall and held it up between the two pictures of their parents. Perfect.

She'd go frame hunting tomorrow, *if . . .*

It was time to fill the emptiness.

55

Annie set the picture on the credenza, then turned her back on her chaotic kitchen, switched off the lights, and walked out. She stood in the living room, surrounded by dark humps of blankets that'd been left behind when the kids went to bed, furniture askew, even a few KFC wrappers and napkins still on the floor. She couldn't bear to clean it up. It was solid evidence of life well lived in this house, of fear sent packing, of imagination taking flight. Annie hoped this memory, regardless of tomorrow's arrival or not, would live in their souls for eternity.

One more look around the beautiful jumble before heading upstairs, and her gaze landed on a bit of orange color under one of the blankets. She recognized it immediately—the delicate figurine of her favorite monarch butterfly.

How did it get in here from the family room?

Annie lifted the corner of Kimmie's quilt and carefully picked it up.

She remembered Nora had been under this very blanket while

they played. She'd said she, the princess, was mixing up her potion to free Annie the Queen.

Annie now noticed something different about the butterfly. She held it up in front of her, catching the glow of the yard light streaming through the window.

The edge of one of the wings was broken off, and about half of it was missing. It must've been stepped on or dropped during the chaos of their play. She was sure no one would've done it on purpose.

The poor thing. It couldn't fly now . . . *Just like me*, Annie thought. Even though she'd learned some things today, she was afraid she'd never really fly again. Just too much brokenness.

Annie sat on the floor, the butterfly nestled in her palm. She stroked the wing. Her memory took her by the hand and walked her backward to when she was a senior in high school.

She was in the school library, sitting at a table surrounded by reference books. She worked it out that it was before she and Roger had met. He hadn't come on the scene until halfway through senior year. What was she trying to remember? Something had happened, or something she'd read . . .

That was it, something about butterflies, but try as she might, she couldn't bring the words into focus.

She turned the marred creature over and over in her hands. She focused on the jagged edge of the broken wing, rubbing her index finger over it. Annie wondered if butterflies felt pain when their wings were broken. She hoped not.

Words finally took shape. Yes, she'd read in an article, all those years ago, that butterflies were often attacked by predator birds midflight.

Just like me . . . I thought I was learning to fly, that my life was just beginning that night. But then it ended behind the gym, or so I thought. If it hadn't been for Ellen—

But now she remembered how that article had ended.

Butterflies, in spite of their delicate features, are tough—they often fly with partial or broken wings.

Annie stood and carefully placed the maimed butterfly on a shelf. She wondered where the broken piece was.

No matter. She'd leave it the way it was. As a reminder to herself that she, too, could fly with broken wings.

After stroking it one more time, she walked upstairs and looked into each room as she crept down the hall.

Smiled at each head on each pillow.

Pulled covers up, kissing each forehead.

Heard again their screams of delight as they'd crawled in and out of their splendid castle rooms made of blankets.

And the bold, commanding voice of Roger the Overlord calling to his miniature army to rescue his queen, taken captive by the evil Squire Bulger.

Saw them coming to take her back to him, plastic cutlery knives in childish hands.

Felt Hank's hand in hers as he gallantly led her back to the dining-room-turned-throne-room, bowing low before Roger as he placed the queen's hand in his.

The army ranged around her—even Mayra. She'd shed her teenaged sophistication and joined in the family hilarity, cast as the wise woman of the castle who'd advised Lord Roger how to get his queen back. It could only be accomplished by feeding Max—Squire Bulger—one of his dog bones, which she'd laced with the special potion mixed by Princess Nora.

Poor Max. She'd laughed when the huge black dog was cast as the evil squire. He'd played his part well though, guarding her as she sat on the floor loosely tied with colorful ribbons from her store of Christmas decorations.

And he'd chomped the bone down, magically distracted as

Queen Annie was triumphantly led away by Hank, Lord Roger's able commander.

And later, the entire royal family—plus Squire Bulger, transformed back into their beloved Max—gobbled chocolate cake together, not caring about smeared frosting, crumbs on the floor, or the shocking lateness of the hour.

All this she remembered as she gazed at each beloved head. What a glorious, untidy evening. The walls would remember the merriment spilled in this house for a long time to come, Annie was sure of it.

She came last to Mayra's room, who lay with her notebook on her chest. Annie picked it up and put it on the nightstand.

Mayra opened one eye. "Mom, it was so fun tonight," she said in her sleep-caked voice. "Can we do it again tomorrow?"

Before Annie could answer, Mayra rolled over and closed her eyes.

Yes, we will. I promise.

Annie slipped quietly into the master bathroom and brushed her teeth. She used a warm washcloth to wipe chocolate frosting from her face and bubble soap out of her hair. The light fragrance lingered as she toweled it off.

She slipped her nightgown off the hook on the door and let it float over her head—still feeling like the noble queen—and knew without a doubt she'd been rescued this night.

Annie lay down next to Roger and rolled over, tucking herself into his back. Her nose rested on the hair curling on the back of his neck. She breathed in the scent of it. Tomorrow she'd give him a haircut . . .

He shifted on the bed, and his hand found hers. The moon bathed them in her bright glow.

"All cleaned up downstairs?" he whispered. "Sorry I didn't help. I was exhausted. It's hard work being Lord Roger." He tenderly brushed hair from her face as he leaned over her and nuzzled her neck. "I can finish up for you tomorrow if you didn't get it all done."

"No, honey. Everything's done. Everything that needed to be done today is done."

He rolled over again and closed his eyes.

Annie fingered the ring under the warm covers. Pulling her hand out, she looked at the words, bold in the moonlight streaming from the window.

She breathed in and out and wondered.

Tomorrow? It was like a half-remembered dream, fading now—unimportant.

Annie listened to Roger's deepening snore—familiar, like a beloved old blanket. What would he do without her?

But the thought floated away through the window. She tried to capture it again, to think about it, to fret over it, to work it out—but it floated beyond the grasp of her mind.

She twisted the ring off and set it on the nightstand with the stone facing her. The moon's smile wrapped the heavy band in bright white light, casting a gleam on the far wall.

She'd done everything that needed doing today.

She'd laughed, she'd made a mess, she'd played. She'd let go of her fear and become a child again for one magic moment in time.

She'd loved. Her husband, her children, her neighbor.

And she'd said goodbye to the best friend she'd ever had . . . but whispered she'd see her again soon.

She'd become a butterfly, soaring on the breeze with beautiful broken wings.

A Note from the Author

Sometimes in this thing we call life, we learn lessons early. Other times, not so much. Some lessons need fifty or sixty years to simmer on the back burner before we can call them Learned.

This story came about because of one of those lessons—one that had escaped the blackboard of my mind, and the flesh of my heart for more years than I can count.

In a group setting about four or five years ago, someone asked, "What if you knew you would die tomorrow?" And then the discussion took off like racehorses out of the gate.

And left me in the dust.

Fear bloomed. My brain expanded ten-fold, then shrank to a pinpoint. *What if?* As you might know, *what if* questions are a staple in the author's toolbox. It's often where we come up with story ideas.

- What if [my character] walks into a robbery-in-progress?

- What if three families are stranded together on a mountain and can't get along—which was my what if question that gave birth to my first novel, The Master's Inn.

- What if you found out, as did Annie Lee in this story, that you had an older sister who was murdered before you were born?

This *what if* question—what if you knew you'd die tomorrow—was one I knew immediately I wouldn't touch with my ten-foot author's pole—no way, no how.

Ahem.

It pestered me. It waylaid me as I wrote other stories—never very far from the forefront of my mind. I pushed it away. I threatened it with grave bodily harm. I contemplated hiring a hit man.

Nothing worked.

Then, the characters started popping up in my dreams, invading my safe spaces where my life was predictable, regimented, and rules ruled.

Hmm . . . sound familiar?

Annie Lee confronted me. She had something to say to me.

I decided the only way to make her stop was to listen.

And I'm so glad I did.

I hope you are, too.

Deb Gorman

https://debggorman.com

A novel of human brokenness and God's still-unfolding drama of redemption . . .

When two wounded and dysfunctional families wind up unexpectedly at the remote Master's Inn during a December snowstorm, it's up to owners Tom and Barb Masters to help—except they're dealing with their own bitter issues. As the winter snowfall confines them, the three families find themselves coping with their crippled relationships and hard emotions . . . and sometimes tearing one another down in the process.

But when a tragic secret is inadvertently revealed and a rebellious teenage girl takes off into the storm, chaos descends. Will they be tossed into more heartbreak, or will the crisis draw them together against a common enemy?

With a forest in Washington state as the backdrop, join Tom and Barb at their B&B as they strive to show Christ's love to all who cross their threshold . . . even when it threatens their own sanity and safety.

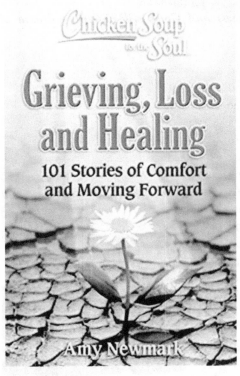

Deb contributed to this Chicken Soup for the Soul anthology, which includes 101 inspirational, compassionate, and empowering stories to help you cope with loss, regain your strength, and find joy in life again.

Losing a loved one is hard. It doesn't matter who it is, it creates a hole in your life.

I lost my only sister to suicide in 1989, and that hole in my heart and in my family is still there.

With these 101 stories, including a short story about my sister, you'll find people just like you who have loved and lost, and have learned how to live, love, and even laugh again.

Encountering Jesus amid our flawed lives, we discover He is bigger than our rebellion, our tragedies, and our confusion.

This devotional plunges you into the lives of twelve biblical characters who are mentioned briefly, almost parenthetically, as the stories of well-known players are told. Several of these obscure individuals aren't even named. But God included them in His Word for a reason, and the reason is us. Author Deb Gorman puts flesh on the bones of these shadow people, to name them, to fill in the canvas of their lives so spiritual truths can be extracted.

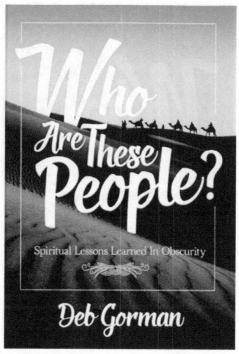

So, get ready to meet these personalities in a new way. And the next time you're tempted to think your life is insignificant, that God can't use such a flawed, mistake-ridden person such as yourself, remember: these twelve people probably thought the same, and here you are reading their stories and learning powerful lessons from their encounters with God. God created you to impact others, and that is definitely not insignificant!

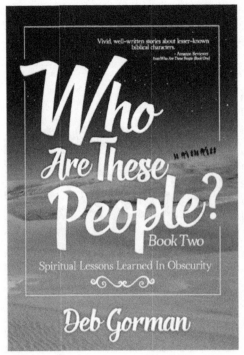

The path of your life will change each time you hold fast to your faith.

This book is about choices. If there is one thing universal in the human experience, it's that we make choices every day. Our choices range from determining how much we'll spend for a cup of coffee to whom we'll spend the rest of our lives with, but only one choice determines where we'll spend eternity.

This devotional immerses you into the lives of six Biblical characters whom God brought to the sharp point of radical decisions— decisions that would change the course of their earthly existences. We might think these six people have nothing to do with us in our century of instant communication, driverless cars, and computers mounted on our wrists, but the earth is old, and humankind hasn't changed.

The choices we make each day still determine the next moment, the next year, the next millennium and have far-reaching consequences for the next generation. God included these characters in His Word for a reason, and the reason is us.

Have you ever confronted a fork in the road of life and paused, wondering which way to go? Or maybe you took the path that seemed most logical, without much thought.

Perhaps the new direction was the correct one...but perhaps not. What do you do if you travel the wrong path?

Read the stories of thirteen people from the Bible who stood at the fork and made a choice. See where their journeys took them.

Pause that the fork in your own road and make the right decision, not just for the here and now but for future generations—your children, grandchildren, and generations beyond, doomed to suffer the consequences of a wrong choice and who scream silently at you to go back.

And if you discover you're on the wrong road, don't believe the lie that you can't turn back.

For the first terror-filled step into the great divide will lay out a cross-shaped bridge before you, stained with holy blood—the sure road that will lead you back to the

Made in the USA
Coppell, TX
07 March 2024